T0381014

THE DEMON, HUNTER'S LOUNGE

ANTHONY WASHINGTON

authorHOUSE®

AuthorHouse™
1663 Liberty Drive
Bloomington, IN 47403
www.authorhouse.com
Phone: 833-262-8899

Published by AuthorHouse 01/11/2024

ISBN: 979-8-8230-2055-8 (sc)
ISBN: 979-8-8230-2054-1 (e)

Library of Congress Control Number: 2024901152

Print information available on the last page.

This book is printed on acid-free paper.

Contents

Contents

PROLOGUE

"I love you son. No matter what." Vincent's father casted a line out into the lake as the fog rolled in, as thick as clouds. The line bobbed, waiting to hook a fish to pass the time. It was Vincent's thirteenth birthday the day after. They were celebrating early.

"I know that, papa." Vincent said, casting his line all the same. "You say the same thing every year."

"That is because it's true. You are a special kid. The only one your mother and I could have. I am proud to be your father." Vincent's father reeled in his line to cast it again. "Tomorrow is a big day for you. For all of us."

The air was calm and quiet aside from some of the seagulls that squawked in the distance. The two went fishing every year before Vincent's birthday. It was their way of bonding for Vincent was an only child. His mother could not bear children. Vincent was their promise to be good for all their days. They etched the memories into time for thirteen years. But time would change due to the family's dark secret.

"What are you going to get me this year, papa? Do I finally get a convertible?"

His father chuckled. "You'd have a better car than I drive." He reeled in his line again for a recast. "No son, this year is going to be better than all the others." He sat and opened a beer after he propped his lure on the edge of the boat. "This year we are going on vacation."

Vincent's eyes lit up. "Where to?"

"That's the surprise. But you are going to love it for sure."

Vincent got a bite. He began to pull and reel. "This is a big one!"

"Be sure to hold it steady, son."

He pulled and pulled but the fish got away. All Vincent was left with was an empty hook. "Damn it. I sure thought I had it."

"Where'd you learn to talk like that?"

"Mom said it. You know I'm old enough to use those big words."

"You think? Maybe you are old enough to pay some bills." His father sighed trying to see the jest in the language.

"As soon as you raise my allowance."

The two drove back home in the blue pick up that housed all the lures, bait, and tackle. The radio played softly. "Why won't you tell me where we are going?" Vincent turned the dial for the volume up.

"I won't say, but there is an amusement park. I'm taking you on your first roller coaster." The road was open, not a car in sight. "I think you are tall enough."

"Sweet! I can't wait. Is mom coming with us?"

"Of course she is. It was her idea. You know your mother likes to get her blood flowing. We met at an amusement park. She figured we'd go as a family. What do you think of that?"

Vincent was elated. Every year the birthday celebrations were increasingly extravagant, little by little. This year was supposed to be at the top of the list. Little did Vincent know, they would never make it to the roller coasters. His parents would meet their end just before midnight.

"I think it's fantastic. I can't wait to see your face in the pictures. You know the one on the ride where you're supposed to keep your eyes open?"

"Yeah son, I know it. I'll be sure to get you some prizes, too. This year will be one to remember."

What Vincent did not know was that his mother and father made a deal with a demon to have him as their child. It was fourteen years ago when they were desperate to start a family. They called upon the nefarious demon that promised them a newborn in exchange for their souls. Vincent's mother practiced the dark arts and did not hesitate when it came to it. She summoned the promise of a family. The price however proved to be a steep one.

They pulled up to the house and parked in the garage. Vincent could smell sweet potatoes brewing in the kitchen from outside. It was his favorite. Vincent walked inside to see his mother pulling food from the oven. She wiped her hands on her apron and hugged him.

"Dinner smells amazing." Vincent's father said. "I can't wait to eat it."

"All that's left is the cake. Caramel, just like he likes it." Vincent's mother turned to whip the batter. "Why don't you two go wash up and get ready to eat. Then we pack for the road."

They spent their last time together eating and telling stories at the dinner table. The promise of a child came with the omen that the demon would return before the child turned thirteen. Vincent's mother and father knew, but they never told him the ominous truth about his origin. They lived with the insidious secret for years. Vincent's father tried to find a way to somehow break the pact, but deals with demons seldom end at the grave.

Vincent slept that night like he never had before. His parents waited up for anything to happen. They knew the demon would return. It was only a matter of time.

"What do we do?" his father asked. "We can't just sit around waiting for someone to take our son."

"I am not sure. Why didn't we tell him? I don't know what to do." his mother said.

"I brought this." Vincent's father pulled out a revolver. "We aren't giving him up without a fight."

"You know that thing is dangerous. Maybe if we pleaded with the demon he may give us more time. I can maybe put up an enchantment to keep him away." She started into her tomes to put up a barrier. "Maybe we can buy more time."

Time lapsed and the barrier was set. It was a mid level charm from an angelic origin designed to halt demon blood. If the demon tried to pass it would be singed at the fray. Time was ticking away and all they could do was wait. Vincent's father loaded the gun in case the barrier did not hold. He was ready to die for his family. And in time he did.

There was a knock on the door that startled the parents. Did the barrier not hold? Vincent's mother sensed no break in her layline. Perhaps the demon had special facets, she just did not know. They did not answer. Vincent's father pointed the gun at the door.

The door burst open. A demon with some nuances of human traipsed in the door with a burned suit and smoke coming from his horns. "Can't say you didn't put up any effort to keep me out. But I always get what I paid for."

Vincent's father opened fire with three rounds from the revolver. The bullets left smoke holes in the suit but the demon did not seem to mind. "You leave this house now. We changed our minds. You won't have our son tonight."

The demon dusted off his sleeves. Billows of smoke upturned from the suit. He flicked embers off of his horns, then shrugged his shoulders in composure. "Why do you have to resist?" The demon's voice was calm and collected. "You see there is a debt to be paid and well, I will see to it that it is paid in full."

Vincent's mother began an incantation, summoning up light to vanquish the demon. In seconds the light burst out into an orb and flew to the demon, to burn him in holy light. The demon caught the orb and it burned his hand. "That is not the way to treat a house guest, is it?"

"What do you want?" Vincent's father asked. "Take anything, just leave us alone."

"I intend to take your souls. But first I have to separate them from your bodies." The demon shot a bone spike from his palm. It pierced Vincent's father in the forehead. He was dead before he hit the ground. "Some things can be solved with a little help from my old friend death."

Vincent's mother dropped to her knees and cradled her husband in her arms. "Are you going to kill him? Are you going to kill my boy?"

The demon's head cocked. "Is that really even a question? Why mutilate my own creation. I have other plans for your child. He will be in servitude for all his days."

She would not have it. She said another incantation. One that would harm the demon if he came near Vincent. "You will never have him. If you touch him you burn."

The demon lifted her by the throat and then began to squeeze. "I always get what I want."

Vincent woke to the commotion in the living room. He sprang out of bed and tightly toed to the living room where he saw the grisly spectacle. His eyes widened in horror. He froze not knowing how to react. The demon's eyes began to glow red.

"So, you are their contract. Shame things had to be the way." the demon muttered. "In time you will see the very nature of making deals with demons." The demon dropped his mother. She was still on the living room floor. "You belong to me now, boy."

Vincent saw the gun by his father's body and grabbed it. He was not experienced with firearms but knew how to point and pull the trigger.

"That won't harm me." the demon said.

Vincent pulled the trigger anyway. The bullet did not phase the demon. Vincent fired the remaining two shots to no avail. The demon walked over to Vincent and grabbed at his arm. But the seal caused the demon's hand to sizzle. It pulled away at the pain. "That witch!" he exclaimed.

"Run!" Vincent's mother yelled. Vincent bolted for the door. The house went up in flames as soon as he was outside. In seconds the house was crumbling with no ordinary flames. Vincent's mother intended to scorch the demon for the sake of her son. With that she died.

But the demon remained. It sat in the center of the flames with the ghostly souls of Vincent's mother and father in his wings. It swallowed the souls then vanished with the flames. Vincent looked on to the ashen remains of his home in disbelief.

A black car pulled up next to him. A dark skinned man with a bald head, a cigar, dressed in all black got out and walked over to him. "Looks like I was too late."

"Who are you?" Vincent asked.

"A friend of your mother's. She said if anything were to happen to her I should take you in."

"All I want is the life of the bastard that did this to my family."

"That is no easy task, kid." The man puffed his cigar. "That is a full fledged demon from the underworld. Those that strike a deal with it usually meet the same end."

"I don't care what it takes."

"I'm Incognito. The name is just for show. Stick with me and I will help you get your revenge."

The two set out into the night. Vincent would pick up the title demon hunter. He opened a hunter's business that answered calls from all over: people who struck deals with demons, were haunted by them, or any that were found in the human realm were eliminated by his hands. He searched high and low for the demon. Vincent and Incognito hunted for seven years with no sign of him. That is when Vincent went solo and opened "The Demon Hunter's Lounge".

CHAPTER ONE

Vincent sat with his legs crossed on the desk. It was hotter than hell. He stared at the ceiling fan as it oscillated back and forth from a few loose screws. Business had been slow for the past couple months. He did not have the funds to pay for the electricity. All he could do was wait for his partner to come back, hopefully of good news with work.

"Man, the author needs to write in some business." he said to himself.

It was mid day. The sun was blazing but it did not stop him from wearing all black. He set out on the road to head to east town Chicago for his favored general tso's chicken from a Chinese takeout spot named "The Asian Counter". He frequented the spot after he was introduced to it by his oriental companion Xiao Lin. He recruited her after she saved his hide from a demon that was eating animals from a binding that went wrong. Lately he did not have the funds to pay her but she remained diligent in the aspects of labor. She was the one that ventured into the fields looking for any odd jobs that came with promises of pay.

Vincent fired up the engine of his mustang and chopped through the busy traffic. He sat his cell phone in the passenger seat in case Xiao Lin found anything that could pay them. They both had the weapon to slay a demon. After he ordered his meal Xiao Lin gave him a ring.

"I found something. It's not going to pay us but I feel you would like it." she said.

"Really? I was beginning to think the author had forgotten all about us. He has me sitting in the heat with nothing to do. He could have least written in a small fortune." Vincent put the phone on speaker mode. "What's the word?"

"It's an ebon." Ebons are weapons that were infused with powers from the underworld. They were crafted by makers down there and were forged to slay powerful demons. Every now and again they made their way to the human world and they promised to inflict fatal wounds to demons where regular weapons would not suffice. "But it is all the way in Egypt."

"That is a long walk from Chicago, Xiao. How do we expect to get all the way to Egypt?"

"We ask Incognito." she responded. "Get him to open the gate and transport us there."

It was no small thing to ask Incognito to pull such a favor. After all he taught Vincent the ways of a demon hunter. If there was any information to be found it was with Incognito. He also had many otherworldly contraptions that could do just about anything. He was a collector as well as a hunter. Many of the other demon hunters came to him when they needed favors. Incognito collected them in full.

"I will meet you tonight." Xiao Lin said. "We will go to him and see what he has to say." With that she hung up the phone. Vincent went back to eating.

Incognito's was an underground nightclub that had its lights lit up with his name. It was a haven for those that did demonic plundering. They gathered there exchanging information as long as they abided by Incognito's rules. One of them was no weapons in his house. The other was no demons allowed. As long as you obeyed there were no troubles.

Vincent pulled into the parking lot and shut out his lights. There was a light rain that night. The lot was packed and bodies were lined up to the end of the block waiting to get in. They were not all hunters. Incognito did let in unsuspecting patrons to pay the bills.

Xiao Lin parked her white motorcycle next to Vincent's mustang. "Try not to get into any fights. We only need him to transport us."

Vincent just drew that kind of attention. Being on the younger side he was edgy. Needless to say other hunters were not so open minded when it came to the choice of verbiage when it came to making small talk. They walked up to the bouncer at the door expecting to get in. The bouncer had other things in mind.

"The line is that way." the bouncer said pointing down the street.

"Come on. We are old friends of the owner. Just let us in and we won't have any trouble." Vincent said dusting off the bouncer's shoulder. It was a threat. Vincent did not mind roughing up a few key holders to get what he wanted.

"Look kid, don't go looking for trouble." the bouncer said.

Just then Incognito showed up. "It's okay Ross. I have been expecting them."

"Amazing what a phone call can do, right Vincent?" Xiao Lin said with a laugh.

The three of them walked inside. The music was playing loudly and bodies were grooving to the tunes. They walked into Incognito's office. It was on the second floor with a window overlooking the dancefloor. It was the only way Incognito could keep an eye on things. He watched like a wolf over his territories. If there was even the slightest threat, he was on it like no other. He was strict when it came to Vincent. It was the only way to keep him from getting killed. Incognito owed Vincent's mother. So he felt a strong sense of obligation when it came to keeping him alive.

"What do you need this time?" Incognito asked. "Little Xiao here was a little skimpy on the details for the favor. All she said was she needed transport."

Xiao Lin spoke. "Well we heard there was an ebon that made its way to the human world. We want to get it before anyone else. Can you open a gate to get us there?"

Incognito sat in his chair at his desk. "Sure thing. I can get you there, but I can't get you back. Why can't you solve this little occurrence with a plane ticket?"

"Money is tight." Vincent chimed. "You are the only one we can rely on at this current junction."

"Is that why you broke away from my authority, Vincent? It would be a lot easier if you just continued to work for me."

"The bird had to move from the nest sometime, Incognito. Just call this a favor and I will owe you one." Vincent moved to the window. "You have a pretty decent crowd rolling in. What's the occasion?"

Incognito pulled a rather large boog from underneath his desk and dropped it on top of it. "Rumor has it that hunts are running dry. Everyone is here celebrating peace times. You could do yourself a real favor by buying a few drinks of your own."

"No need to advertise here." He turned back to Incognito. "What's with the bible?" He was referring to the book. "Looking to save my soul? Jesus, it's just Egypt."

"This here is a compendium of various artifacts known throughout all of demonology. It has the known locations of ebon and other trinkets that prove to be valuable in its necessities. I send you to where you need to go and you bring back something for me."

It was the status quo in the business. It all depended on the risk. But something so simple as an ebon could not have been so much trouble, could it? Bringing back a trinket was nothing more than going to the gift shop as far as Vincent was concerned. Incognito flipped the pages.

"Here it is. Promise to bring this puppy back and I will send you on your way." It was an ankh. Such a valuable artifact was used in ancient times. The pharaohs used them to tread between realms. "I need it for another client. It is supposed to help souls cross over from the other side back to the human world."

"You don't plan on dying, do you?" Xiao Lin asked.

"If I do it won't be for long."

"Fine." Vincent said. "It's yours. When can we depart?"

"The gate won't open for another day or so. If you could find another way there it would save me some trouble."

"What about the ankh?" Xiao asked.

"I can find other ways to the afterlife. That one is just a convenience. Don't be late when the time comes. The gate won't open again for another month or so."

Vincent and Xiao Lin went to the dance floor. They weaved their way through thick sweat and jumbling bodies to get to one of the couches that lined the area. They wanted to get a gameplan on the ebon. They needed to know if there were any dangers that lurked while they looked for the demon slaying weapon. Chances are where there was an ebon there was trouble.

Vincent ordered rum. Xiao Lin did not drink, but stayed for the company. She did not mind hitting the dance floor a little later on. "So what do you know about the ebon, Xiao? Can't imagine there won't be trouble."

"It is supposed to have been used by a hunter that went to the other side and didn't make it back. The Egyptians are known for opening those kinds of doors. You know, the kind that spit something out if you aren't careful." Xiao Lin kicked up her feet and nodded her head to the beat. "I already have a few ebons. Yours is the one that needs to be replaced.

The last ebon Vincent held was a sword that he wielded. It was given to him by Incognito when he became the drinking age. Ultimately the sword was broken when the gate he jumped into collapsed as he was escaping from a giant mantis demon. It was not too long ago. Xiao chalked it up to poor planning. This time around she wanted to be ahead in the game.

Xiao Lin rose up. She could not contain herself. She needed to dance. She was off before Vincent could finish his drink. He ordered another before a familiar figure sat her waistline down next to him. It was Veronica. She still worked for Incognito and every now and again she would kiss the young demon hunter. She had no intention on being with him, but every now and again she sated her urges with Vincent. Vincent did not mind as she is his first love. He always kissed back.

"Long time no see, sweet thing." he said. "Looks like you guys have it all here. What brings you to me?"

"Vincent, you know why I am here. I heard you broke your sword. I wanted to know if you required one of mine?"

"You would do that? I do need something a little sporty. What do you have in mind?"

She climbed into his lap and kissed him deep. Her lips tasted like cherries. Vincent grabbed her waist and pulled her down. The music was not enough to stop Incognito form showing up.

"You two need to tie the knot already. This isn't the place to go on and make kiddies." Incognito said breaking the two up.

Before they knew it Vincent and Veronica were outside sitting on the roof of the mustang. Veronica specialized in bewitching tattoos that carried ebon. It was much easier to summon a sword than carry one. Veronica was giving Vincent the latest ink job that carried an ebon on his forearm.

"You need to be careful with these." she said. "If they break so does your soul."

"You do care about me. I am not just your sex toy?" Vincent jested.

"If I ever settled down Vincent, you are the man I would be with. But for now I am a little high strung. Don't do anything with any of those other women. I am the one for you, just you wait." When she finished she kissed her handywork, then Vincent on the mouth. She hopped off the mustang and blew him a kiss. "See you around, tiger." she said as she swayed her hips in a dramatic exit.

Vincent looked at his new tattoo. It was an alchemic shrinking rune with latin written in a circle to encase an ebon. He would wait until the moment he needed it before calling it forth. But for now he wanted to get back inside to where Xiao Lin was to tell her we was preparing to leave. He did not want to vanish without saying anything.

It took him a while to find her in the mass of bodies. She was dancing with a woman and even kissing her on the mouth. Vincent was amused. It was no secret that Xiao Lin had a lot of energy. Her once secluded self was now tearing the world a new one, one fresh pair of lips at a time. Vincent caught her eyes and waved goodbye. No sense in interrupting a good thing.

Vincent hit the streets, reving the mustang and enjoying Chicago. It was his city. There were not many hunters that would cross over into his turf without a purpose. He smelled like Veronica and he liked it. He did not sleep that night and it was just a few short hours before the jump to Egypt. Heaven knew what lay in store for the trigger-happy huntsman. Xiao Lin had not returned. That made Vincent just a little anxious. It was not like her to miss a beat. Just a few moments into the worry, Vincent's phone rang. It was a rare call from Incognito.

"Vincent, you get your ass back here. It is almost time to jump and I want that relic."

"Geez, no hey. How are you doing?"

"I just saw you a few hours ago. No need to go on with pleasantries. You know you used to live in my house. Was I ever so cordial?"

"No, If I remember you were not. Maybe that's where I get my bad attitude."

"If you want a positive role model you go to fucking Disney Land."

"Yeah yeah, on my way." Vincent Paused. "Is Xiao there with you? I haven't heard from her since your nightclub."

"She's here. We are waiting for you. You miss this jump there won't be another."

Incognito hung up. Vincent sped through the back streets. It was a little ways longer but at least he could go fast. In a way it cut down on the time. The lot to Incognito's was empty in the daytime. There were no people inside either aside from the help Incognito kept to keep the place clean. Vincent walked inside and went straight to the basement. There he saw Incognito, Xiao Lin, and Veronica standing next to a large brick ring. It was the gate that would be used to transport Vincent and Xiao Lin directly into the heart of Egypt.

"Let's fire this bad boy up." Vincent started, not wanting to waste time. He removed his leather coat anticipating the desert. The last thing he wanted to do was to die a sizzling piece of bacon all over the desert sands.

"I'm going with you." Veronica said.

"Oh, no you aren't." Vincent contested. "You aren't a hunter. The last thing we need is a casualty. I'll be damned if anything were to happen to you."

"I'm not a hunter but I do have ties all around the world. What are you going to do, walk back to Chicago?" Veronica began to tune the gate. "Just sit back and shut it. Let mama take care of you."

"Is she going to be the mother of your children?" Xiao Lin asked.

"Ha ha." Vincent said sardonically.

"You all stand back. This thing is going to rip a hole in space. If you go in before the thing opens you will be a frappe and that will be the story of you." Incognito lit a cigar and began to puff. "I don't feel like mopping hunters."

The bricks began to glow blue. Sparks started kicking out of the circular framework. The gate began to float and spin. It sounded like a racecar humming down the daytona tack. When it stabilized it was just floating. It was harmless and safe to step through.

"After you." Vincent said to Xiao Lin.

Xiao Lin sighed and stepped through. She readied her two pistols just in case they would land where there was trouble. Veronica followed shortly after. Last was Vincent. He looked down at his ebon mark and smiled. He just could not wait for something to stir. It was shoot first, shoot some more, then when everything is dead ask a couple questions. He stepped through the gate. When he was through the gate's bricks fell to the floor in a pile.

Incognito took a puff of his cigar once more. "Kids these days."

When the dust settled Veronica was nowhere to be found. She had disappeared without a word. That was exactly what Vincent did not want. He knew she was a firecracker but this was a bit much. They arrived on the outskirts of a market square, just atop a roof looking over merchants that sold food, blades, anything that explorers needed on their journey. There were even guns available. The funds were tight with The Demon Hunter's Lounge, so Vincent and Xiao Lin only carried what they brought with them, which was not much.

Xiao Lin put her ebon pistols in their sheaths and began rummaging through her backpack in search of a paper that had what exactly they were looking for on it. When she found it she crouched.

"This is it." she said. On the paper there was a drawing of a shotgun that had more of the alchemic runed inscribed on it, signifying that it was in fact and indeed an ebon.

"That looks wicked." Vincent said peering at the ebon. "What exactly is so special about it?"

"It was made from an Egyptian demon. It is from an Ammit."

"The fucks an Ammit?"

"A half human half alligator demon. It eats the souls of people who died. Not really sure how such a thing gets up for grabs though."

"Where do we begin, you being the brains and all." Vincent stood and looked onto the market. "Maybe those arms men would have an idea on where to find this Ammit."

"My thoughts exactly." Xiao Lin rolled up the paper and they made their way to the center square.

There were so many people crowding the square that there was a line that moved in one direction. Vincent and Xiao Lin had to walk in that line that moved in a circle until they arrived at the shop that they wanted to inspect. They had to be very careful not to bump into any of the patrons as pick pockets were something to caution against. The sun was beating down in beams that made them feel like they were ants on the business end of a magnifying glass. They approached a gun shop run by a woman with wraps that covered her face.

Vincent spoke first. "Do you have any peculiar weapons around here? I'm looking for something a little off the beaten path." The woman ushered Vincent towards the guns but spoke an Egyptian language that he did not understand. "Look lady, we are looking for Ammit. Get it? Ammit." She seemed surprised and put her hands up. Then she reached under the counter and pulled out magazines filled with bullets. "Damn it, not ammo. Am-MIT." Vincent said feeling frustrations like he never felt before.

Vincent had just about given up. None of the weapons appear to have ebonic origin. It was not not as if he intended on buying Ammit to begin with. He just was not sure what he would do when he found it. He could not kill for it as killing humans was just beyond the code of the demon hunters. But there was something that caught his attention. A short old woman sauntered over to him. She was hunched over and carrying something that looked like a baby held in her arms.

"You are looking for a demon's weapon, are you?" she said. Her voice was dry. Vincent could tell she lived in the deserts her entire life. Her skin was dark from the sun and wrinkled from the sands. "I have it here but I will need something in return."

Vincent sighed. "What do you need?" he asked in ambivalence.

"In time you will need another weapon. All demon hunters need someone to supply them with those kinds of goods. Just remember me in your hour of need." The old woman handed Vincent the Ammit. "Give these old bones a reason to keep going."

Vincent held Ammit out, checking the weight of it against his arm. "Tell me, what do you know of an Ankh? Know where I can find one?"

"The Ankh is a precious relic, made to have someone traverse between this life and the next. There is only one left. The others buried deep within the dunes of the desert." She pointed at a distant pyramid. "The pharaoh has it in his tomb."

"Thanks. Nothing like old fashioned grave robbing to keep me on my toes."

"Be warned traveler." the old woman said. "To disturb the pharaoh is to awaken the wrath of the Egyptian gods."

"I think I will take my chances." Vincent then went to look for Xioa Lin. He found her eating a broth from a clay bowl with some of the other patrons in the marketplace. He never really knew how Xiao Lin was so chum with people. Here he was starving without a penny and she managed to become the center of attention and acquire free food. He held up Ammit to show her and she nearly shot broth from her nose in excitement. "Fancy that, huh?"

"That was fast." Xiao Lin said, slurping the broth from the bowl. "Now all we have to do is find the Ankh. With that Veronica should have us a way home."

"I have the location already. It's in the tomb of some pharaoh. All we have to do is pillage the remains and then we can get out of this god forsaken desert."

"We need to figure out a way there. I did some research before we came and it is said that we could be buried if we walk on loose sand."

Veronica pulled up with a desert jeep, kicking up sand as she parked next to the two. "You know you need me, Vincent." she said getting out.

"Maybe I should recruit you. Seems as the author gave you all the resources. If things continue like this I may need you for future chapters." Vincent hopped into the front seat of the windowless jeep and revved the engine. Xiao Lin got into the back seat with a more than chipper attitude and saw a supply bag next to her.

"What's in the goodie bag?" Xiao Lin asked.

"We are going to need it." Veronica stated. "We are going to need it if we are going grave robbing."

"How do you know about that? I just found that out." Vincent asked.

"I told you," said Veronica. "I have ties all over the world. Is that the ebon you have there?"

"Oh yeah. It is a full snapjaw rocket. I can't wait to give this baby a whirl."

"I am going to give that an ebon mark. The last thing you should be doing is laboring an ebon. I brought my tattoo kit as well."

After Veronica stapled the ebon to Vincent's skin they were off in the desert jeep towards the ancient pyramid. They did not know what was in store. They had seen plenty of movies to know it could be a showcase death charge, filled with traps and potentially far worse. However they remained adamant in finding the Ankh for Incognito. It was the remainder of their scavenger hunt in Egypt. They could do without the sun and finding sand in places where sand should not have been.

The jeep came with only one disc. They listened to it. It was Egyptian drums that were to be played in times of war. It was fitting for the travelers since they would battle against the tomb of a pharaoh. It certainly got them into the mood to face a mummy. It was what they were expecting. The only thing that stood in their way was to find a quicksilver way back to Chicago and head back to the office. The trick was making it back alive.

CHAPTER TWO

The jeep was parked outside of a large dune that was to be crossed on foot. There was no way it would climb the sand hill without tipping over. The crew ran out of water but made it just before nightfall, which worked out better since the sun would no longer be present.

Veronica circled the pyramid looking for an entrance. There was not one to be found. This particular tomb was built against grave robbers. It was sealed with that in mind. And since the roster of grave robbing aspired to keep the three of them out an alternative sure needed to be found. What was an excavation without a few explosives?

"We need to blast a hole in the wall. It is the only way in." Veronica said with c4 and wires. She set them on a sealed wall that looked like it was closed off at the finish of the pyramid's construction. "The natives aren't going to like this."

"Whatever. As long as we get the damn thing. This desert is starting to give me hives." Vincent grabbed some more of the explosives and helped set the charges. "Whatever gets us home faster."

They stood a good distance away, ready to make a hole in desert brick. "Fire in the hole!" Xiao Lin screamed. She always wanted to say that. Who knew when she would get the chance again? There was a loud "boom" and the seal of the wall gave way. There was a lot of sand and debri at the detonation zone. A strong wind that sounded like screams came roaring through the opening.

"Yay!" Xiao Lin acclaimed. "It's like an ancient haunted house!"

The three moved in a triangle formation to cover all peripherals. If anything made a move there were no reactions, only shoot to kill. An anticipation that Veronica would have weapons was the expectation. Vincent discovered shortly that this was not the case.

"You don't have ANY weapons?" he said.

"I'm a lover not a fighter." said shrugging him off.

"But you can get explosives? Seriously woman you are ass backwards. How are we going to rob a tomb if we aren't synchronized?" Vincent said. "I'm going to have a word with the editors."

"I guess you're just going to have to put up with me, honey. You just have to accept what you cannot change."

There were carvings on the walls, ancient hieroglyphs. It was too dark for Xiao Lin to read as she was the only one in this tale who could somehow read the ancient text. Veronica tossed the self judge overly excited Xiao Lin a flashlight, shedding literal and metaphorical light on the situation. Took her a moment of muttering ancient Egyptian before she could decrypt the nature of the text.

"What does it say?" Vincent asked, becoming impatient. "I don't want to stay in this place a second longer than I have to."

"It's a warning. It says, "Let those who come to steal the Pharaoh's purse beware the god of jackal's curse." Then there are some inscriptions that show Anubis and an army of his warriors protecting the pharaoh sarcophagus."

"So on our first trip together, Vincent, we have to awaken an Egyption god?" Veronica went ahead, down into the crypt of the pyramid. "I don't approve. You had better plan a decent honeymoon."

"I wanna go!" Xiao Lin said trailing after Veronica. "Let's go to Paris."

"That's not how honeymoons work!" Vincent said, trying to catch up to the two women that sounded more threatening than an egyptian god.

They reached a drop. At the very bottom they could see the sarcophagus of the pharaoh, the very tomb of an ancient king. It was a reflection of mirrors that reflected moonlight into the tomb. There was a statue of Anubis in an annex just a few feet away. It was so that the gods could keep watch, harmless. Or so they assumed.

"Any clue as to how to get down there?" Vincent said, starting to feel wear and tear. "Jumping is suicide."

"There." Veronica pointed to a pillar that was fastened with rope. "It looks like it is held together with rope and bags of sand. Cut the rope, the sandbags will fall, then we swing across." She points across the drop with the flashlight. "There is an opening. Looks like it's our only ticket to the loot. Getting back up is going to be a real bitch."

"Looks like this is a one way ticket." Xiao Lin chirped. "Those who come in weren't made to get out."

"Onward then, kittens." Vincent gestured the two ladies onto the pillar. He climbed on. Veronica handed Vincent a knife with a serrated edge to cut the rope. When the rope was cut the pillar swung them across like a pendulum. They hopped across before it lost momentum and landed safely on the other side.

They went down winding stairs and through long hallways. There were no traps so far. They did however come to a dead end. It was an opening in a room that had four statues that were the body of a man and head of a jackal, partially wrapped in mummy bandages.

Vincent took the flashlight and inspected them closely. "If I had to say it, those teeth look real."

The statue Vincent was closest to roared. It then swung a rounded axe in his direction. He dodged it. The shock from its awakening sent him doping back. "Ladies?" he shouted. The jackal brought the axe down but Vincent spread his legs, making the jackal guard miss. "Run!"

The two of them darted in the direction form which they came. One of the guards roared and shambled after them, axe in hand and duty in mind. They were to kill any of whom entered the pyramid, all that disturbed their slumber.

Vincent summoned Ammit and shot it into the gaping mouth of the guard. It went down. The remaining two moved slowly but Vincent did not waste any time. He pointed Ammit and started to fire. The jackal guard swiped and knocked him on his ass. Ammit slid across the floor.

Then Vincent remembered he had another ebon. The one to replace his sword. He held out his arm to summon it, anxious to see the prize in the Cracker Jack box. Black smoke swirled from his arm and suddenly a scythe appeared.

"Daddy likes it." He said. He spun the scythe displaying combative form, then motioned the guards to him. "Let's dance!"

One of the guards swung its axe. Vincent countered by sidestepping and slicing it in two. The other swung from the side. Vincent blocked the advancement then severed its head. He then flourished at the victory. "No task too sweet." he said over the corpses.

One thing to always note when it comes to Egypt. There was never a time when the gods did not return for the Egyptians were the first to delve into the afterlife. Before Vincent could go to help those he considered the fairer sex the jackals reassembled themselves from sand and gave a battle cry. It was Anubis that made them immortal. What better way to protect ancient artifacts?

"Shit, that's not very fair at all." Vincent said to the guards. Then he bolted from the room to find and help his well endangered companions.

Vincent ran but the guards were not far off. He called Ammit back to him and shot at the demon jackal's legs to slow the chase. He followed the sound of Mogui, the ebon that Xiao Lin wielded that came in the form of pistols. Vincent saw them on a lower level, shooting with no avail.

Vincent saw as Veronica artfully swung from a rope down to the pharaoh's tomb. He wondered why they did not just do that in the first place. He grabbed one of the ropes and shot it free as he slid down it to the very bottom of the tomb. Xiao Lin shortly followed.

"We have to get the ankh and get the hell out of here." Veronica shouted.

"Hey missy, you're preaching to the choir."

Xiao Lin tried lifting the lid with her skinny arms. "It won't budge."

It took the three of them to open the lid of the sarcophagy. There in the pharaoh's well decorated corpse they found what they were looking for. There in the moonlight, the artifact that allowed one to walk between one life and the next, sat in the glow of mirrors.

Veronica was the one to take it, prying it from the stale hands of the ancient king.

"Should we say a prayer?" Xiao Lin asked. The jackal demons leaped from the higher levels and surrounded the amatuer escavationists.

"No time!" Vincent shouted. "Let's get the hell out of Egypt!"

They ran swiftly trying to find an exit. The jackal demons were on their tails. They climbed up the side wall. The demons did the same. They figured they would head out of the top of the pyramid, following the moonlight that trailed in with the night sky.

When they climbed out of the narrow hole they saw there were more of the demons waiting for them at the base of the pyramid. "You two aren't going to believe this." Veronica said, catching the first glimpse of what looked to be an army protecting the dead.

"Ah crap." Vincent said, second out of the hole.

Xiao Lin climbed out last. "We should have said a prayer."

The demons came up from the pyramid after the three grave robbers bagan sliding down the pyramid. If they could make it to the jeep, they would put a large distance between them and certain demise. The other demons began to close in. The jeep was the only way to live.

Bullets rang out left and right as they fought their way through the sands. The feeble attempt to kill something that would never die was evened out by ebon never needing to be reloaded or sharpened. They made it to the jeep and climbed in expeditiously. Vincent put the pedal to the metal and ass was hauled to make a daring escape.

"How in the hell are we going to get us out of here?" Vincent asked Veronica. "What else do you have that can do it with fervor?."

"Remember the old woman?" Veronica asked.

"You mean the evil witchy woman that doubles as an arms dealer? What about her?"

Veronica pulled out a glowing blue crystal. "This thing transports us anywhere we want to go. It's a one time use. She gave it to me because I once did her a favor."

"You really do have friends in high places." Xiao Lin laughed.

The jackal demons were closing in. They were surprisingly fast for five-thousand something year old monsters. But it is stated that wine gets better with age.

"Well can you move it along, we are running out of road."

There was a flash of blue. They were in Chicago, again. Half of the Jeep was missing, however. What was not stated was that if you did not keep all limbs within the vehicle on was liable to come up missing. Vincent looked at the wreckage parked just outside of Incognito's.

"That was a close one." he said

"Let's do that again!" Xiao Lin said with giddy excitement.

"Let's not and say we did."

Incognito was standing just short from the damaged jeep smoking a cigar. "You aren't planning on leaving this heaping junk in my lot are you? I would charge you for parking but I know you can't afford it."

Veronica got out of the mangle machine. "Here is the Ankh."

"My girl." Incognito said, exhaling as he spoke. "I have a little extra pay for its recovery."

"What about us? We risked our lives for that thing." Vincent said in protest of being left out of the spoils of war. "Don't we at least get a thank you?"

"You get your thanks when you get that junk mobile out of my sight."

"See you around, tiger." Veronica said as she went into the nightclub. "Let's put time between you and our next adventure, ok?"

"Damn it. She gets treated like a princess and I get stuck with heavy lifting."

Xiao Lin was singing in chinese. "I can't wait for our next gig. Hopefully it's a paying one." She left Vincent alone in the parking lot. He felt cheated that he had to clean up the bucket of bolts. Such is the life of a demon hunter. Sometimes you barely escape Egypt and others you are left holding the bags.

A few moments later a tow truck hauled the jeep away. Vincent ws handed a bill that he could not afford. It was going to take some real work to get things back up to speed. Not that he wanted people to trade their lives for his selfish gain, but a couple thousand would really soften these hard times. He went into the nightclub to find Veronica and Xiao Lin sitting on one of the couches. They were the only persons giving patronage to the abode. Incognito retreated into his office and did not want to be disturbed.

Vincent walked over to the young ladies and plopped himself into the seat, right in between them. "I suppose you don't have any friends willing to pay for a demon executioner do you?" he said to Veronica. "I could really use the money so I can flush my own toilet."

"I may have something." She pulled out an envelope from her bra. It had a few hundred dollar bills in it. "There are no demons but if you are willing to put in the work you will find that this is only half the pay, up front, too."

"We're all ears." Xiao Lin said, not really wanting to take a break from the desert. "Where in the world do we go this time. I have always wanted to visit Japan."

"It's right here in Chicago, a missing object." Veronica unfolded a piece of paper that had a drawing of a jewel that looked like a hairpin and cabochon. "The one who this baby belongs to is quite wealthy. I am sure they would give you a little extra for your troubles."

"Missing object? Not really my style." said Vincent kicking his feet up on the wooden table. "I need a little something that lets me dig into my repertoire."

"Beggars can't be choosers, Vincent." Xiao Lin said sipping orange juice from a juicebox. "Besides, I need a new outfit. I have a date soon."

"A date!?" Vincent shrieked. "With who?"

"She isn't someone you know."

"She?" Vincent and Veronica both said simultaneously.

Xiao Lin ignored the passive excitement. "I will do research on the missing object. I will let you know if I run into any trouble. We need the money, Vinny."

"Fine." Vincent caved. "Just do it as quickly as possible, and don't call me Vinny. I don't need readers thinking I'm a mobster."

Xiao Lin laughed. "Your new shotgun doesn't do that kind of justice. We should change the business name to "Demon Hunter's Mob"."

Veronica game Xiao Lin the details as to where to find the proprietor of said missing cabochon. Vincent went for some chinese take out. He did not think she would run into trouble. However, if it were anything like Egypt he would have to prepare for the worst.

It was a couple of days before Vincent heard from his oriental companion. The trouble with the trinket was there were tons of help that could have stolen it. Xiao Lin gave her investigation skills a whirl and what she found was nothing short of an entreat to her friend Vincent. There was an auction to be held. It would sell many fashionable paintings and jewels. The thief had already fenced the cabochon and it would be resold by the auctioneer. All Vincent had to do was help to get it back.

"I don't know what to do here, Xiao." Vincent held the phone to his ear as he sat in the office with his feet kicked up upon the desk with a battery operated radio playing classic 80's rock. "I don't think we could steal it. It's not like we could purchase the damned thing."

"That is just it." Xiao Lin began. "There is one suspicious character that is going to be at the auction. It's a person that Elise had recently done business with and he wants the jewel for himself, reasons unknown."

"Who is Elise?"

"The person who hired us."

"What does this person have to do with the cabochon? If he buys it, it will belong to him."

"He is a demon."

Vincent jumped out of his seat. "A demon? Are you sure?"

"I tailed him myself. It looks like he is in league with a shady bunch. I tapped a payphone that he frequented and overheard a conversation that stated they would meet at the auction. Chances are there is going to be trouble. Bring your best game face, ok?"

Xiao Lin hung up the phone. A few minutes later Vincent received a text that told him where to meet her. It did not take him long to have the roar of his mustang in the streets. Though the Xiao Lin forgot to mention the huge mansion in which the auction was being held. Maybe he would do well as a monster after all. He could extort all the military funds he would need in just one job.

There were tons of people that helped with the moving of such valued objects. They used large moving trucks to move some large, well thought out paintings. They wore white gloves not to tarnish the goods. But he did not see Xiao Lin anywhere. He looked at his cell phone and saw that he had arrived an hour before the auction began. He figured he would hit the food before the face of otherworldly bounties reared their god forsaken faces.

He bit his way into fingers full of shrimp and sandwich halves. After he was finished filling his face he wanted to see if he could find the cabochon before the auction started, at least catch a glimpse of it before any commotion started.

Come to think of it Vincent did not really have a plan for acquiring it. He could alway hold the place up at gunpoint. It would definitely give his trigger happy sense a boost. He decided against it because Incognito would never let him live it down. He could steal it. Before Xiao Lin arrived? She would kill him. The plan, after much self deliberation, was to wait for the demon to have it in its clutches, he would shake him down for what it was worth. Elise was sure to pay extra for a timely return. Or so the demon wanted to believe. There was only one way to be sure.

Vincent waited for his opportunity to look at all the goods that were being hauled in by the couriers. He stealthily maneuvered behind a large oil painting that depicted a woman with angel wings in a bathtub, blowing bubbles as he lounged in cool looking waters. Then he ducked under a table that took two men to carry it. "That one doesn't even look fancy." he said out loud.

He then found himself in a large room that looked as if it was where the auction was to be held. There were rows of chairs set up and a podium on the stage. There would be no fortune if he did not press on. Vincent wormed his way passed a few more men carrying lots with no suspicions being alarmed. Then he saw it, the cabochon from the picture. It was then he became slightly discouraged for it was behind a small glass box marked "unbreakable".

Xiao Lin appeared like an apparition from behind him. "Looks like you and I have similar thought patterns."

Vincent was startled. "All for good fortune, lolita."

The two of them lifted the glass box, attempting to free the cabochon. The box however was bolted down. It was not to be opened without a key. Neither of them knew where such a thing would be. It would take all day to search for it and Vincent saw it as he did not have the patience nor time to participate in such a scavenger hunt.

"Why don't we just wait for the auction, then pretend to buy it?" Xiao Lin asked, with hopelessness in her eyes. "No sense in causing a commotion, right?"

"Why don't we just wait for your mystery demon to get it then jump him in the back alley. You know, flex some of those mob muscles you were going on about."

"Brilliant!"

The auction was starting. Bodies filled the empty seats and soon the gavel for the first item was banging against the podium. Vincent and Xiao Lin took seats in the back of the room and waited for the demon to show his face. It could not have been hard to spot a demon. Something about them always stood out. All they had to do was wait and see if the cabochon would flow in his direction then hit him like a ton of bricks.

Hours went by. Items were sold. There was no telling when the cabochon was going up for sale. "What did this demon of yours look like?" Vincent asked, leaning in for a whisper, careful not to make a disturbance.

"He looks like a scarecrow." Xiao Lin said.

"Are you sure he is going to be here? I don't want to wait all day to be stood up in a good old fashioned mugging."

Then a man with a hood up from underneath a fancy coat sauntered from behind the crowd and sat dead center in the first row. "That's him!" Xiao Lin exclaimed. Then the jewel was brought from stage right and the auction would continue with the duo's promise of fortune.

The auctioneer began, "Here we have a priceless artifact brought from an ancient ruin. It is rumored to be the key to a ghostly prison.

Legends state that its wielder is the warden of countless entities imprisoned for all of time. We begin the bid at one hundred million."

"Key?" Vincent asked.

"Who knew?" Xiao Lin replied.

The demon in the front took the opening bid. The calls came from left and right but the demon seemed to have more money than any human Vincent had ever known. Though all in good time it would be safe in his hands and so would the reward for returning it to its rightful owner.

Yet, something did not sit right with Vincent. It was a key to a prison. What would that demon need with that sort of thing? How did it fall into the hands of Elise? Was there more to this than he knew? Did he even want to find out?

"Sold! To the man in the front row."

The bidding was done and it was time to ask some questions. The two would corner the scarecrow and get the answers that they wanted. But first they need to follow the demon. The rest was demon hunter's business. And that was what Vincent had always done best.

CHAPTER THREE

The demon was trailed down quiet corridors in the mansion. Most of it was empty due to the stirrings of the sales at the auction. Fine bits of straw made it easy to tail a scarecrow. Vincent and Xiao Lin were quiet and stuck to the quieted shadows, careful not to give away their position. That key was a ticket to hot meals and electricity. It was prudent that they recovered it. It made it easy that the key's current holder was a demon. Killing it was an option that was accepted with grace.

The demon did not seem to notice the two muggers as they enclosed on it. It knelt down and broke the glass case. It was far away enough from the crowds of people not to cause a disturbance. Vincent summoned his scythe and coiled the hook around the demon's neck.

"That's enough." he said. "We'll be taking it from here."

The demon shrieked as its mouth opened wide. It looked like it was held together by a cotton sack with twine. Vincent slashed at it out of reflex but the demon was ever so agile. It ducked and a plume of straw kicked up from the demon's seams. From underneath its overcoat sprang four legs on stilts. It was so much taller than initially anticipated. It crouched on the wall and let out another scream. It ran along the wall down the hall, attempting to make off with the goods.

Vincently was shortly after it. Xiao Lin summoned her pistols and fired at the quick demon, trying to slow it down. "Don't break the key!" Vincent called. If anything were to happen to it, there went their meal ticket.

The demon was hit with the bullets but it did not slow it down.

It did not have flesh the way other demons did, that was unexpected. The demon leapt through a window and ran with incredulous speed. They were on the fourth floor, a jump that would surely break a bone or two. That did not stop Vincent's ingenuity from throwing his scythe and severing the demon's arm on the way down. He clipped the limb that was holding the key. The demon escaped leaving it behind.

The two made their way outside and picked up the key. With it in their clutches they inspected the scarecrow's limb. "Maybe we should take it back to Incognito, see if he knows anything about it." Xiao Lin said, picking up the remnant. "It's important to do a thorough investigation on who wanted the key and why."

"Maybe there will be some cash in finding out."

They were on the road back to Elise to collect their prize. It was a handsome sum, too. They would have food and electricity for the months ahead. However that was not the end of their journey when it came to the key. A series of events would unfold that would cause terror to demon hunters around the world. The prison housed elite warlocks and witches that practiced magics that were less than savory against mankind. Incognito did not have the slightest clue as to who would want the key. After Xiao Lin explained the nature of the demon Veronica shed some light on the situation.

"It is a cucumerario formido. The scarecrow demon." she said. She carried a large tome and dropped in on the center table in Incognito's office. "Those things are not to be trifled with."

"What's so special about it?" Xiao Lin said, slurping a juice box.

"They have human souls trapped within them. The souls act as fuel to keep them operational. They aren't alive, one could say they are immortal."

"Who makes these things?" Vincent asked.

"I only know of one witch." Veronica opened the tome to a criminal witch. "Her name is Beatrix." The drawing showed a woman with short dark hair and what looked like a smile of stitches on her face. She had stitches all over her body. "She is a dangerous one indeed."

"Her demon wanted the key. What for?" Vincent continued.

"It is the key of Solomon. It opens the gates to a verse that holds the most notorious of magic practitioners. Beatrix is held there for waging war on demon hunters. What for is beyond me."

"So no money on someone that is already captured." Vincent hung his head low. "Good thing we returned the key of Solomon to its rightful owner."

Incognito chimed in. "There may be one little obstacle that may have gone overlooked. If the demon knew where to find the key, it may return to find it again."

Xiao Lin gasped. "Is Elise in danger?"

"Possibly." Incognito continued. "You had better go to retrieve it just in case. Solomon does not need to be opened. Who knows what may come crawling out."

"Look," Vincent said, "We already got paid and we don't work for free."

"But think of poor Elise!" Xiao Lin chimed. "I'm going to go and warn her." She stormed out of the nightclub and sped away on her motorcycle.

"That woman sure can be stubborn." Incognito said. "A lot of firepower for someone that is four feet, three inches."

Vincent went back to his well heated lounge and waited for a phone call that would allow him to get paid for the miraculous job of demon hunting. He sat with chinese fried rice and had a sense of accomplishment written on his face. It had been months since the water and electricity had been paid. He had money to spare.

Night fell and he wanted to go to Incognito's to see Veronica. He had a craving for those plump lips of hers. He was craving her like no other. With no calls coming in it was the way to spend the night, with the woman of his dreams and sometimes nightmares. He was off in his mustang without a hitch, though traffic was slow. It came to a screeching halt at a red light. There was commotion.

A body jumped in front of the car, breaking the windshields. It was the scarecrow. It came looking for the key of Solomon. It screeched with a new limb that was a hooked blade. Soon the demon was on the hood of Vincent's mustang.

"Oh no you don'!" he said, throwing the engine into reverse. Smoke burned from his tires. The demon pierced the windshield of his car. "Son of a bitch." He spun the car with the demon dangling from the hood. He immediately called Xiao Lin. "Hey, I have a problem here."

"Elise is dead, the key is missing. I'm being chased by a scarecrow." she said.

"Damn it. Just make it back to me in one piece."

The scarecrow demon scrambled to its feet on the car then struck again. Vincent summoned Ammit and shot the demon off the hood of his car. He ran it over and bits of straw got stuck in his tires. He veered off the road and crashed into a mailbox. Smoke came from the crinkled hood. He got out, bleeding from the forehead.

Vincent did not have time to get his bearings, the demon was making its way through his blurred vision. He held up Ammit and fired. The demon staggered but it did not stop. "Damn these demons, ruined my ride." He sent Ammit back into its tattoo and called out the scythe. Sparks sprang loose as Vincent and the scarecrow crossed blades. The demon did not have the strength but it was, however, fast in its dowsing of blades. Vincent slashed and straw fell to the ground.

What Vincent did not know about the ebonic scythe was it once belonged to the grim reaper. If he could slice the souls from the scarecrow it would fall dead, a heaping pile of straw and cloth sack. He could see glowing white in its eyes and target them. It was the only semblance of life the demon had. With skill he sliced the demon in two. A man stood behind the demon with stitching, the same as Beatrix.

"She will return. And when she does it will be the end of you demon hunters." he said.

"What the hell?" Vincent said, wiping blood from his face. "You bastards are going to open that prison?"

"All in good time hunter. When it is opened Beatrix will be sure to put you hunters in the grave." He vanished before Vincent could make a move.

Xiao Lin pulled up next to the wreckage of Vincent and his car. "We have trouble. If the prison is opened who knows what we will be up against?"

"Look at what they did to my ride. I want to get even with the lot of them. Someone is going to pay for this."

Veronica patched up Vincent at the lounge. She came running as soon as she heard there was an incident. The three of them looked over pages in old tomes to see if there was some way to permanently dispel the soul written scarecrows.

"Fire will do the trick." Xiao Lin said. "It will dispel the soul and burn the straw."

"Good to know. But what am I going to do about wheels?"

"You worry too much." Veronica said. "Why don't you just buy a new car?"

"It's not like that thing did not have sentiment. I am not going to buy a new car every time a demon sees fit to run a blade through my windshield and run me off the road." he said, slightly agitated. "That's not how this is going to work. I don't have the funding for that kind of trauma."

"I'm sure you'll figure something out, sweetheart. It's not the end of the road."

"It's the end of my mustang."

The chief concern of the hunters was to recover the key before anyone with cruel intentions used it to release any prisoners. Vincent and his cunning mind wanted them to be released so he could charge a hefty sum for their capture. What was a little elbow grease on this ever so dry demon hunting world. He thought it would be fun or at least a payday. With a threat of his life upon Beatrix's return, Vincent wanted the opportunity to deal a blow for his lost ride.

"I was coming to see you, you know." Vincent said to Veronica.

"Is that so?" she said. "You keep me in mind? What were you expecting, puppy love?"

"You know you don't have to be so hurtful." he joked.

"Now here I am patching you up. Don't you go dying before the wedding."

"You should die after." Xiao Lin said mockingly. "We can bring you back with that artifact from Egypt."

"I am not going to die just so you can see if there are gift shops in the afterlife!"

"You're no fun." Xiao said pouting. "You won't even take me to Paris with you."

"You're not coming on the honeymoon!"

Veronic stood up and threw on her jacket. "Looks like you two need to work on a few things."

"Where are you going?" Vincent asked.

"Back to the nightclub. I need a drink or seven."

"Take me with you!" Xiao Lin said, grabbing her coat. "I wanna dance." With that the two women were out the door with the car at full throttle.

"Thanks for the invite." Vincent said to an empty room. He did not have any plans and the two women in his life had abandoned him for the evening to do whatever it was that women like themselves did. Xiao Lin would probably be tangled lips with a secret lover that shared the same bathroom and, well Veronica felt like being alone that night. There was not much to do and no calls came in. Perhaps he would find the key of Solomon for himself, dabble in the dark side of demon hunting.

There was a knock on his door. It was after hours but no job was too small as long as it was a paying one. A man with long black hair and spanish descent walked in after Vincent opened the door. "Can I help you?"

"Ah, but it is I who am here to help you." he said with an accent. "The name is Dimitri, I too am a demon hunter. I see you have your hands full with a witch in Solomon." Dimitri sat down on the couch in the lounge. "It seems you will need this." He held out the key of Solomon.

"Where did you get that? You know it's against the rules to kill humans."

"Elise? The poor woman was already dead when I found this trinket. I managed to tail the mystery man from your accident after Elise was killed while they were searching for it. I am crafty in those arts, you see."

"Why do I need the key?"

"To go to Solomon and kill the demon that killed your parents."

The room took a deep shift in tone. "How do you know about me?"

"How do you not know yourself?" Dimitri lit a cigarette. "The demon that is in question has a rather nasty habit of creating promises that end in paying with the lives that are under its contract. I was hired to eliminate it."

"That still does not explain why you came to me. Why not just kill it and claim the bounty. Not that I am not excited about getting well deserved revenge."

"I need to gain entrance to Solomon. You will double as my prisoner. It is the perfect crime. I will split the profits with you evenly. All we have to do is make sure the bounty on this demon is a resounding success."

"Alright, you have me. I don't mind money, that is the bonus."

The two set out in Dimitri's car to the gate of Solomon. The night air was crisp. The anticipation was eating away at Vincent. His chest burned with the memories of that night in which his parents were killed. He was haunted by it for years, Now he would finally get his chance.

"What can you tell me about this demon?" Vincent asked in the passenger side of a two seating camaro. "How do you know about it?"

"I have been tracking it for some months now. He now has a contract with Beatrix for her freedom. She promises souls for that kind of leverage. She doesn't mind killing humans to pay the debt."

"So he plans to free her, right? What got her in such a foul mood?"

"Who knows? Maybe it is just a domination sequence. One never really knows why one would practice such magic. It is the same as your mother. I say this as the story goes with you."

"What do you mean? What does my mother have to do with this?"

"She was a witch as well, and a famous one at that. She battled against demons in a war what rages in the afterlife. There was only sentiment when it came to having a child. She knew the risks when it came to making deals with demons. Apparently you were worth the trade of her life."

Vincent stared out of the passenger window. "This demon have a name?"

"Of course. It is Xagos. He used to be human, or so the rumors go. It is apparent that he has been around for longer than a human's lifespan, but that is just the extension he gets from devouring human souls."

They veered onto a road that was less traveled by commoners. It was shrouded by trees that blocked the view of the horizon. The sun was coming up and the day anew. It was not uncommon for demon hunters to link up for a bounty, though the business was usually a race in competition for the prize. The only reason Vincent took the partnership with Dimitri was to settle a grievance that was long overdue.

They parked and climbed out of the fancy sports car. "I don't see a prison here." Vincent said. "You sure we are in the right spot?"

"You cannot be deceived by your eyes, seniour. Solomon is a place that is hidden because of all of the inmates. Some of them have immense dominion. Solomon is not even on an earthly plain." Dimitri took the key of Solomon and put it in a stone keep that jutted from the ground. The stone began to glow red and open a doorway that led to a runic enclosure. "I should know, I specialize in capturing demons alive."

"Whatever you say, pal."

They stepped through and saw a gargantuan building. The sky was red and there were some flying demons circling some of the watchtowers that had guards overlooking any prisoner escape plan. Dimitri summoned an ebon that took the form of a rifle with a scope.

"Just in time." Dimitri said looking through the scope. "Take a look." Vincent looked through the scope and saw Xagos mincing words with what appeared to be a warden. He wanted to go and take the demon under right then and there. But Dimitri put a hand on his shoulder. "We don't want to fight the entire compound, seniour. We must tread softly."

"So what, we wait for him to free the prisoner?"

Dimitri put handcuffs on Vincent. "We follow him in."

They followed a trail that led to the entrance. A hulking demon that was half man, half boar watched the front gate in heavy armor that looked like it could withstand a barrage from Ammit. "State your business." Its voice was heavy and monotone.

"I have captured a criminal and wish to trade him for the collection of extradition."

"Nature of the crime?" the demon asked.

"Demonic lithomancy and the murder of humans."

The demon opened the gate to Solomon. "Collect your reward inside."

Diitri removed the handcuffs after they were a safe distance away. "What is lithomancy?"

"Runic use. It is the charm that houses ebon."

"That is illegal?"

"Demons don't take too kindly to weapons that kill their kind."

"Ah, so they abhor exterminators."

"You could say that. Now back to the task at hand."

They began to sneak around looking for traces of Xagos. Solomon was a maze of confusion. It was built in a fashion that did not allow for an easy escape, not to mention the amblings of the guards that were strong demons to begin with. To escape one needed large amounts of fire power.

"How did Beatrix get out one of her minions? Do you know anything about her?" Vincent asked.

"It is the other way around. Someone else is trying to break her out. But due to the key being missing she was willing to make a deal for her freedom."

They traveled in the heart of Solomon. They found Xagos at the cell that kept Beatrix held and stripped dof her unearthly powers. Vincent summoned Ammit and fired it out of impulse. He kept firing like a madman. The bullets seemed to dissipate before they reached the demon.

Xagos stood in its suit with a large smile etched into his wicked face. "I have been expecting you, Vincent. Who knew that you would find me here?" Vincent charged at Xagos with the scythe ebon and slashed, but the blade seemed to pass through the demon without so much as brushing its skin. "You cannot harm me as long as they curse protects you, the one your mother gave before I ate her soul."

"You bastard!" Vincent shouted. He continued to slash with no avail.

The barred door that kept Beatrix at bay opened and her powers were restored. "She on the other hand," Xagos said, "Will have the luxury of killing you. One could say I came prepared to our reunion, wouldn't you say?"

The stitched Beatrix summoned two large needles and held them by their eye. "As my first task of freedom, you will learn why they call me the suture priestess." she said. She leapt with great speed at the demon hunter and they traded blows of bade and steel. Dimitri shot from his ebon but Beatrix blocked the barrage with her needled arms.

Xagos slid his heel across the floor and large flames billowed in a tunnel at the two hunters. Vincent was protected by his mother's dying charm. Xagos could not hurt him as long as the charm was in place. Vincent could not hurt the demon in turn. Dimitri was not so lucky. His arm was singed as he attempted to dodge the flame. Beatrix was on him and pierced the shoulder of Dimitri, pulled the needle through his body and stitched him to the wall.

The other prisoners were chanting in a riot. Beatrix charged at Vincent and pierced his leg, then used that stitch to tie him to the bar. The prisoner that those bars housed grabbed him and began to choke him. Xagos, with a sadistic smile on his face, stepped inches away from the suffocating hunter. "You want me dead, you will face me as a mortal. There will be no protection. I will have your soul, hunter."

Xagos transported Beatrix from the prison with its demonic powers. The bars opened that kept the prisoners. Solomon was in mayhem. Vincent cut the threads that bound him and Dimitri. "We have to get the hell out of here."

"Agreed." said Dimitri. "I put most of these prisoners in here. Looks like they have their chance to get even."

They made their way through winding halls while fighting prisoners and guards alike. When they made it back to the entrance where the boar demon stood blocking their escape. "No one has ever escaped Solomon. You will not be the firsts."

"This just keeps getting better and better." Vincent said to Dimitri. "You have any ebon that can take down this big guy?"

Dimitri summoned an ebon bolas that tied the boar demon to itself. They made a run for the entrance from which they came. "We had better move quickly. If the prisoners find their way to the human world there will be trouble on the streets of Chicago."

"With Beatrix free, there is already trouble. Let's get a move on."

They closed the gate behind them. They were in aches and pains from the daring escape from the prison. They sat catching their breath and licking their wounds. Vincent was defeated at the idea of not killing the one that killed his parents. Not only were they invincible to each other, but they managed to let a witch escape with promises to end the lives of hunters everywhere.

There was nothing to do but return to the lounge. With defeat fresh on the brim of his brow there was nothing to do but brood over their losses. The two hunters sat in a funk of despair while news was spreading across the hunter universe that the notorious hunter killer was now free again. Time was not wasted when it came to fulfilling her promise to collect hunter souls. In time Beatrix would come for Vincent. There was nothing to do but try to free himself from his mother's protection. In time he would kill the demon that killed his parents.

CHAPTER FOUR

News spread all over of Solomon opening and a ruthless witch was freed. Beatrix had already claimed the souls of a few demon hunters. A bounty was put out for her capture. Demon hunters were to be on their toes for the dangerous witch moved with a sense for destruction to all hunters. No one would be given quarter nor knew the extent of her power. If one's soul was captured, it would undoubtedly serve as one of her scarecrow minions.

Vincent sat with a wanted poster in his lap reading the terrors he had unleashed from the prison. He felt obligated to recapture her but was geared more towards the wayward sum for her capture. Xiao Lin called the lounge ready to break the news but Vincent had already known the blunder of the evil witch's release.

"What do you mean you know?" she said, surprised and angry.

"I may have accidentally been there when she escaped." he said reluctantly.

"You helped release a powerful witch and failed to inform me?" Xiao Lin was furious. "And how, pray tell, did you manage that?"

"I was hunting the demon that killed my parents. You know the author wrote me in as the vengeful type, right?" Vincent sat in his armchair, sweating in his set. If anything made him uncomfortable, it was setting off the tiny asian. "All we have to do is recapture her. All will be made right in the world."

"She is a killer. Not like demons. If she finds us, who will protect me?"

"Don't worry." Xiao Lin hung up. "Geez, that woman can be so uptight."

It was time for Vincent to replace his ride. There was a special encampment that housed the specialized motor vehicles for demon hunters. He wanted another mustang and it was one he would get. This one was electric blue with a black racing stripe. It was promised to be reinforced to withstand the barrage of any demon. He drove it with pride. The license plate read "Hunter" just to show his supreme nature when it came to the gig.

The days were turning into months. No one had seen Beatrix and lived. Hunters were missing left and right, turning up in the hunter's newspaper or vanishing into thin air. There had to be a way to stop her, if there was, Vincent would find out. He went to see Veronica in her expertise to find any information that would lead to her capture.

"You expect me to know where to find her?"

"I thought you had connections?"

"It's not like my sources are cohorting with a bloodthirsty witch."

"I'm sure they could find something. Just give it a try."

"Vincent, you asked too much from me. I don't dabble in those kinds of affairs, I thought that was your gimmick. What has you attached to her anyway?"

"She teamed up with the demon that killed my parents. They are out there harvesting souls together. If need be I would end them both."

"What is the demon's name?"

"Xagos."

"You are hunting the reaper king? You are going to get yourself killed."

"Where is the faith?" he jested.

"At your cremation." She turned and went into the nightclub of Incognito. Vincent followed her in. Patrons were beginning to swarm the place in a night of revelry. "Vincent, I'm not going to help you do something you might regret."

Vincent sighed. "Can you at least tell me where Xiao Lin is?"

"I don't know. She left with a woman arm in arm. It was the last I have seen of her."

The music began to play a jazzy mix. Veronica kissed Vincent like she missed him. It was a kiss that she let swell from within in the event the demon hunter would meet an untimely end. She took him by the hand and dragged him to the dance floor. She swayed in his arm and twirled between his fingers. "I don't want to lose you, you idiot."

"I can handle this."

"Then don't be so careless. Take your partner with you. Beatrix is an act of war. Don't you know she kills hunters indiscriminately? Xiao could be very much in danger right now."

Vincent tore away from the dance floor and was on the phone dialing Xiao Lin. There was no answer. He dialed again and only got her message inbox. Here she had the nerve to bite off his head for being occupationally careless but did not answer his call when he was concerned. Hunters filled Incognito's and she was not one of them.

Vincent sped back to the lounge to see if she had returned. He burst open the empty lounge and he began to worry beyond belief. Where could she have gone? He would have to enforce a strict "call often" order in these hours of peril. Xiao Lin was not going to die on his watch. At least not without a life insurance policy. Just then the office phone rang.

"The Demon Hunter's Lounge," he answered "you name them, we slay them."

It was a call from a priest in Japan. "I hear you take care of otherworldly aspects? Have I called the right place?" The man had a very heavy accent. Vincent could barely understand his english.

"Oh yeah, you have the right number. We are like exterminators here. What is the nature of your demonic infestation?"

"A hunter was killed in my province. His body was possessed and he kills people in the walk of night."

"So, he's a demon. This is no easy plight, my friend. It's going to cost you. Japan isn't exactly an average road trip."

"Whatever you need." the priest assured.

Vincent just needed to get a hold of Xiao Lin. She would kill him if he took another job without her. If the little oriental just answered her phone. All he could do was wait. But the longer he waited the more people would die. The last place he could check was her apartment which was not too far from the lounge. He was well on his way there.

He knocked on the door and a brunette scantily clad in nothing but her underwear answered the door.

"Can I help you?" the brunette asked.

"Oh sugar, I am quite sure you can." Vincent said eyeing her curves in manish delight. "You see an asian about this tall with two very dangerous pistols here?"

Xiao Lin appeared in her underwear prompting Vincent's imagination. "You rang?" she asked.

"Remember that time you said you wanted to go to Japan?"

Xiao Lin's eyes lit up. "You finally tied the knot with Veronica!?" She began to dress before Vincent could say another word.

"This one is more business. We leave as soon as possible."

"Will we be taking the gate? I love taking the gate."

"With luck, Incognito will let us jump from his nightclub."

Incognito's was as packed as it had ever been. The hunters that gathered were enough to start an army. Maybe one day they would form a coalition and fight, but money always superseded camaraderie.

The demon of japan skulked an empty field and murdered all who came to slay it. It started with rice field workers armed with pitchforks and farming tools. It was a samurai hired to protect the rice workers that turned deadly when a prayer that was said to bring a good harvest brought mayhem to the honorable lands. Who was responsible for the tickery was never discovered. The soul of the samurai had already perished and was beyond saving. The two hunters had never been to such a land with twisted reasoning.

When they arrived from the gate, they were greeted by the priest that called. He held a talisman that was said to ward off evil and was saying a prayer over the hunters so that they may bring peace to the land once more. He was accompanied by his daughter who held a rod with spell tags on it that brought their ancestors with battle in their memories.

Xiao Lin spoke with them in their native tongue and exchanged greeting as well as information on the whereabouts of the demon. To Vincent it was another day's work. Though to the natives it was blasphemy for such evils to lurk in the body of one of their beloved.

"Just point us in the direction, we will take care of the demon for you." Vincent said, interrupting pleasantries.

"Don't forget to bow." Xiao Lin said, lowering her head in ceremonial efforts.

"Is he a king?" Vincent wondered.

"I am not. My name is Torune. My daughter will accompany you on your endeavour."

"Like hell she will."

Torune was demanding. "It was her idea to call you, the least you could do is accept her help."

"What is with everyone wanting to tag along? This is not a "bring your child to work" day."

"We will accept her help." Xiao Lin said, settling the air. "We would be honored."

"Hey kid, what's your name?" Vincent commanded.

"I am Sakura. It was I that summoned the demon."

"You ought to be more careful when saying prayers. How long has it been since it was summoned?"

Sakura was bashful in her answer. "Three weeks. Twenty have fallen to the blade of the demon. We cannot waste another second."

They were off to the rice field. There was a waterflow amongst the field that gave nourishment to the grain. They traveled throughout the field looking for signs of the demon. Vincent had battled many demonkind before, but he was in for a real treat when it came to battling one that was skilled in the art of the samurai. Sakura told them the man tales of warriors from her homeland. She warned them that it would not be an easy battle.

Sakura was dressed in samurai gear as well. She held a naginata: a japanese spear that samurai used against multiple opponents. Xiao Lin was impressed by the preparation that Sakura yielded and by the tenacity of such a young huntress that mimicked her own.

"What do you know of the one that gave you the prayer?" Xiao Lin asked.

"She tricked me. I brought great warrior shame and dismay to a samurai's honor."

"She is most likely a witch." Vincent chimed. "You can't have demons without a puppeteer."

Sakura's face grew stoic. "She will pay with her life." Hot blood flowed through her veins. She wanted to restore peace to her land. The only way to defeat the evil she had brought to her prosperitus land was to atone for the trouble she caused.

The path of Vincent was the same in comparison only to the recent plight in Solomon. The hunter could relate, but with information small on Beatrix there was nothing he could do but continue the wares of a demon hunter. In time, he would settle the score with Xagos as well. That was after he made himself vulnerable to the demon's touch. That itself was a danger for the power of Xagos was not yet calculated to any certain extent.

Sakura gestured for the three of them to quiet their chattering. She lowered herself into the tall grass and pointed to a figure moving in the distance. "There, look." Someone was moving in the rice field. It looked like another worker. Soon a suit of armor was on him, blade first into his chest. "The demon is here." Sakura whispered.

"What are we waiting for?" Vincent started towards the demon with a freshly dabbed with blood blade. "Hey ugly, you caused enough trouble. I think it's about time you and I had a long talk about how to treat the living."

The demon's eyes were glowing a purple hue. It raised its blade and slashed at the wind to clear it of blood. It lowered the cold steel slowly and locked its demonic eyes on Vincent. Vincent called forth the scythe looking for a workout with the hooked blade. He whirled it, cutting the wind. They clashed blades and sparks flew. The demon was fast. Faster than Vincent has anticipated. He received a cut on his arm. The demon was clearly a skilled warrior, but possessed enhanced talents.

Sakura charged the demon with her spear, but the demon parried and slashed her leg. The demon's eyes flowed behind the hanya mask. Xiao Lin summoned her pistols and joined the fray, shooting relentlessly. The demon rolled onto the earth dodging and blocked bullets with the back of its blade.

Vincent surprised it from behind and pierced through its armor.

The demon went limp, buckling at the knee. It then grabbed the blade and pushed itself free. The nature of this demon was set at immortal Vincent figured. It would fight until its foe was defeated. That was perhaps so many farmers had fallen to its malicious tendency.

"What the hell kind of prayer did you use to call this thing, anyway?" Vincent said to Sakura. The demon slashed faster and faster, Vincent could barely keep up.

"I was told it was prayer for the harvest."

Maybe we should find the witch." Xiao Lin said, still shooting.

"We can't just leave this thing here." Sakura said, contesting leaving the demon there to slay more people.

Vincent summoned Ammit and shot the samurai at point blank range in the face. Its head shot back and its mask went flying. When the dust from the gunfire cleared they saw its face. The skin was gray, its eyes were sunken in as if the life force of the samurai had been drained. The spray of bullets from Ammit did not slow the demon in the least bit. It raised its sword to strike Vincent a lethal blow.

Sakura severed the demon's head. It fell to the ground but the body kept on swinging. Vincent cut off the arm that had the sword in it, then it was off with its legs. The demon fell to the ground, twitching for more combat.

"That is one plucky demon." Vincent said, recalling his ebons. "We will be taking our payment now.

It was then, just over the horizon, there were ten more samurai demons inching closer to the three hunters. "We had better get out of here." Xiao Lin said. "We can't take on them like this."

"You will get your pay when we get out of here alive." Sakura said with fleet in her foot.

They escaped from the rice fields and went back to the temple. There were signs of a struggle. Torune, in his white robes, was stained with blood and lying at the gate. "Papa!" Sakura shouted. She rushed over to his side. Vincent and Xiao Lin were shortly after her. "What happened here?"

"The demons," Torune said, spitting up blood. "They followed the two hunters here. They killed everyone in the village. All I could do was defend us, barely."

"There has to be a way to defeat them." Xiao Lin said, somberly.

Torune shuffled to his feet. "There is only one way. Defeat the witch that keeps them using this." He summoned an ebon. It was a katana named Yatagarasu. Then he passed away in the arms of his daughter.

"Papa!" Sakura shouted. "Papa, no!"

Torune's eyes rolled into the back of his head when he died. Though the end of his life was prematurely determined. His eyes began to glow with demonic rebirth. He grabbed Xiao Lin by the neck with both hands and began to choke her. Vincent severed his head, then Torune's body fell to the temple floor.

"You killed my father!" Sakura shouted. She charged Vincent with the naginata.

"What are you doing, woman!" Vincent shouted back. "He was already gone."

Sakura slashed and slashed. Vincent dodge trying to calm her down. Xiao Lin would have died if he had not delivered the blow to the shinto monk Torune. Xiao Lin was trying to stop Sakura from killing her partner. After Sakura accepted the death of her father she fell to the temple floor in tears. She held up Yatagarasu, her eyes in the reflection of the blade. "We must kill the witch." she whispered. "I will avenge my father."

Vincent put his hand on her shoulder. "We will be right there with you."

Days passed with no clue as to where to find the witch. There was no way of telling where she would appear or what she wanted. If they knew they could set a trap and lure her out into the open. There were only skirmishes with more samurai demons. They showed every night. That was the only occurrence that was promised to the hunters. Villagers would die, they would always arrive a few moments too late.

They paused to take a break from all the fighting at a tea house, sat in official robes and everything. It was Xiao Lin's idea to decide to start taking in the site. Sakura needed time to mourn her father's death and the recovery of her new ebon Yatagarasu needed some figuring out.

Yatagarasu was a unique weapon passed down from the gods Izanami and Izanagi: the mother and father of the creation of Japan. It was a useful tool in the regards that it could summon shinobi warriors crafted of pure stealth and shadow. It was used to battle the great and terrible Nobunaga Oda in his return in the 1800's. There was another ebon called the Onimusha that aided in vanquishing the demon warlord.

"We must summon the witch to kill her. It is the only way." Sakura said, brooding over some herbal tea. "I will save the Shinto Province of Japan."

"How did you come across the witch the first time?" Xiao Lin asked humbly, not to set off the rage of Sakura. Xiao wanted nothing but to befriend her as she empathized with the sentiment of losing her caretaker. Vincent on the other hand was chomping noodles and enjoyed fighting in the endless war.

The tea shop was quiet. There were other ronin enjoying the patronage as well as the three demon hunters. "I said a prayer I found on an ancient scroll and suddenly she appeared from the shadows. The prayer was encoded with a demonic essence that released the witch's power. She was waiting for someone foolish enough to tap into her realm. My father is dead because of me."

WItches were powerful. Dealing with them came at costly prices. No one was ever free of guilt when it came to them. Some were tethered to them by the oaths that were sworn to summon them. Though not all witches were that of the dark path. This just so happened to be one that brought all hell with her.

"I know what you seek." a man said with his head lowered, sipping tea. "What you want can be accomplished through a power I am familiar with."

"You're looking to kill the witch as well, eh?" Vincent said, finishing his bowl. "Tell you what, the bounty is already ours."

"I have no need for your money. I am the one who sealed the witch away. It was a duty passed down through the bloodline. One could say your friend encroached on my family's affairs."

Sakura welled with tears. "What do you know."

"I know you now wield the Yatagarsu." He pointed to the sheathed sword that leaned against the table. "That is a powerful ebon able to command an army."

"I am not worthy." Sakura said, her face drippied in a sombre reconciliation. "I must clear my aura."

Xaio Lin attempted to console the warrior's regret. The wound cut so deeply to the huntress for bringing about such a trial to her path. Sakura's Japanese pride was wounded. "We will get her. All we have to do is try."

"We aren't exactly on our heels. It can't be so hard to kill a witch." Vincent said, trying to ease the dark tension in the tea shop. "We just call her up and boom, one for the books."

"I am Shin." the man said from a table over. I believe I can help you." He summoned an ebon that was a samurai sword. "But first we take care of these demons."

"What demons?" Vincent asked.

The ronin in the shop all drew their blades. More of the samurai demons were just out in the dirt road, blades were everywhere. The witch was collecting the bodies of the warriors she had killed, replenishing her ranks. Her motives were unknown. There were dozens of the raised demons. This would be a battle that had not been seen since the resurrection of the Oda clan.

A few demons made their way into the tea shop. Some of them had bows and arrows. An arrow sailed towards Shin. He flipped the tea tale up on its side and blocked the projectile. The three hunters all drew their weapons, readying for the advancement. Demons climbed through the tea shop window and soon the shop was doused in blades.

Xiao Lin fired a flurry of bullets. Vincent was blade locked with two demons. Sakura used the Yatagarsu, which gave her partial armor, and it gave her the power that was needed to kill the demons. Shin was an elegant warrior. It was later discovered that he used the ebon Onimusha, a link passed down in his bloodline. He was a hunter of

Japan. Sakura would later team up with him and occupy the Shinto Province officially.

The ronin and hunters battled in the road for the freedom of their province. Vincent and Xiao Lin aided the warrior land with valor. As soon as the last demon was eliminated the warriors let out a victory shout. Vincent's blood never ran so hot. He felt it was a scene from a movie. Xiao Lin was elated just to be a part of the macabrey.

Shin led the trio of hunters to his temple where the bloodline of his clan participated in the practice of what they call "Katas": the form of combat. Since both the Yatagarasu and the Onimusha were once allied in previous wars, Shin felt Sakura was obligatory to his clan and in exchange he saw an opportunity to vanquish an ancient evil.

"How long have demons been in Japan?" Vincent asked Shin.

"Since Izanagi's first son, Susano." Shin said. "At the union of Izanagi and Izanami there was an error, causing their first born to become a demon. The Onimusha have been vanquishing the demonic kind ever since. I am the current proprietor of the ancient code."

"How are we going to go about this witch thing. She has not shown her face. What are the terms of summoning her?"

"She is elusive, sure. She comes preying on the prayers of the innocent. We call her offering ourselves as a sacrifice. Then we kill her." Shin said while preparing white sand. It would be used to trap the witch and prevent escape.

Sakura chimed in through her gloom. "How long will it take?"

"Shin said, unaware of the troubles that ached Sakura. "We execute her at midnight. We go to the mountains, away from the villagers so there are no more casualties."

The four of them made their way up the hills and through sacred forests so that the spread of the dominion of the witch was limited. To summon this particular witch meant to call upon her powers by coaxing part of her land to a certain area. They would encircle her with blessed sand so that she could not escape and she would be rendered at mercy to the will of the ebon that would be used to vanquish her. Then Vincent would collect his pay and then it was back to Chicago where he had to deal with the Witch Beatrix.

CHAPTER FIVE

The moon was lit the way that was the stuff of dreams. It was a high full orb that made the bamboo forest at the top of the Shin's mountain temple. There they would summon the witch that left a torrent of terror across Japan. Sakura would be the one to resummon the witch. She wanted to as she felt responsible for her release. She stood readily in the center of a transcribed circle of white sand while focusing her energies on the task at hand.

The air was tinted with a purple hue as she said the words that would conjure an evil of evils. She had done so once before and it cost the many lives of fallen warriors and villagers. Vincent, Xiao Lin, and Shin hid in the forest awaiting the opportune time to strike. It would not be long before the witches reckoned. Soon, Japan would be free of an evil reign.

Sakura's eyes cut to a shadowy figure that moved elegantly with the essence of beauty. A woman with a missing lower jaw stood nude as she sauntered to the warrior Sakura. The hair was long and she wore bandages over her eyes. Sakura did not hesitate as she drew Yatagarasu ready to kill the evil that which walked toward her.

"You beckoned me." the witch said. "To what do I owe this ritual?"

Sakura was filled with a passionate rage. "I am Sakura Tanaka. You are responsible for my father's death. I am here to kill you."

"Was it not you that called me? You are responsible. Your hand is the guilty one." The witch's voice was choked. "You cannot kill me. My power is beyond your reasoning."

"Prepare yourself." Sakara said. Her right arm was clad in black and red armor from her ebon. Her hair was pulled back in a ponytail to keep it from blocking her vision. She was ready to trade her life for this moment.

The witch's tongue that hung from her missing jaw slithered from her mouth. It was ten feet long before she used it to loop a hand blade. "You weak fool. Now you suffer at the hands of Ren, the blood priestess."

"Do you think it's a little arrogant to say your own name before a fight?" Xiao Lin asked Vincent from the shadows.

"I would never do it." he said. "God forbid I add any negative aspects like that to the story."

Sakura moved slowly toward Ren, keeping a watchful eye on the blade in case the witch decided to strike. She then charged and gave a slash that was perfect in its form. Ren simply ducked and whipped her tongue so that the blade would pierce the dark haired warrior. Sakura took a blow to the shoulder and bled warm blood. She slashed at the tongue to free the witch from the burden of a weapon but Ren coiled it in reprieve. She then pounced to Sakura and flew overhead and wrapped her tongue around her throat.

Sakura felt the life slipping from her. Shin came from the flank and severed Ren's tongue. "Are you alright?" he asked the fainting Sakura.

"I will be fine. But we have trouble."

Samurai demons emerged from the thicket of the bamboo forest. There were at least twenty in total that surrounded them. Ren hissed and took off in a rolling fog in an attempt to escape.

Vincent stopped her at the gunpoint of Ammit. "Why don't you slow down there, little lady." he said with a finger on the hair trigger. Before he could deliver the fatal blow an arrow came and shot him through the forearm. "God damn it!" he shouted. "Who in the hell writes these kinds of surprises!?"

Xiao Lin's ebon fired at the demons rapidly. She aimed for the joints to at least immobilize the immortal creatures. Shin locked swords with three of them, showing off his skill for combat. Vincent yanked the arrow from his arm. Ren was already speeding away and Sakura trailed behind her.

Vincent used Ammit to shoot the limbs from the samurai demons. No matter how many were slain, more seemed to appear in their place. Shin darted to the ones that had arrows and diced them with extreme speed.

"Should one of us go and help Sakura?" Xiao lin asked.

"She is on her own path." Shin said. "She must recover her honor and slay the witch with Yatagarau."

"Yea." Vincent said. "We have our own troubles." He blocked the blade of one of the demons with his scythe, then whirled it splitting one of the samurai in two.

Xiao Lin was surrounded but was kept out of danger by the swiftness of Shin's Onimusha. He unleashed its full power becoming regaled in red insect armor. Wings beat with a hum as he flew around the battlefield chopping and slicing. His hair grew long and white and followed him like a tiger with a tail.

When the air was quiet and the last demon was slain, all ebon were called away. "Now, about that witch." Vincent trailed his words.

That was not the end of the demon encroachment, however. The earth began to tremble beneath their feet. A giant four armed oni had shown itself with a large iron club with spiked decorating along the neck of the weapon. Despite its large size it moves swift enough to bash Shin a good distance away. He was knocked unconscious and laid there in danger. More samurai emerged from behind the oni, firing arrows and advancing with swords.

"Son of a bitch, you have to be fucking kidding me." Vincent said about the events to come.

He resummoned his blade and attempted to cut the oni. Its thick skin prevented it from harm. He was swatted like a fly. Xiao Lin galloped backwards while firing her ebon at the samurai. "We have to go." she said.

"Yea, no kidding." Vincent said scrambling to his feet. "I think I broke a rib. Veronica is not going to like this."

"Where is Shin?"

"Hell if I know."

Xiao Lin spotted him a little ways into the forest. "There!" They rushed over to him laying on the forest floor. He was still breathing. Vincent hoisted him up and leveraged him over his shoulder.

"We must make it to the edge of the sand." Shin said, weakened.

"You don't have to tell me twice, come on." They rushed uneasily as quickly as their bodies would allow them. As they ran, arrows pierced them in the back. Perhaps they had bitten off more than they could chew. They were being tailed by demons that they simply did not have the strength to conquer anymore. One of their warriors at arms were down and all they could do was run. It would be up to Sakura to kill the witch and release the demons back to the underworld from which they came.

They made a mad dash to the outer edge of the sand. Xiao Lin crossed it to safety. Vincent stumbled carrying the heavy weight of Shin and fell. An arrow sailed it way to him and he blocked it with his sword. The oni was upon Vincent. It grabbed his leg and slammed him to the ground. Xiao Lin gave as much cover fire as she could. The samurai were just too much.

Vincent limped to safety. The three of them sat outside the sand circle where the demons could not tread. "What about Sakura?" Xiao Lin asked, full of worry and concern. "We can't just leave her in there."

"We must put trust in her." Shin said. "She is the last line so that Shinto can persevere."

The forest was quiet around Sakura. Her mind was sharp and focused. She did not let the witch slip from her site until Ren hid in the fog. It was thick but she could hear the witch. Ren stopped running because she reached the end of the sand circle. It was time to finish what Sakura started.

"You have reached your end, witch!" Sakura called out. "It is time you have paid for what you have done to these lands." Sakura used Yatagarasu to call forth shadow shinobi to comb the area. "You can not hide from me forever."

A kunai sliced through the fog. Sakura caught it just before it reached her. The blade gave away the witch's location. Sakura moved swiftly as if she was the wind itself. Her vision tunnel as she caught sight of Ren. Then she commanded her shinobi and they converged on the witch with their blades. Ren was pierced from all sides.

"I will return." Ren said. "I will bring the underworld with." Then her body went out in purple flames.

The demons that followed Vincent and the others died out as well. Sakura walked past the three, very weary and stoic. "It is done." she said. "Time to collect your pay."

It was two weeks time before they were ready to travel back to Chicago. Broken ribs, arrow holes, and deep bruises all took time to heal. They stayed in Shin's temple where the medics tended to their wounds.

"I think it's time we head back home." Vincent said, pulling his clothes over his bandages. "I'd say we are all done here."

"You always have a home here in Japan." Shin said, patting him on the shoulder.

"Do you have any clue as to where my partner went?"

"If I am not mistaken, she went with Sakura to the river. I believe she was saying goodbye."

Vincent krept behind some trees. He saw Xiao Lin and Sakura kissing. Leave it to Xiao to have all the charms to swoon another woman. When he finally decided to break the intimate moment, Sakura jumped as if she were doing something shameful.

"Sorry to break up this heated moment but it is high time we made it back home."

"So soon?" Xiao Lin said, disappointed. "We haven't even gone shopping."

"Make a special trip here to see me." Sakura said. "I will show you all of the sites."

"That'd be wonderful." Xiao Lin said in excitement. "I can't wait to see all of Japan."

"Hopefully I can call you at my pleasure. Now that I am an official demon huntress there is bound to be trouble."

Vincent said "Call us if you need us. And don't skip out on the check.

Soon they were back in Chicago. Veronica was furious that Vincent almost got himself killed. She was worried sick. They spent their first night back together up in arms over the tale of Ren. Ultimately Veronica kissed his wounds. She forgave him for his recklessness. She went with him back to the Demon Hunter's Lounge and they spent the night without their clothes. Xiao Lin told Incognito about her new Japanese lover. For his strictest of way he sure did fancy the idea of two women going at it.

Days went by and the demon hunting world had its feathers ruffles. A few hunters went missing, probably by the hands of Xagos and Beatrix. Either way the hunters put out an all points bulletin that no demon hunter should travel no less than four. With more scarecrows lurking about to capture their souls, it was a defensive measure should the need to do battle should ever arise. This meant that it was time for Vincent to find some new recruits. There was only one place to find such initiates.

There was a famed demon hunter academy where the ones who attended were usually orphaned by the makings of those of other worldly origin that had nefarious tendencies. It was where Vincent found his illustrious partner of chinese descent. The world's top notch class of hunters were groomed there and usually lived to tell the tale. It was time to recruit once more. With Beatrix on the loose, the need to expand the Demon Hunter's Lounge became a paramount necessity.

Xiao Lin was ecstatic that she could get a few new partners to help with the tidings of the Lounge. Vincent was just happy that he had made enough money to embark on such an endeavour. Though, one would have to pass a series of tests to officially become a demon hunter. The time to have a pick of the graduating class was at hand. Beatrix needed to be stopped. Though Vincent's selfish plans to slay Xagos could never be revealed to the administration. The personal vendetta would surely deny him of initiates as such tendencies were forbidden. Never hunt a demon with personal motives.

Veronica sat looking for the number to Eros Academy, the suite that housed the finest hunters to be. It was lost in a stack of papers that Incognito kept in his office. It would be hours before she could put a dent in the search. Incognito never really took apprentices but every now and again he could pass off assignments to the class to show some alumni ties to the place from which he graduated himself. Vincent did not partake in the Eros Academy. Instead he was personally trained by the dark skinned hunter Incognito, thus taking on some of his best traits.

Xiao Lin specialized in gathering information and was awarded her ebon upon graduation. Needless to say she took them with a flirt of fancy and adapted rather quickly to the routine that Vincent proposed. She never complained about the money when they were short of it. She was chipper when it came to her duties. "I wonder what this year's students are like." she said to Veronica, helping search the phone books and sifted through some of the papers. "If they are anything like what I sat through it's going to be a real treat."

"If we can just find that number we will be in business." Veronica said, feeling the weight of stress from rummaging for hours on end. "Where is Vincent? Shouldn't he be helping us?"

"The boss is ordering chinese take out. You know how he gets when he is in the mood for something oriental."

"Is that why he hired you?"

"Don't be silly. He hired me because I am the best at what I do."

"What do you do exactly?" Veronica said, flustered.

"I find us work and every now and again track down ebon that are up for grabs." Xiao Lin was sensing a bit of feminie jealousy. Maybe it was because she worked so closely with the person that Veronica doted on.

"Well, whoever he hires better not be snot nosed brats with god complexes. That is one sure fire way to get yourself killed, or worse release a blood crazed witch with a soul stealing demon."

"Don't be so hard on him. I'm sure it was just an accident."

"I'm sure it was."

Vincent sat in the seating area of his favorite chinese restaurant. He waited patiently for his name to be called on so he could drive back to the nightclub and chow down. He had not been to the academy in some years, not since Xiao Lin. The application would bind the students to him financially. With all the work he had been putting in, there was no problem in the monetary department. All that mattered was that his rookies did not die.

It was not long before he was on the road in his mustang. Chicago, and the crisp air, was all he needed to ease his mind after the troubles in Japan. All he needed was good food and even better company. He could not ask for more than this.

When he arrived at Incognito's night had fallen and the club was doing its song and dance of patrons filling the dance floor. Xiao Lin was feeling her groove and Veronica, well she was still looking for that all important number. Incognito met Vincent outside with his signature cigar and was smoking like a freight train.

"Are you treating her right?" Incognito asked, billowing.

"Uh, what?"

"Veronica. Are you upholding the standards of a gentleman?"

"I like to think that I don't cause her too much trauma. She is a tough cookie at times. Why do you ask?"

"She has been working all day for you. Make sure you do something nice for her. I like my staff to be happy."

"You know I'm going to marry her someday. I like her happiness, too."

"If you don't perform as the man you are going to be, I will kick your ass myself." Incognito took the chinese food and began to head inside his nightclub. "I will keep my eye on you, son."

"Of course, asshole."

The four of them sat in the office with the walls beating to the music just outside the office. Veronica took a break on that number. She was not sure she would ever find it. Though the time eating with ones she was familiar with gave her a sense of happiness and ease.

"What are we looking for in terms of new members, boss?" Xiao Lin asked with a mouth full of noodles.

"Don't hire any women." Veronica said, reaching for spring rolls.

"I have no idea." Vincent said. "Maybe some folks with a good mode of transportation. Ebon specialists are not bad either."

Xiao Lin teemed with enthusiasm. "Oooh, I hope they have cool weapons. I am a sucker for things that go "boom" when there's stuff."

"Don't hire any women." Veronica repeated.

"Whoever it is had better like chinese food." Incognito said.

Vincent laughed. "Oh they will. It is definitely a fan favorite around here."

"Vincent, what is up with Veronica. She seems a little on edge lately." Xiao Lin whispered to Vincent, hoping that Veronica did not hear.

Vincent wondered what the deal was. Everyone was worried about Veronica. Incognito basically said he was neglecting her. Xiao Lin was now probing him. Was there something he was missing. She did not chew him out like she usually does. He thought maybe she was giving him a break. He would take her out that night and give her some extra love and attention.

He drove her to Lake Michigan. She was quiet in the car. The music on the radio was low and was all that cluttered the silent drive. He bought her ice cream and a teddy bear. She had not said a word the entirety of the trip. He held her hand and even cracked a few jokes. There was nothing that seemed to sway her from the funk that she was in.

The truth is Veronica carried secrets within her. There were things that ate away at her daily that made her unsure she wanted to be close with anyone. She found solace in the company of the man she wanted to be with. She was even grateful for the bear that Vincent named Soap. He named it that so that it could wash away whatever was ailing her.

"You have been quiet all night, my dear. Is there something you want to say? What is bothering you?"

"Vincent, I'm bad."

"I know, it's one of the reasons I like you."

"No, I mean really bad."

"It can't be so bad that you can't tell me. I am here for you and always will be. Come on, you can tell me anything. I don't want you to feel like you can't tell me something that bothers you. What bothers you bothers me, too."

"It has a lot to do with my family. My father in particular. There is a lot that I have not told you about the woman I am to be. It is the future that frightens me, Vincent. A future I am not sure you can handle."

"I can handle just about anything. Remember that time in Egypt?"

Veronica smiled. "I know, lover boy. I was there."

"Something about the gods really puts hair on the chest."

She chuckled. "I don't want the image in my mind of you having a hairy chest."

"It's a turn of phrase."

"No it bloody well isn't."

They sat on the roof of the mustang. Veronica clutched Soap in her arms. The lights from the mall district lit up the area in a sepia style ambience. It had been a while since the two of them had spent time like this together. It was usually work and slaying demons. It was time well spent. With Veronica, and her shy and timid side, it was what she needed but could not rely on. The secrets that she kept were a threat to all humankind. It would be too long coming when events that would shape the foundation of her and Vincent's relationship took hold. But what could she tell the man she loved?

Vincent drove her back to her apartment and kissed her goodnight. "You know, about you recruiting new hunters?"

"Yeah, I am looking forward to it actually."

"Don't hire any women."

She turned and left him without a word after that. He drove back to the lounge waiting on calls from people that had work for him. His mind settled on Veronica. He could see that she was hiding something. He felt it best not to press the matter. He was the type to wait and let her say the truth when she wanted to. It was like everyone could sense that air about her. The air that brought doom and gloom to the ones around her. He texted Xiao Lin.

Xiao Lin did not reply and he figured she had another lady over at her apartment. He would definitely have to impede on her when it came to the work initiative. Vincent usually let it slide but this was a bit much. She would have to answer him or he would have to come up with some sort of penalty system. That asian was definitely a wild thing.

Vincent then got a text from Veronica. The message had the number to Eros Academy and the words "You're welcome" underneath. He would wait to call the Academy the following morning. He and Xiao Lin would go to check out what new talents awaited The Demon Hunter's Lounge. It would be the first time more than the two of them worked officially on demon hunting.

Vincent decided to sleep in the lounge and it was some of the best sleep he had gotten in his life. He dreamt of his mother and her delicious meals. He dreamt of his father and them fishing. Then he dreamt of Xagos killing his parents. It was as if he was reliving that night all those years ago. He was stirred awake after he fired Ammit at the wall in attempts to kill the demon in his slumber.

"Wicked." he said to the empty room.

He had to be careful. More shocks like that, he would never be able to move in with Veronica.

CHAPTER SIX

The bridge between worlds was all that separated Eros Academy from the sullen streets of Chicago. When one controls an Ebon as large as an entire school, one would need to keep it veiled with a certain spell to keep the norm from one's own intentions. Vincent was nothing short of a phone call away in his demon killing mustang. Xiao Lin trailed loosely behind him on her motor bike. They were on their way to collect graduates from the academy. How else did they plan on taking on a bitter heart witch and a blood thirsty demon that preyed upon the wishes of those lesser to it.

Traces of Beatrix haunted the mind of the demon hunter Vincent. Stories of hunters going missing was just the least of his worries. As long as he could keep his initiates alive, he would be better for increasing the work when it came to the lounge. The bind that his mother sealed upon him kept Xagos from touching him. In return, Xagos put a bind on himself that kept Vincent from doing the same. Somehow the bind must be broken, making Vincent vulnerable to the demon, yet freed him to exact bloody vengeance on the demon that killed his parents.

All it took was the flip of a switch on the dashboard to open the bridge between realms. The academy was a massive construct that housed thousands of potential applicants. Vincent only needed two. What would he find there at the academy? Only processing the initiates with demon hunting collaborations would find the seemingly worthy.

Vincent parked at the front gate and walked the extra mile to the front door with Xiao Lin at his side. There were two students manning the front gate in the uniforms of those chosen to work the grounds. It was not likely that the Eros Academy would be attacked, but the walls were reinforced with demon killing weapons. Not to mention the fact that all in attendance was enough to say that there was an army on standby.

Xiao Lin felt waves of nostalgia upon returning to the academy. It had been a few years since she set foot in the great hall. There was a kiosk that held all the paperwork for applying for graduates. Vincent took two identical forms and filled out the requirements for who he was looking for, that is to say he applied for a certain skill set.

He was looking for someone well endowed in charms and someone that had an ebon that was good for transportation. They would accept anyone that could break his family bind and someone that made it easier to jump around the planet in the search for any demonic affairs or newly crafted ebon. They would have to wait a week before they received an answer. Any student that fit the requirement could apply, so long as they were ready to graduate from practice to practicality.

Xiao Lin took the lead when it came to advocating the positions at the Demon Hunter's Lounge. She held seminars in which students interested in moving to the human world's Chicago to amp up their tutelage into full on demon hunting. Vincent spent time dueling with the students to see if they were ready to sample the life and limb aspect when it came to battle. Most of them put up a good fight. Not all were classified as "ready for war with Xagos." Though in time there was a shining star when it came to judging aptitude for battle. His name was Louis. He was the proprietor of a charmbreaker sword. He held his own in combat and was skilled in severing ties that bound human and demonkind.

"What makes you want to join the Lounge?" Vincent asked Louis. They sat on the center circle of the charm circle that Louis crafted to keep the sound out. He was a private and quiet and smoked a cigarette to keep his nerves calm.

"I know it sounds bland, but I have never been in a large city. I want to explore while killing off those that would bind humans to bogus contracts that costs lives, or worse."

"What is the nature of your ebon?"

Louis inhaled long and dryly his tobacco. "Demons have the binding contracts sey in their bones. Many use souls to prolong their life. They can not establish a connection with the human world without being bound by the contracts. I sever them, freeing the soul of the victim."

The questioning led Vincent to his own ambition. He wanted to know if he could sever the bond that kept him from killing Xagos. "And what do you know of bindings made of holy light?"

"It's not as simple as killing a demon, my ebon. That sort of thing can kill the human that it is bound to. The only way to remove such a bind is to have the person who cast it remove it or one could have real trouble staying all kinds of alive."

That was quite a shame. If such a thing were true Vincent could never kill Xagos, for his mother was already dead. "Any other ebon?"

Louis rolled up his sleeve. "Tons."

"Looks like we will be taking you on our next adventure, Louis. Welcome aboard."

It would be some time before he could find the next candidate, or at least one that fit the needs of the crew. Vincent figures he would expand the Lounge into something sporty to make more money to pay his underlings. He thought of a restaurant where demon hunters could gather and exchange information. He was not ready to cook however. He settled it in his mind that the Lounge would become a guild. There hunters would pay for information and exchange temporary contracts in the expedition of hunting occupation.

Finally after a month of interviews Xiao Lin brought forth a candidate that she thought was perfect for the Lounge. Her name was Rachel. She specializes in tuning gates and drove an ebon that was classified as a war machine. It was equipped with a gatling gun, a few rocket launchers, spiked tires, and radio com frequencies that traced magic from all sorts of directions. It was primarily based on hunting witches. Demons were extra on her hunting radar. All of this was inside an iron reinforced van.

"There is a witch on the loose in the windy city. How would you say, likely of you tracing her before she kills every hunter in the area?"

"All I would need to do is catch her using her powers and I could easily trace her leyline to her exact location. My van is like a spider web. All we would need to do is drive around the city and place ebon markers in prime locations and it would be like waiting for a spider to catch a fly. Could take a couple days to set up, but once the jet in fueled we could find her in seconds."

"Do you have any other ebon?"

"The van is my only ebon. It is stocked with all the weaponey needed to stop an army of demons."

Vincent smiled. "We could have used you back in Japan."

"Why?" Rachel asked. "What happened in Japan?"

"You ever face a demon samurai army that never went down unless you had an ebon that seemed to be made of demons themselves?"

"I reckon I can't say that I have."

"Stick with us and it will be the only tune you sing to. You're hired."

The last words of veronica stuck out in his mind. He did not want to go against her wishes, for what lover intentionally stepped on the toes of his infatuation. It could not be helped. The new team would set a course back to the streets of Chicago. He would just have to be hated when it came to showing the new team at the nightclub.

Louis and Rachel drove the van they named Tags; for collecting the official bodies of demons and witches, like military trophies. Vincent led the caravan. Xiao Lin weaved between them at her leisure on the motorbike. They were off to Incognito's to commemorate the new beginnings of the Demon Hunter's Lounge latest expansion. Veronica, after she saw Rachel, left and soon Vincent would pay for not heeding her cry.

The new crew all sat in the nightclub during the day when it was empty, sipping on brandy and whatever else Incognito would let them get away with. Rachel sat in denim shorts and a cowgirl hat. Louis sat in all black cloth with a scarf wrapped around his neck. It seemed he was high strung and edgy. Incognito saw a little bit of Vincent in him and thought they could have been brothers.

"So Incognito, what exactly do you bring to the table when it comes to our occupation?" Rachel asked, her voice heavy with a southern accent.

"I used to be a hunter just like you four set out to be. I have retired and opened this nightclub and serve as a veteran. This is my haven for the demon hunter kind. Now I just collect relics and other demon hunter tools that serve humankind to the best of my capabilities."

"You sure are my type." Rachel said. "If you were a few years younger I would have you wrapped around my finger."

Incognito chucked. "Careful, it is never too old to learn a new trick."

They chatted and drank until it was time to open the club. Hunters came from all over the way they usually did when it came to Incognito's. The crew danced and mingled. Surprisingly Louis flirted all over when it came to huntresses. Xiao Lin had her hands all over Rachel, even wore her cowgirl hat to mark her territory. Vincent spent the time in a stupor trying to get a hold of Veronica by phone.

He felt like an idiot. However, work was work. She had nothing to worry about. It was not as if Vincent was going to put the moves of his underling. Xiao Lin had already smoothed her way up Rachel's shorts. They even smeared lipstick across each other's face. No matter what though Vincent felt a sense of guilt. His hands were tied. He pissed off the woman he cared about. He had no idea how he would make it up to her.

After a night out on the town Vincent and the crew stepped foot in the Lounge for the first time. Tags was parked on the street since the garage only fit Xiao Lin's motorbike and the mustang. The crew stepped inside and eyes were wide at the lack of space. There was room for expansion. After all with the new initiates it was time to grow. Vincent put in the lookout for larger facilities.

"So cramped." Louis said, dropping his mystery bag on the love seat that sat in the corner. "How much are you going to be paying us?"

It was a manner of nerve to answer. "You get paid a partial amount based on the work we find. Put a hand in and you will find this is quite the profit." Vincent said.

Rachel spent time outside fine tuning Tags. It had to be maintained in order for optimal functionality. She set up the tracers for around the city. It was the only way to set the parameters to trace Beatrix. Vincent assigned her the role to trace that witch. It was her first and prudent order of business. The phone did not ring so she had plenty of time for the set up. It took a few hours but in time the crew took the van and it was the enthusiastic Xiao Lin that got to fire the tracers around the city.

Louis began looking for charm breakers at Vincent's request. He searched his laptop on demonic wares that may have led to any clue as to that which he was tasked with. Vincent of course did not tell the whole truth about his past. It was the only way to ensure progress was made on eliminating Xagos, the demon that was free to do as he pleased. There was never any real notifications on Xagos' ongoings. It was hit or miss. Vincent kept Dimitri's number in case Xagos reared his ugly head.

The crew worked diligently day in and day out on the static assignments. Xiao Lin never stopped flirting with Rachel. It was rather odd for Rachel to take a liking to the ambitious Xiao Lin. Xiao Lin was very persuasive when it came to flirting with the female component. SOmehow she always got what she wanted without breaking any hearts. Louis was impressed with the progress Xiao Lin made with the now bisexaul cowgirl.

Things were quiet in Chicago. No real threats were reported, at least any that would be considered non-amatuer. Vincent only took jobs that paid large amounts. He had to start thinking even bigger because of the new team. Veronica did not answer any of his calls. She had to be let down. Vincent wondered if it was jealousy. However, when duty called....

There was a call that tempted the newly found hunter coalition. It was a call from Arlington, Texas. There was a murder of a demon hunter and it was to be investigated by someone that was considered an outside source. A warlock had gone rogue and was to be captured alive. That was a little outside the box for the demon hunters, but who could deny a clever, well advertised 1.2million? Vincent accepted without hesitation. That money would sponsor a new and larger headquarters. Who in their right mind would pass up the notion? No one, that is who.

Rachel had a portal in the back of Tags. They could be anywhere in the world in a moment's notice. Rachel had all the knowledge when it came to Texas, her home state. So it was nothing short of a hop, skip, and jump when it came to transportation. She could not, however, transport any other vehicles. The demon hunting crew would have to pile in the back of Tags where the machine works of the ebon held the operating systems. That was no matter as Tags was spacious. It would be the quickest road trip of their lives. Naturally Xiao Lin road shotgun as Louis and Vincent sat attentively in the back of the demon hunting warmachine.

They set out as soon as everyone was loaded. Vincent was distracted with his phone and the absence of his lady lover. It brought him down but there was no time to dawdle. Such distractions would only cause calamities that no one needed in their operations. That was something to keep in mind, that is if one intended to stay alive. Vincent would just have to go on with the silent treatment.

First they were to meet with a certain Jonathan, the man that placed the bounty on the warlock that had slain the demon hunter. It was just a phone call when they reached the Lone Star State. Jonathan was a short haired stout sort of gentleman that swooned southern hospitality.

"Thank you for coming." Jonathan said. "The situation is that of a devastating circumstance. The loss of our very own protector will leave these lands vulnerable to those of the unsavory kind." He had a heavy accent, the same as Rachel.

The crew stood outside the white manor just in front of Tags with red dirt under their heels. "We generally deal with demons. A warlock is a little out of the way, especially wanting to catch him alive. When was the last you heard of this warlock?" Vincent said, gathering what information he could. It was not often the opportunity presented itself with a live bounty.

"It was just a week ago. The demon hunter whose name was Clide attended the warlock in a business that would call for closing a gate that let little pyro imps run free and burn crops. Lord knows how said gate was opened but the coalition of the ministry insisted on bringing in an outside source to deal with such provocations swiftly. Clide was dead seven days later and the warlock simply vanished. We want the warlock for questioning."

"Do we have to worry about little fire imps, that would cost extra on the bounty. I do have to think about the well being of my crew."

"Well as time would have it, the gate that let those little rascals roam free had been closed. That is the peculiar part. The job was finished but the warlock never arrived to collect his reward." Jonathan explained.

"How do you know the warlock killed him?" Louis chimed. "Was Clide burned to death, it could have been a work hazard."

"The warlock uses a whip. Clide has tell tale signs of strangulation and the whip has the same pattern as the bruises around Clide's neck. Simple as that."

"Alright." Vincent said. "I think we have enough to get started. Can you point us in the direction of the gate? That is where we will start our investigation."

Jonathan gave them a map that had a trail of red marker on it that would lead the crew to the origin of the overly complicated demon gate. They would drive uphill to a secluded location where sat a large ring marked with ebonic scribe that signified the gate was opened by someone who knew what they were doing. The markings were determined by ebon specialist Louis to be formed by a magic wielder with intentions unknown.

"We should get rid of the aftermath of the gate. If it opens up again there could be trouble in Texas." Louis said.

"Not a bad call." Vincent responded. "Rachel, what do we have for demolitions?"

"I have runic marked dynamite. My sticks are potent so it's best we keep a good distance at detonation."

A bundle was set at the base of the circular gate and the crew watched a few hundred feet away as red dust kicked up after the explosion rang in the hills. That gate would not be settled by regular dynamite. Most powers that were based in runic markings were to be treated like they were the source of demonic origin. Louis hypothesized that the warlock may have had something to do with the opening of the gate. An outsider may have had motive which led to its creation. Quite the underhanded tactic.

The crew returned to Jonathan looking for information as to the headquarters of Clide the demon hunter. He worked in a strip that seemed to be straight out of a western film, with a saloon and casino just on opposite ends of a single road. Tags was parked at the end of the road and the crew traveled on foot to snoop the locals under cover. It was cowboys that ran vice, even had horses to match the scenery. Rachel was right at home.

"Alright team, we split up to search for clues. We meet at Tags in an hour." Vincent ordered.

They began to look for any persons of suspicion. They looked for rnic tattoos, glowing weapons, anyone that just did not seem to fit in. Forty five minutes and all they found was Texans looking tough. Vincent took to the saloons and sipped whiskey to blend in. Rachel minded the dirt road and asked the ladies if they knew Clide. Louis asked coercing questions. Xiao Lin managed a cowgirl hat and sang on stage at a brothel. She managed to make herself at home.

Vincent sat at a table to a game of poker, wagering the table minimum. He did so after he saw a man light a cigar with his thumb, a rather curious trick that stood out among the crowd. "What is the big blind?" he asked.

"Big blind is fifty, small twenty five." the man dressed in black leather said. "I reckon you here to play bold the way you are dressed in them there vests."

"I do alright. Where'd you get that cigar?" Vincent asked, attempting to lure the man into a sense of false security to derive just where that man was from.

"Won it in a low stakes gamble. A simple game of hold'em." He exhaled a large cloud of smoke and blew it upright.

The first hand was dealt. It was just the two of them at the table. The bets were down and they both filled the pot with one-hundred dollars. It was the flop that caught Vincent's attention. He pocketed a pair of fours and one was turned up on the table giving him three of a kind. Vincent knew what he was doing when it came to gambling. Instead of raising the stakes he would lay low and play the field, covering what was most likely a win when the turn was finally flipped.

A jack came with the river. The man dressed in black raised the tables two hundred. Vincent made due with a call. The odds of losing to jacks at three of a kind were slim, but the odds were in Vincent's favor. The river was played and there was another four. Vincent had four of a kind, an easy win.

"You aren't here to play cards, are you pilgrim?" the man asked.

"Are you saying that because you know I have you?"

"The marks on your arm then are nothing short of ebon alchemy. I know a bounty hunter when I see one. You are looking for a man, aren't you?" He laid down his cards. "Three of a kind."

"I tell you what Vincent said. "You tell me what happened to Clide and I may just forget the whole thing." Vincent wanted the story out of him, not bluffing in cards but at the hunt of a warlock.

"That man had no idea what he was in bed with. I killed him for wanting to close off my leyline. Why don't you show your cards. Then I will kill you, too."

Vincent laughed. "Four of a kind. I win. And you will be taken in." Vincent pulled out Ammit at a quickdraw but the man lashed a whip that caught his arm and before Vincent knew what hit him he was pulled to the floor.

The whip was a vine that had thorns that dug into the ambitious demon hunter's skin. He was scratched all the way up to his elbow. The poker table was flipped over in the prazen upstart and the man in black stood way taller than anticipated.

Vincent stood. "So what do I have the pleasure of calling you, Mr....?"

"The name is Barrel. Not that you will live long enough to remember it."

"I beg to differ." Vincent raised his hand and lowered it signaling to his team that were waiting just outside. It was a signal to move in on Barrel for his capture so that they could collect him and then the bounty.

Bullets turned the walls and the swing door into swiss cheese in a matter of seconds. Rachel had misunderstood the signal and Xiao Lin was on the gatling gun spraying bullets like she was a cloud made of lead.

"What the hell, guys!?" Vincent shouted.

"Was that not an execution order?" Louis shouted back.

Vincent took cover behind the bar. "We are supposed to capture him. ALIVE!"

"We have to work signals. We weren't briefed. These things should be covered in the briefing." Rachel said. Barrel made his way on horseback out of the saloon. "Our cowboy is kicking up dust. Come on boss. We had better get after him." Vincent quickly joined the crew in Tags and they made tracks after their bounty.

Barrel's horse was fast. It was presumed otherworldly. They made their way past a field of cacti. They trailed a ways behind the speeding warlock. "We need to capture him. What does this thing have for non-lethals?" Vincent asked Rachel as she struggled to keep up with their target.

"I have nets and a few bolas. They shoot pretty good but every attempt needs to count."

Vincent settled in the rising chair that rose through the roof. Replacing the gatling gun with something that promised to pay this mission was an easy switch. He aimed down the sites of the scope to the backside of a galloping Barrel and he was confident in the first netting. When he pulled the trigger a net blasted from the gun and wrapped itself around the bounty. "Bull's eye." Barrel though apparently had other tricks up his sleeve. He lit up in flames, burning away the intended capture. "What in the hell is this guy?"

The chase lasted a while longer. A barrage of nets and bolas were not enough to wrangle the on the run Barrel. Vincent figured he was to take down the horse if he wanted to end the chase and get paid. He ordered Louis to switch the gun cartridge to something that would bring down the hoofed mount. There was a sniper rifle that would do the trick. Tags was an armory of goods that supplied it as an intricate war machine. All it took was a little patience in the leading of the kill.

The shot was fired and the horse went down. Tags came to a treading halt and when the dust settled the crew hopped out to deal with the ever so difficult warlock out in the red clay desert. Xiao Lin however stayed behind, readying another net in the event it would prove useful. They just needed to douse the flames and capture their prey. All it would take was a little convincing of the team's ebon.

"What do you have for flames?" Vincent said to Louis.

"Oh I have a nice seal

CHAPTER SEVEN

The red clay served as the edge of the battleground in the mountains in the horizon. Tumbleweed skipped between the hunters and the prey. "You suckers are barking up the wrong tree." Barrel said. He lit a cigar with a flame from his gloved thumb. Then his face flushed with flame and blackened. "I won't let you fools take me in. Your grave is here."

"Will he ever shut up?" Rachel said. She fancied a six shooter ebon, though now they were mostly for ploy. Bringing in a bounty alive was the most difficult thing the crew was about to embark on. But when the price on a hog tie was too good to be true, anything was possible.

"That's one for the editors." Vincent said as he called his scythe.

Louis called a runic rod forth. It had a vacuum cutter that syphoned off elements but only if they were in their simplistic form. Fire would be the target. He would have to suck all the energy from Barrel so that he could be caught in the net that Xiao Lin sat at, waiting to pull the trigger. The plan was to tire him out, then drag him in.

Vincent made the first move. He made his motions obvious as he could not consciously perform a non-lethal without putting in the extra effort. Maybe the crew would disarm Barrel. That whip could do some real damage. Especially if Barrel went for the eyes. Vincent sluggishly moved towards his bounty looking to lead him in. Barrel cracked the whip, attempting to catch the hunter by his ankle, failing to do so as Vincent lifted his heel.

Rachel pulled her revolver from the holster and shot at Barrel attempting to wing him. Barrel saw it coming and performed a combat roll and the shot hit the gravel road. She needed to be careful not to do too much damage to the target. Practice from the range at the academy prepared her for this particular endeavour.

Barrel was quick to his feet before he realized that Louis had already closed the distance. The rod syphoned some of the flame from Barrel's face. It pulled the billows directly into its end, the Louis bashed Barrel over the head knocking him into a stumble. Barrel grabbed his jaw in pain, then set out the whip to lash at the triumphant Louis. Louis let the whip catch onto the rod and countered it as a snare that let Vincent cut the whip in half.

Barrel was without weapon save for whatever else he could do with fire. The crew was only moments short of finding out exactly what that was. Barrel raised his hands and there to their astonished amazement came lava balls the size of baseballs. They were thrown like clockwork. Louis sent some flying back after hitting them with the rod. They may not have burned the target, but getting hit by one definitely stung the surface.

Vincent ordered the crew to surround Barrel. They got into position. Xiao Lin fired the net shortly after Louis began to syphon off more of the flames. They tied him up and dragged him a few miles back to Jonathan off the back hitch of tags.

The crew received their payment and Vincent divided the sum so that everyone got paid under half the collection. The rest would be saved to expand an annex onto the lounge. Everyone voted that they needed the space.

The first mission of the crew in the field was a resounding success. It would be a while before they found another demon. Beatrix was now working in obscure patterns. That was because Xagos spread his dominion into the human world. The more binds that he made the longer he could sustain his presence. With Beatrix collecting souls it was easier for him to stay. Their whereabouts were still unknown. It was only known that the demon hunters kept dying out. Who knew how long it would be before Beatrix and Xagos came for them.

Of course they had to do something. It was even suggested that they use themselves as bait, but the rate at which the witch was growing, she had to have amassed an army by now. It was voted out until something could be done by her expanding powers. Who knew what Xagos was planning as well. He was strong before but now he really had to be the pits.

Veronica had not returned any of Vincent's calls or messages. It had been weeks. He could only assume the worst. Maybe she hated him now. That was all that kept popping into that fevered mind of his. He knew she could hold a grudge, but this was pushing it. She was all he could think about while the crew ordered from catalogs the new expansion onto the lounge.

Rachel came in quietly as Vincent sat with a magazine over his eyes. "Something bothering you, boss? You have been all kinds of quiet since we came back from Texas."

"I would rather not talk about it." He said rising out of his chair. "It is no one's problem but my own."

"You sure you want to limit your inner demons to what goes on in that head of yours? There is a good chance letting some of that stuff out would make you feel better." she said. "We would make a well oiled team that way."

"My oh my, your character design is very persuasive."

"I am the middle child of seventeen kids. I know my way around those campfire troubles."

"I have to introduce you to my troubles sometime. Maybe you and her can work out hers."

"A woman?"

"You'd better believe it."

There was not much to do at The Demon Hunter's Lounge besides get to know more about your battle mates. The only way to do that was to engage in a little sparring practice. They would hold a house tournament where the number one would be the keeper of the latest ebon that was called in. They would go to Athens where a chain was found. It was rumored to be able to capture targets because of its endless links. All in all they would at the very least be used to do some decent melee damage.

It was Louis against Xiao Lin for starters. Louis would use the rod. It was special because it could spit out whatever was sucked in. He could use it to spit out the flames he acquired back in Texas. It was not unlimited however. He could only dish out what he picked up. Xiao Lin was not a close ranged fighter but she did have a long sword ebon that she would use every now and again. They clashed weapons in the back of the lounge in which would eventually become a parking lot to house the other vehicle.

Xiao Lin conceded to defeat after Louis aimed for her bones and sought to bruise them. Xiao Lin was more a lover than a fighter and Louis had just a little more experience fighting. In the academy he specialized in taking on multiple opponents. Xiao Lin was unworthy of the talents of the young hunter.

Next up it was Rachel and Vincent. Now Vincent had the advantage when it came to the way of the blade. His scythe was massive and had a hooked blade while Rachel only had a dirk to be her weapon of choice. Vincent would become the victor after only a few swift movements.

Louis with his honor when it came to battle did not see it proper to battle his boss for all supremacy. That meant Vincent was in the running for an ebon made of steel chains which would come in handy if they ever needed to capture another bounty alive.

The crew went to Incognito's to find out more about the new ebon listed halfway around the world. They did not need the transport as Tags had its own, but it never hurt to educate oneself of the tools for demon hunting.

"It was once used to chain a cyclops to the mountain." Incognito said. "They could change in size, one link could be as big as a building."

"What did the cyclops do to deserve such treatment?" Xiao Lin asked with a juicebox.

"Beats me. The gods of those kinds of tales did whatever they thought was necessary. Be careful over there. Recklessness may prompt imprisonment."

Vincent, not taking this seriously, said, "I always wanted a police record in another country."

The night was quiet. Louis stayed behind in the lounge for reasons he kept to himself. Vincent and Veronica were not the only ones harboring secrets. He pulled a yellow stone from his pocket. It began to glow and a projection shot onto the wall. A hooded figure posed like a shadow began to speak. "How is the plan coming along? We are a few short months before our arrival."

"I need more time." Louis said. "I don't have the resources to build a bridge of that size."

"If you keep the plan low and to the ground there should not be much trouble. We only intend to kill the one they call Veronica. The progression is most paramount."

"I know. She is immune to most if not all magic thanks to her father's bind. If he was to be released there would be an apocalypse that would end all of Chicago thanks to his dominion." Louis heard a sound and decided it would be best if he kept his voice down.

"It would be best if we captured her and delivered her to the council. It is a great reprieve but there is to be no hold up." the projected figure said.

"I will not fail you."

"You are correct in saying so. You must figure out her whereabouts, befriend her if need be."

"My loyalty is not to Vincent but the council."

"We live on." The projection ended. The stone was placed back into Louis's pocket. There began so many plots that there was no telling who would strike first. Vincent, if he knew the truth, would not stand for the capture of the one he loved. Louis was a well placed tactical insurgent that promised to stop the end of the world. What was the truth about Veronica? Did anyone besides Vincent promise to aid her? Her secrets were too much to keep to herself.

Vincent still could not get a hold of the soon to be endangered love of his. He needed her to make another alchemic rune to house the new ebon. He should find her before they set off to Athens. Who knew what they would encounter? The stories of their gods were all in place. Their demons must have been of the dame accord. The only difference was the gods directly protected the populace. There were no hunters in those lands that ran a demon hunting business accordingly. Vincent thought it would be an interesting turn of ambience.

He began to read up on the ancient stories and what it took to run into one of the giant deities. The books in which he read led him to believe that the gods would present themselves to those on one of their racing labors. He wanted the ebon that tethered giants to mountains and wanted their blessing for it. He was not in the least bit suspecting the stirrings of one of his underlings. Stopping an apocalypse was one thing, but he would never settle for harming Veronica.

The truth about Louis was he was a relic hunter. His mission was to collect the three pieces of an ancient relic and use it to kill off the demon spawn before the overlord could be resurrected. He did know of the bond between Vincent and Veronica. He was well placed when it came to being chosen at the academy. He was to move in absolute secrecy. Had Vincent found out, who knows what turnabout would have surfaced.

Veronica knew of her father's imminent return. That was what she wanted to tell Vincent the day they visited Lake Michigan. She did not have the nerve to tell him the whole truth. She choked because of the demon hunting business. The truth was she was half demon. Her father would be the dark secret she carried within her. She was the gate that would bring about destruction. Her rage meter was the teetering scale that would open the door to desolation.

That was why she did not want Vincent to hire a woman into The Demon Hunter's Lounge. Her jealousy was something she could not control. The gate was sealed on her heart. Love would slow down the process of her father's return but rage on the other hand only made imminent destruction occur at a pace she could not control.

Rachel was tasked with finding out more about the leyline of Beatrix. She would not visit Athens for the ebon. Vincent suspected they would not need such heavy weaponry and devised that someone stay on the homefront to progress the many secrets of a bitter heart witch. She agreed happily and worked closely with Incognito in research to find out the origin of Beatrix's power. Maybe then they could find out what she wanted. Maybe then she could be trapped.

Xiao Lin and Vincent went out for food when Vincent finally got a call from Veronica. She had to cool her head. The gate on her heart would threaten to be broken if she had not. She had to find her inner center so that she could face the new crew.

"Veronica, baby. You can't just disappear on me like that."

"I know. There was something I needed to take care of. How are things going?" she said. Vincent did not know it but she was wiping away some tears.

"We are headed out of the country again. A new ebon has shown itself. I need you to come along."

"Is it going to be anything like Egypt?"

"No, we aren't waking any pharaohs this time. Just a simple extraction of some chains. I need your tattooing handiwork. You in?"

"Is SHE going along?"

"Rachel? No, she is performing a witch hunt with Incognito."

"I will go anywhere she isn't."

It unsettled Vincent the way she apple of Rachel. He had to commemorate the new huntress and Veronica just made things difficult. He was unsure how to handle the situation. Should he keep the two separate? It was not the first time he had to balance work with personal ongoings. That is to mention Beatrix and the choosing at the academy. Why were things so difficult?

The crew began to prepare for Athens. Who knew how long they would be there? Vincent suspected a simple smash and grab, but anything could happen when they were out in the field. It would not be the first time they ran into gods but it was a first for some.

Louis prepared by packing extra tools they thought they might need. Chain cutters were at the very least mandatory. Xiao Lin and her excitement to visit new places blew bubblegum bubbles while reading Anne Rice's "The Vampire Lestat". She was impatiently waiting to see the new land. As she always was and always will be.

Vincent sat in his own amusements when he finally heard from his symbol of affections. It was weight off of his shoulders but it was out of the frying pan and into the fire. Veronica sat with him on the love seat and they were quiet as the trials of love took Vincent's mind. He was happy she was around again, but stressed when it came to her behavior. He did not know of the coming prophecy. Perhaps he would have let things go if he did. Only time would tell. Time always had a fancy way of doing so.

The gate that would transfer them needed special augmentations before they could make the jumps to Athens. There was a barrier that needed to be overcome. The gods of Athens were sure to keep out any magic of any variety with the dominion of godly presence in the area. It was because the gods took care of any worldly bindings themselves. They were powerful as they were giant. There was sure to be a way but it would not be easy. It only took a little extra tweaking. Rachel tinkered away at the gate's preparation. It was her specialty.

Domain kept a watchful eye on his secret target. In his mind he referred to Veronica as the gate and knew the parameters of evoking and loosening the portal that would transport evil into the realm of man. He approached Vincent and Veronica on the couch just to probe how loose the gate was. He had to do anything to stop it from opening.

"Do I get to know the pleasure of the name of such a dame." Louis was deceptive. He knew of Veronica, but this was the first time they would interact. He had to keep his true intentions hidden.

"Shouldn't you be working?" Vincent said. "It is almost time to go."

"I was just wondering who this is. You can't knock my curiosity. I am way ahead in the preparation for Athens." Louis lowered his head trying to give the visual queue of obedience though his intentions were a little less than honorable.

Veronica extended her hand to shake Louis's. "I am Veronica." She said.

"Are you a demon hunter as well?" Louis asked, carrying the conversation.

"I am not. I handle ebon and what I call carrying tattoos. Makes it easier than lugging them around in the traditional sense."

"I handle binds like that myself." Louis extended his rod. "This one is a creation of my own design. Can swallow up magics and spit them back out. Took me a year to figure that one out."

Veronica took the rod and closely examined it. "Looks like a tetra seal. That one is a little unorthodox for a vacuum seal."

"It was a matter of reaction and residual suction. This was originally used to steal souls. I refined it for a practical use a little less morbid."

Veronica was impressed. It was not often that she was. "We should definitely get together sometime and talk shop."

Louis let a thin smile creep across his face. "I look forward to working with you."

"Alright." Vincent said. "Why don't you go see if Rachel needs any help. The sooner we leave the sooner we can get back."

"Ah, yes. There is a matter of the witch Beatrix. I have been inspecting her profile." Louis said after securing his rod and the future close workings of the gate Veronica. "It seems her powers are of an ancient origin. She works from a phylactery that houses the center of her leyline. If we destroy her lab she loses a majority of her powers."

"She can tussle, too." Vincent said, unaware of what the ardent Louis was planning. "She is nothing to take lightly."

"What are her skill sets?" Louis asked, still concealing his intention. "You sound as if you experienced her first hand."

"A demon hunter and myself went toe to toe with her and a demon that sought to free her from her prison. She uses stitching needles as if they were rapier. She also has scarecrow puppets that are crafted from hunter souls. If we aren't careful she could easily convert any of us to do her bidding."

"Sounds like there is work to do, indeed." Louis turned and went to see if Rachel needed a hand.

Veronica lifted her head from Vincent's lap and sat up next to him. "He seems like a real charmer."

"He is the best at binds. He steals demon power and uses it against them. With any luck he could help free the souls that Beatrix has captured."

"That would be the day." Veronica said.

Later that night Vincent treated the entire crew and his lady to chinese food, the traditional anthem of any hungry stomach in the lounge. Incognito paid the lounge a visit with information on how to proceed on official business in Athens. If they were not careful they would set off the gods and could very easily start a war. Tensions were high in the crowned city as one of the gods had a plot to take over Olympia.

The story of how that came about was because one lone warrior killed the god of war and took his seat on the fabled mountain. His skin was ashen and he wore a red tribal tattoo across his eye. That same warrior had two blades on the end of two chains that spit fire when swung. Hades had plans to take over and that warrior was the center of such a devious plot. The crew listened intently as they heard the rules on how they should operate. They sat and filled their bellies on spring rolls as they let the rules and how to set in.

They would leave in three days time. Veronica chose to approach Rachel to settle her jealousy. She did not want any woman working closely with the man she loved. However, when life hands you lemons one may as well quench the thirst. She did not sense a romantic threat when it came to Rachel. She rather fancied her southern accent. She settled on her mind and heart being over reactive. Just a chat with Rachel soothed her ever so spiking temperament.

It was just a short while of a construction crew's work to expand the lounge into a more spacious construct. A bunker was added with caged walls in the basement with demon tracking computers in the event that work favored a close to home radius. The garage was expanded and so was the office area which was now fit for ten people. No more shoulder rubbing in the lounge. Each worker even got their own desk where they could research and expand their influence when it came to exploring knowledge. A bulletin board with Beatrix's face on a wanted poster sat in the front on the wall as she was their primary concern.

A kitchen was even added. That was the private domain of the ambitious Xiao Lin. She wanted to master the art of Chinese Cooking. The lounge would save money if she cooked the food herself. She wanted to serve her boss better than any takeout joint could. In time the oriental huntress would accomplish this goal. It was even better that the funds for the ingredients did not come from her own pocket.

Louis and his surreptitious plotting were better concealed in the larger facility. The projection of the yellow stone was hidden by his desk. He chatted with Veronica on and off but could not tell the status of the gate that she held within. He would have to craft a meter and use it to probe her every so often. He would have to move expeditiously in the event the seal on her heart weakened.

News was spreading. The crew was getting calls from all over. Most of the work was denied due to lack of pay or after greater research proved to be hoaxes. One had to be very careful not to get caught up in mundane affairs. If one was unlucky the only thing that would be spent was precious supplies and much needed time. One should never waste time. Jobs of the lower class were redirected to the academy. It was nice of Vincent to show a little support of those demon hunters to be. He received high praises from the crew for that sense in business.

The lounge was promised supplies for that search in low end jobs. The academy sent over parcels of money as the students weren't to be paid in other than work experience. It was a rather well paying arrangement since there was no danger or risk in setting out low class demons.

The day of Athens approached rather quickly. The crew all stood at the tailgate of Tags, eagerly awaiting the jump to the city of the gods. "Just a few minutes." Rachel said, putting the finishing touches on the coordinates. "Hold on to your gears, it's going to be a nasty one."

"How will we get back?" Vincent asked. "Can this thing do round trips?"

"I have that taken care of." Louis said in response. "All we have to do is appease Athena. I am sure there is something we can do to get her aid."

"Maybe you could seduce her." Xiao Li jested.

Louis looked to her with unease in his eyes. "That woman is at least six hundred stores tall."

They all laughed. "I'm sure you can figure something out." Vincent said.

"Alright," Rachel said. "You're all set to go."

CHAPTER EIGHT

Athens, it was a glorious sight to see. The crew arrived just on the outskirts of the city and it would be a titanic walk before they reached anyone that could help them affirm their mission. The chains of Athens was the ebon they were to collect. Little did they know of what would lie in store for them. Xiao Lin was already snapping photos of the city. To her it was like a vacation. She was always the eager one.

Louis held out a probe to see if they were near any magic that would cause them harm. Who knew the enemies of the gods? One wrong move and wrath could be set upon them. "We are in the clear." he said with the meter ticking.

"Then there isn't any time to waste." Veronica said. She was the first to move. Xiao Lin, still snapping pictures followed just after her.

"Is this going to be like Egypt?" Xiao Lin asked.

"Hopefully with less beings pissed off at us." Vincent joined the line through the mountains. "We shouldn't run into any trouble as we are not disturbing any ancient tombs."

"We are just here to steal from the goddess Athena, right?" Veronica said, gauging the parameters of the mission.

"What do you mean to steal from the goddess? It is just a simple ebon." Vincent trailed in front of the eager Veronica.

"We are here to get some chains. Who knows why the cyclops is chained up. I am sure we are going to ruin the plans of the divine." Veronica halted in front of the questioning of her mate. "I'm sorry, am I slowing you down?"

"So we could piss off more gods?"

"A knack you certainly prove time and time again."

The meter bagan to fade. Louis was certain that there were no demons nor gods in their vacinity. They marched and argued about the temperament of the mission. Only time would tell if they would invoke the wrath of Olympus. Vincent was enthusiastic about the run. He did not mind proving he was worth the godly aggravation.

When they were a few miles out a scout was appointed to go ahead and assess the nature of what they would encounter. Xiao Lin volunteered as the noble sacrifice. She was not likely to find trouble as she turned trouble into a pet that she could cuddle and turn into her own plaything. Louis was accompanying her should anything go south outside of their favor. This gave Vincent and Veronica time alone to patch over any wounds left in their minds and hearts.

"I burned your teddy bear." Veronica said.

"That bad?"

"I took its embers as an apology." Veronica sat on a jagged rock. "I feel better now."

"Harsh. That's the last time I get you one."

Veronica and Vincent sat on the tip of tense negotiations when it came to them being bound together. She settled on her emotions and Vincent paid the price. It was one thing to ignore her preference when it came to hiring Rachel, she felt like getting even. It would be two hours before Louis would return without Xiao Lin. The news in which he brought back was a little surprising.

"She took over." Domain said out of breath.

"Athena!" Vincent shouted. He summoned his scythe, readying for an imaginary assault.

"No, Xiao Lin." Louis explained. "She took over an entire house of gladiators. She sits atop a throne as their queen regent."

That was the nature of the Xioa Lin parade. Her nature was unpredictable. The crew made the march to the edge of the city where they met a gate that had two men armed with shields and swords. Vincent thought he would be the one to get them past the gladiators and into the presence of the one they now served. It would be a little more difficult as they were open to a fight more than mincing words.

"We are here to see your leader." One of the men opened his mouth for a long yawn. They were both silent. "Uh, knock knock. Anyone home?"

"We are only open to fighters that would exist for the games." the gladiator on the left said. "Anyone else can buzz off."

"We are here for the games." Veronica said. "These two men are my slaves. I want them trained and ready for battle."

"That is a bit much." Vincent whispered to Veronica.

"Silence, slave!" She hit Vincent on the head, commanding that he obey.

Louis lowered his head. "It's best we do as she says."

"The things that get through editing." Vincent said to himself.

"Do you pledge your slave's lives to the house of Xiao Lin, warden of this ludus?"

"For the right price." Veronica said. They were shown in and taken to the seat of Xiao Lin. She was being fed grapes and being fanned by house slaves. The take Veronica would send was to gain access to the house so that she could infiltrate the city to find what they were looking for. Vincent saw this as nothing more than a waste of time.

"We are deviating from the story's main plot." he said to Louis.

"Let's just see how it goes." Louis said with a smile.

Xiao Lin gestured her new slaves away. "Who dares interrupt my sunbathing? State your guise for I am easily tempered."

"Uh, your grace," Vincent started. "How is this going to help us get the ebon we have come to collect?"

"Such a manifesto is beneath me. I am now heir to creating the finest gladiators this ludus has ever seen. Such governing requires my undivided attention. Away with this fool."

"Hey, I pay your salary."

"You there, woman." Xiao Lin started at Veronica. "Is this chattering animal your slave?"

"He knows not his place." Veronica said. "Perhaps time in your training field would set him straight."

"You offer your man as an offering to my ludus? Is he worthy of such transgressions?"

"What the hell is going on here?" Vincent said trying to grasp hold of what these two ladies were up to. He was in the dog house with one and the other had gone mad with power. "Don't you think the readers will wonder why we stray so far from why we are in Athens to begin with?"

"Silence!" Xiao and Veronica said in unison.

At Xiao Lin's command Louis and Vincent were stripped and dressed in a gladiator's regalia. They were sent into the holding cells awaiting their trial to see if they would be deemed worthy to fight for the house of Lin, a ceremonious name given to the ludus that was taken over in just a few short hours.

Vincent was put in a cell with a man that sat in similar leather garbs. He apparently was a fighter that had not been up to Xiao Lin's standards. He was awaiting a verdict that would send him to the mines. It was a place that tortured any gladiator that did not perform at optimal capacity.

"The gods will smile on us." the man said.

"I wish they had stopped the passive takeover of your ludus." Vincent said. "I could do without a power stricken leader," he said referring to Xiao Lin.

"She is wise as she is dangerous. Tell me your name warrior."

"The name is Vincent."

"You lack the sun. You are not from around here. Which god do you serve?"

"Currently up for debate. I'm sorry, who are you?"

"I am Adras, the name is one that all of Athens will know."

"Is that right?"

"Ah yes, but of course. I am to be the most renowned gladiator in these lands. The games will prove to be good with this year's prize at hand."

"And what is the prize?" Vincent did not really care. He had to first deliver a stern word to the women that settled him into this predicament.

"Athena herself will grant you one favor." Adras said, smiling through his beard.

A favor from a goddess? That would be their ticket home. It was why Xiao Lin decided to take over. Once word hit that Athena would grant them any one favor it was sure to be the one that needed.

When the cell door was opened Vincent was led to the training grounds where any that sought out the favor of the goddess would set blood and bone to purpose. "Which one, would you say is the toughest, Adras?" The men were mid battle in the sun with sand at their feet. "I want to do a little take over of my own."

"That would be me." A man in a helmet with a wooden sword and shield stood towering over the demon hunter. "The name is Faustas. I will be your tour guide."

"You don't look so tough." Vincent wagered his words. "I bet I can floor you in seconds."

"Care to make a demonstration?" Faustas cleared the field.

"Don't mind if I do."

Vincent was handed a sword and shield. Faustas was given the same. Though Vincnent being ever so confident exchanged his shield for a second sword, seeking to make a barrage of daggers to win the contest. The other gladiators went into a house war change meant to startle any of their opponents. Domain joined in the chant nervously, trying to blend in.

Faustas banged his shield with his sword, entreating the very essence of gladiator warfare. Vincent made the first move. He charged the warrior without taking in the anticipation of what it meant to serve in a ludus. He was certainly the best when it came to battling demons, but this was not the tainted streets of Chicago. This was a world of blood and sand. Faustus blocked the flurry of Vincent's strikes like it was the breeze on blades of grass.

"You are too eager, tiny man." Faustas said with the grit of tutelage. "The sun will tire you out and I will break your excessive force."

"What can I say, it is my first time." Vincent was on Faustas again. This time he aimed for around the shield. When he made a sweep for the legs it was easily countered with a simple lift. Vincent was out of his league and did not know it. It would be time and sweat before he was ready to enter the arena.

Faustas saw an opportunity to end the contest. The others were chanting his name. So was Louis who only bet against his boss in the uproar. He would never do so under normal circumstances. Vincent caught a glimpse of the balcony that overlooked the training field. Xiao Loin was fanning herself with Veronica at her side. Not paying attention he was knocked to the sand and nearly unconscious, a clever tactic used to subdue the opponent.

The other gladiators fell silent. Faustas stood over Vincent with his eyes to Xiao Lin, waiting for the verdict of life or death. Xiao Lin held out her thumb sideways, divining the outcome of her boss' life. "Are you kidding me?" He said out loud.

He thumb went up. Faustus threw his arm out and helped Vincent from the ground. "You fight like a wild man. That is no good for the arena. You must build your muscles to break your foe."

"I will keep that in mind the next time you bash me in the skull."

"Thank the gods for the rock hard appendage."

Vincent spent hours drilling the gladiator code into his bones. If they were going to get home he needed to win the games. He refined hid strikes and tuned his agility. He was doing backflips off of shields and diving from them into a lethal tempo. Louis was upgraded to the field trainer and set up skirmishes between the gladiators so that only the top chosen could be sifted out for the games. Adras, Faustas, and Vincent were put on a team to face ten gladiators. It was the best and the worst. Adras needed to be covered if they all were to make it out alive.

Vincent dodged a net that was meant for him but Adras was caught in it. He really was the worst of the three. Faustas held back a group of their opponents while Adras attempted to free himself. Vincent scurried into weak points that Faustas' defensive form created. They really were a working team. Perhaps they would use Adras as bait for the self refining team tactic.

They ate as brothers in their cells. The top two contenders were promised special treatment for their efforts in satisfying the whim of combat from the house leader Xiao Lin. Faustas would have wine and extra food. Vincent had one request; Veronica.

Veronica came in clad in sultry undergarments. The mood was correct but Vincent had some complaining to do. "How long are we going to go with this farce?"

"Just win the games so we can go home."

"We haven't recovered the ebon yet." Vincent was a one track mind.

"The chains of Olympus? None of us knows where they are." Veronica began to belly dance.

"Would you quit fooling around, woman. I got my ass handed to me by a guy twice my size. Let's just focus on the task at hand."

"Why are you so boring? I am enjoying the life of luxury." she said, swirling her hips.

"Alright, I give. I need you to find out how to contact Athena."

"If I refuse to help you?"

"I go hog wild and burn your newly found fortress to the ground. Then it's back to work for all of you."

That set Veronica off. "You are no fun. I am not even employed by you."

"You don't have to be to have your luxuries burned to crisps."

The next day Xiao Lin approached Vincent on the fields. He was chosen along with Adras and Faustas and a few other gladiators to perform in the games. There was no doubt the progress that was made on Vincent's behalf. He just worked better in a team, though his original crew had gone mad with power. They strayed so far from their goal that it was impossible to have order.

Louis called the busy Vincent aside. "You have a message from the keeper of the house."

"So you're buying into this ludus deal, too?"

Louis winked. "It is an information gathering strategy."

"Find that ebon."

"You got it, boss."

Vincent approached the pampered Xiao Lin. "You summoned me, your grace?"

"Yes, I have. You have shown the most progress when it comes to training. This much is true. I have a special request that I hope would suit your warrior class."

"I am all ears, though you aren't the one that should be giving orders Xiao."

"Just stick to the new pecking order."

Vincent rolled his eyes. "Whatever, let's just get on with it."

"Upon your victory in the games, you will be sold into the army of Athens to slay the foe of the goddess Athena."

"Will I be any closer to getting the ebon?"

"Yes, actually. The army will lay siege to the mountain of hades, there is where the chains of Olympus dwell."

"So all i have to do is not die and we can get back to business?"

"Correct."

Vincent was dismissed. It was back to the gladiator regiment. It was news that a gladiator would serve a purpose to the army of Athens. The news spread like wildfire. Not only would one sustain glory, but they would also gain promise to the lands that granted social freedoms. This only brought a sense of gloom though, since Vincent lost control of his team and was essentially put at the bottom of the barrel.

Later that night Louis snuck into the cell where Vincent slept with stirring news. He found a source that would boost his speed in the field of combat. They sauntered into the city where they would meet the old woman from Egypt. She gave Vincent some sandals that had wings on them. It was said they belonged to the messenger of Zeus. To be honest it was whatever brought them out of the crazy that was brought upon even visiting Athens.

"Should I consider you to be my arms dealer?" Vincent said to the old woman.

"You could consider me such."

"You have a number? A name? Anything that would let me know where you are?"

"I am Agatha Goodwitch. I used to be like you."

"Dashingly good looking and jumping head first into danger."

"Oh, those were the good days of demon hunting. That was before your time."

"Do you know the status of the ebon Chains of Olympus? My team has gone stir crazy and aren't really looking to do the work of a demon hunter."

"The chains will be revealed to you all in good time, young one. Patience must be practiced." Agatha disappeared rather cryptically in a mirage of smoke.

Vincent thought it was more than less than useless. As much as he loved the thrill of battle, killing humans was against the demon hunter code. Why Xiao Lin enlisted him in the servitude of the ludus was beyond him. He fancied himself more a general, but that was in the commonplace sobriquet of the norm.

It was the day before the games when he slipped on the sandals and moved with a hasty speed. He could even fly when he got the balance right. Faustas made Vincent run primary battle drills in preparation for the battle to come. It would be two rounds in the arena. The first bunch would be weeded out by animals that were enraged and the second against another ludus. The victor would be visited by Athena in a rather dramatic encounter. The rest was history.

Vincent had a dream that night. It was another of Xagos. This time Xagos sat on the balcony of the arena and Beatrix was at his side. He battled a titan and he was no match. Faustas and Adras lay slain in the sands, covered in scars and broken bones. Vincent stood alone and Xagos sat with that sinister smile carved into his face. Vincent was defeated. Xagos revealed the souls of his mother and father. They were at its whims and suffering. The titan crushed his limbs so that he could not move. Vincent looked over and his crew was dead as well, including Veronica, his love.

Vincent woke with his scythe summoned and at the end of its point was Adras, slowly bleeding out. Vincent reacted in his sleep the way he had before. This time it would cost him the life of one of his brothers at arms.

He had killed a human. The council of demon hunters would surely hear of this mishap. It would be the end of the lounge if they had. Vincent would be stripped of his demon hunting license. The business would be in ruin.

Xiao Lin was lenient, as well she should have been. Had it not been for the antics maybe Adras would still be alive. The other gladiators put up a wooden sword and shield to remember their fallen comrade. Louis gave a small speech before the games were to start.

Vincent was transported by wooden carriage to the arena. He was side by side with the leather clad Fautas, of whom seemed a little on edge as one of his sparring partners had fallen. But these were no times to cry over spilled milk. Adras was left to the afterlife. The time to claim glory upon the sands was at hand. A warrior must keep his mind sharp lest he give way to the unfortunate.

Vincent was behind bars when Veronica came to him, a few hours remained before the slaughter would begin. "Why am I doing this again?" he asked her.

"Because no one else could ensure victory, it is our only way home."

"And if I die?"

"I will divorce you. I am not into dead men."

"So you admit to still loving me?" Vincent said, gauging her emotions.

"I admit to my whims and my whims only. I am only here to give you a ribbon so that you return to me without missing any limbs."

"Like the one that counts?"

"You lose that and you are less of a man. You might as well die." She tied a ribbon to his wrist. Ultimately she was there for him. That is what mattered. The useless bickering was just an insult to injury. Vincent wondered if she would ever let Rachel go. After all his life and their way home was on the line. Not the first time Vincent really risked it all.

He could hear the crowd going wild, chanting the names of the ludus that they gamle their fortunes on. He wondered if they were ready for quite the show. His handcuffs were removed and two swords were placed in his hands.

"Let the games begin." Faustas said, to the right of him.

CHAPTER NINE

They stood upon the sands with the crowd in an uproar. There was only leather and steel that promised them a road to glory. The first round of the gladiator games were at hand. A beast was promised to deliver them the renown that prefaced the winners to the goddess Athena. Faustas and Vincent were ready to claim all that was promised.

Xiao Lin and Veronica sat on the balcony, viewing the match with the other keepers of the ludus. Wagers were placed on the lives of the gladiators. Those that had shown skill promised a better yield in gold and glory.

"You think your boss is up for these kinds of battles?" Veronica asked. Xiao Lin sat with a bronze mask fanning herself against the sun. "It would be a shame if we lost such a fierce leader."

"I am sure he can handle it. How else would you marry him?" Xiao said, assuring herself for the prize money.

"He went against my wishes. I feel this is a purgatory nothing less than rendered."

There was a pair of glowing eyes just behind the gate that kept their opponent at bay. Soon the chains wheeled and out came the snarl of a beast that Vincent had never seen in all his days as a demon hunter. It had the body of a tiger and the tail of a scorpion. Such a beast was not native to these lands but somehow it was there in front of them. Was Vincent's training enough to slay the beast?

"What in the hell is that?" he said to Faustas. "That's one mean looking kitten."

"I believe that is a manticore. Better watch out for that tail. It is ripe with poison." Faustas began to sway. He let out a battle shout that was to inspire the others to battle.

The beast first set its claws into a gladiator that seemed all too eager to press the attack. Another threw a net over the beast and a few others attempted to swarm the manticore. Its agility however allowed it to pounce from beneath the netting and sink the barb of its tail into the chest of an unsuspecting warrior. Despite its massive size, it was fast and apparently smart.

"Looks like this is going to be some trouble for Vincent. That looks like a bit more than he is used to." Veronica said to Xiao Lin.

"He better not die. Who is going to pay my salary?"

With both swords ready Vincent closed in on the manticore. The beast lowered its head with its fangs bared, taunting the demon hunter. Vincent swiped at the beast, gauging its reaction reflex. It jumped onto its hind legs, dodging the blade. It turned to swipe with its tail but Vincent simply rolled out of range.

Faustas was underneath the manticore and knocked it over with his shield. He put it up above his head. He was good for rushing onslaughts considering his size. It was definitely an asset in battle. If they could keep up the volley they would surely win in no time.

Another gladiator rushed in for the kill. He was not expecting the beast to pierce his chest from being knocked over. The manticore was extremely reflexive. Something that the demon hunter had to keep in mind if he wanted to win the favor of the goddess of Athens.

Another gladiator hopped on the back of the beast before it could rise from the sands. The manticore was up and shook him like a bull would a cowboy at a rodeo. He was toppled to the ground before the manticore gripped him in his jaws and shook him until he was two halves of an Athenian corpse. Vincent was rather impressed by the tenacity of the beast as he had only battled demons before. This was just an entertaining feat to him.

Soon only Faustas and Vincent remained along with the roar of the crowd. The crowd did not favor the hunter as they wanted to see human blood shed. That is why they came to see such a sport. They were chanting in favor of the mythical beast, though Vincent paid it no mind. His only objective was to clear the field of the hulking manticore and secure the favor of the goddess.

The manticore began to run at Faustus. It pounced upright but he propped his shield into the manticore's mouth before he could close in for a bite. Faustas then stabbed the beast in the eye. It doppled backward as he rushed a flurry of cuts to its eyes and paws. Vincent ran and saw his chance to strike. He severed the tail of the beast so that it was just a little less lethal than it was before. Now all they had to do was tame the kitten to death.

"Let's see them cut that out in editing." he said, triumphantly.

"What are your words?" Faustas asked in genuine confusion.

"I believe my parables are the work of a stricken and mad author that favors the use of omnipotence to cast the story as a classic tale of adventure."

"Does this author foresee our victory of the games?"

"The story would be cut rather short if I, the main character, found an untimely end."

"You sure are a funny one."

"I chalk that up to the ambient sense of humor."

The manticore was bleeding and tired. The two gladiators saw this as the opportunity to win the first match. The simultaneously charged the beast and in unison severed its front paws. Then Vincent drove his blade in the neck of the beast and pulled the blade out, severing all that he could that kept the manticore alive. It fell to the sands and moaned as it bled to death. The crowd was in an uproar, gravely disappointed at the turnabout in the arena.

"There, you see?" Veronica said. "Nothing to worry about."

The first match was a complete success. All that remained for their favor of Athena was to commit another victory in the second round. They would face other gladiators this time. Ones that held a renown as some of the most brutal. Nothing scared the demon hunter. It would be another battle that he saw as an easy one. Years of demonic conquest had prepared him for battles to come.

Vincent sat in his cell sharpening his swords with stone when Veronica came with a daft touch. She kissed him on the lips, of which was a shock because Vincent was not sure just how long she would begrudge him. There was temperament to her that Vincent just could not figure out. He liked her all the same.

"You did not bet against me did you?" he asked her as she caressed his chin. "It would be a shame if you lost out because you played against my skills."

"I know better than that. You know I don't want you dead."

"You also needn't be so cruel to me."

"I think I like this cruelty. Maybe you shouldn't be so bold."

"Bold is why you love me." He gripped her hips and pulled her close. "Will you hate me forever?"

"Not forever. And I would not go so far to say hate. I think I want to torture you just a little. I would love to see you squirm."

"If I could handle a manticore, I think I could handle you." He kissed her and she kissed back. There was only a slight quarrel between the two lovers but passion would prove stronger as a bond.

"Xiao Lin would like to see you." she said, pulling away. "Not that I didn't want to see the champion of Athens after his hot blooded victory."

"What now? Has she thought up new ways to take advantage of me as her temporary slave?"

"Who knows what she wants."

"Fine, let's go see her."

They moved through the ludus to the bath house where Xiao Lin sat in the tub with a few naked women as they combed her hair and washed her. Vincent was absolutely certain she was enjoying Athens way more than she should have been. They were only there to collect an ebon. It had turned into something way off the beaten path.

"Vincent, champion of Athens, I trust I can expect the same in the second round?" Xiao Lin said.

"How did we even come across you being the queen here? WHat exactly did I miss?"

"Oh you know, I am persuasive. I'm sure you will get used to my surprises, boss."

"What is it that you want?"

"I heard we are in for a rude surprise when it comes to the next round. Hades is sending a few warriors from the afterlife to serve as your next opponents."

"So, they are demons?"

"Does Olympus have that kind of power?"

"Nothing would surprise me if they did."

"There is something else." Xiao Lin said. "The chains of Olympus will be in the next match. So there is the chance to collect what we came for."

"The sooner we get them and win the next match, the sooner we can get back to good old Chicago." Veronica said, breaking her silence.

"I am sure I'm going to miss Faustas." Vincent said. "He is quite the fighter."

Vincent was dismissed back to his cell but went to the training fields instead. The gladiators that were lost in the arena were replaced by warriors that seemed to hold their own against the human class. Vincent would be sure to bring those magic sandals with him to the next round. Anything to ensure a swift victory.

That night the gladiators gathered outside their cells in a sense of brotherhood to welcome the new combatants. They also celebrated the victory in the arena as such a deed brought favor to the ludus. Louis used the yellow projection stone in secret while everyone was distracted by the festivities. "They suspect nothing." He said to the being at the other end of the line. "I have no way of knowing how stable the gate is."

"The council will send tools to aid with such details. Keep an eye on her and we will tell you when to capture her."

"What of the demon hunter Vincent? He won't let her go without a fight. It would only provoke him."

"Deal with him accordingly. Though if you can capture Veronica without him knowing, it would be a more favored outcome."

"The council's wish is my command." Louis pocketed the stone and then joined the ludus in their uproar as cover. The less he was suspected the better off his mission would be. He decided to approach Veronica after all his intentions were in favor of humankind. Should he address the gate as a gambit to prevent its opening? Or should he stick to the shadows in favor of her capture. Either way no one could know of his intent.

Veronica was overlooking the training sands when he found her. She was contemplating the end of the world at the destructive hand of her father. Only time was standing in the way of his desolate arrival. She was just a means to her father's glorified end. She caught Louis sneaking around.

"Are you going to weasel your way around forever?' she said, addressing him. "Such a quality does not look good on a man." She turned to him from the gladiators basking in brotherhood outside. AMong them was Vincent who led skirmishes to test the mettle of the new additions.

"I was simply looking to talk. No need to be so abrasive." Louis stepped onto the balcony and viewed the skirmishes alongside her. "What do you know of demon gates?" he said probing. He was not sure if she would react in favor of his mission.

"I know they don't open without blood in mind."

"So you are familiar with them?"

"I have had my fair share of experiences." She paid the questioning no mind. Her arms were folded while she watched her lover topple a few good men. "None of which are worth mentioning as they are all somber tales."

"I am on the hunt for one, one in particular."

"You plan on ending the world. Does your boss know about this?"

"I don't think that he does. Elseways you wouldn't be so close to him, would you?" There was a sense of conviction in the observation. Veronica was pulling away from Vincent knowing well the impending doom that her father would deliver. It was the reason she burned the teddy bear. It was the reason she kept him in the dog house. "Does he know of your father?"

Veronica furled her brow and turned to the coercion of Louis. "What do you know?" she asked with demand in her persona.

"I know you are the key to the apocalypse. I was sent-"

"Sent? You know nothing. If you were smart you would stay as far away from me as possible." The wild nature of Veronica sat like a spire in the conversation. "I don't like the way you have been sneaking about."

"I am only here to help." Louis tried to assure her of something auspicious. Though there was no settling this without setting her off. If she told Vincent he would lose his position. He did not tell her that he was to capture her. Who knew how she would react? For now he would settle on being the savior to her problems. "I know your father will return and with him destruction."

"And you can stop him?"

"I may be able to delay the gate from opening, I only need your cooperation."

"And if I decide to go along with what you are planning and it doesn't work?"

"Then you can kill me."

"I am not the killing type."

"Well, I don't want to die so I guess you will just have to trust me."

Veronica leaned on the balcony. "What do you need?"

"Just a little bit of blood. It will help me check the status of the gate's opening and in time I can devise a solution to the whole damn problem."

Veronica was a little hesitant. She did not want to trust someone who was keeping a secret as dark as hers from the people he worked with. "Why haven't you told anyone?" she asked him. It was rather peculiar that he did not. It was a very serious ordeal not to be trifled with.

"I have my orders. I don't particularly have a limit when it comes to the range of my operation."

"Who exactly do you work for if not Vincent?" she asked.

"That is a need to know basis."

They talked for a while longer before she agreed to give him blood. The council which remained hidden was updated on the ongoings that would in theory save a lot of lives. The truth, in whole, was to kill Veronica. The council hoped that it would stop the procession of the gate that was bound to her. Louis, if ordered, would be the assassin in the quiet night that would deliver the lethal strike.

The blood was put into a catalyst stone and with a simple cast of enchantment could show the swirling runes of the gate that encircled Veronica's heart. The council was pleased by the ingenuity of their agent. Now they had a visal in which they could put on a timeline. All that remained was the council's orders to capture her but Louis did not see the need if he could remove the gate from her person. Of course he would keep that portion of his plan to himself.

Xiao Lin sat in a luxury chair with harems keeping her attention. She mostly basked in the glory of her trappings as she was head of the ludus. She was in charge of recruiting gladiators and preparing them for the battles that would keep all of Athens in a frenzy of excitement and gore. She loved the new role of being in charge and pitied the day when she would have to give up her power and return to the lounge as an information gatherer.

And she still had her cell phone. Of which she had a phone call from Incognito on the whereabouts of the witch Beatrix. "Why the hell isn't Vincent picking up his phone?" the former demon hunter asked.

"He is currently doing some sparring with some gladiators as we prepare to take on the ludus of Hades."

"Do I even want to know?"

"It is a rather inspiring tale of triumph in the arena. You sure you don't want to know?"

"Just tell him we found out where Beatrix is going to strike next. You all better make it back here in one piece if he is going to capture her."

"I will be sure to tell him." The phone clicked as it was hung up.

Beatrix had been busy collecting souls for puppets as she prepared to strike out against the world of the demon hunters. Her malicious tidings were the only mark she had left to be tracked. It seems Rachel and Incognito made some headway into stopping her. The ebon paled in comparison to the turmoil that was caused back in Chicago. But there was no getting around what the crew had gotten themselves into.

They would battle the realm of Hades and if they were victorious they would be hot into the pursuit of the devilish witch.

Vincent was adamant when he heard the news. There was no guarantee that Xagos would be sited. There was after all no reason for him not to show and Vincent wanted the first pick when it came to the ravenous demon. There was a score to settle and it was high time it was resolved. There was that pesky bind that made Xagos immune to the demon hunter. He wondered if Louis could be of any use in that department.

"Louis, you are good with binds, no?" he asked.

"I thought it was the reason you recruited me."

"That and your kick ass hair."

Louis stoked his dark hair. "It is rather luxurious, is it not?"

"I need one broken so that we can stop a demon from capturing hunter's souls."

"That can be really tricky." Louis said, unsure of the bind and the demon involved. "You have to have been the one that casted the bind and even then they are rarely undone. Have you been doing some work without telling us?"

"It was before your time. The one that put the bind on said demon has passed away. Are there no other options?"

"Depends on the demon. If it is weaker, I don't see why there would be a bind. But a more powerful one might just cause trouble."

"Yep, this is complete bullshit." Vincent said. He kept the origin of his mother at bay. Personal motives against demons were frowned upon and Vincent was not quite ready to divulge all of his secrets to his underling. "I will show you when we get back to Chicago. The demon is running amok and I can't kill it because it has a protection bind on me."

"I could kill your demon." Louis said as innocent as he was unaware of the vendetta. "It is why you pay me after all."

"I kind of want this one for myself. When we get back I will fill you in on the details."

Faustas interrupted the chat as it was time for Vincent and himself to face off in the house skirmish. Vincent slipped on those magic sandals and equipped himself with the wooden apparels. The two circled each other and the other gladiators were in full chant. The two would spar to claim the top gladiator of the ludus of Xiao Lin. She herself joined Veronica on the balcony to oversee the final match.

"We have some news about the witch of Chicago." Xiao said to Veronica.

Veronica had her mind on her family stirrings, she was not yet convinced that Louis could help. For now she would keep that conversation out of the rest of the Demon Hunter's Lounge's light. The last thing she wanted to do was cause more trouble than she felt she was worth. "Anything worth my time?"

"We are one step closer to finding Beatrix, or so your favored Incognito tells me. How exactly did you two meet?"

Veronica did not want to be rude but her mind was elsewhere. "It is not something I usually tell. I don't really want to get into it Xiao, you have to forgive me. It is an uneasy tale."

"You know you can confide in me. I would never reveal what you don't want me to."

"What if I told you I knew how the world was going to end?" Veronica said, testing the waters.

"I would say that is not something you should keep in. Should I be worried?"

Veronica sighed. "What do you know of Louis? He seems to know more than he lets on."

"I don't know much." Xiao said. She was unaware of Veronica changing the subject. "He is still relatively new to us." Xiao Lin gasped "Is he a demon overlord?"

"Not that I can tell." Veronica laughed. "I will do my research on him when we arrive in Chicago. I sense intentions in him that aren't the most savory."

"Should we tell Vincent?"

"No need to worry him with what is probably nothing. I may just be over reacting."

No one slept. Their energies were high as the next round of the games were at hand. Vincent was sure he could conquer Hades, especially with a gladiator like Faustas at his side. The others put up a good fight as well. There was sure to be less casualties when it came to the arena. Xiao Lin had done a wonderful job in hand picking her crops when it came to the warriors. Vincent only played along for the ebon which was promised to make an appearance in the next match.

Were they ready to face what the gods of Olympus had to offer? There was only one way to find out.

CHAPTER TEN

House Xiao Lin stood in the arena with purple flames torches lighting the night sky. It was the beckoning of the underworld; the odd colored fire. The Athenians were in favor of the gladiator as Hades was a bitter rival of Athena. Hades wanted to topple the city and cast the underworld upon it and claim dominion over it. Such ambitions were the reason for the games in which the ardent demon hunter Vincent now participated in.

"Your author will tell of our victory tonight and it shall ring throughout history for many years to come." Faustas said to Vincent, readying his sword and shield.

"No matter the outcome, it was a pleasure battling at your side." Vincent said in return.

The gladiators deployed by Xiao Lin stood in a circle with shields in a sort of phalanx. They would be surrounded on all sides by the demonic hoard that Hades would send in the battle to win Athena's favor. What they saw a few moments later was nothing the likes of Faustas had ever seen.

Bone and armor rose from the sand. The skeletal demons had swords and shields as well, the catch was that House Xiao Lin was outnumbered. It was less than favorable and the odds of Vincent surviving was dwindle down to a "very unlikely". The demon hunter implored the challenge. It was not everyday the odds were stacked against him. He held up his swords and roared and the other roared behind him.

The demon hoard shambled their way with fervor towards the

gladiators and were met with a metal wall that stopped their advance. Spears jutted out from behind the shields and pierced the demons. What the gladiators did not expect was that demons did not fall to regular weapons. They were in fact and indeed in peril as the wall of shields fell and they began to die one by one.

If their immortality was not enough, the entrance gate opened and there stood the cyclops wrapped in the chains of Olympus hulking with its gargantuan one eye. Vincent gazed at the demon with delight. "That's one big baby."

The cyclops whipped the chains into some of the defending shields, knocking some of the warriors aside. They recovered quickly as they were better trained than the last bunch. But they were no match overall. Vincent had to react quickly. He three his swords into some of the skeletal demons and summoned his famous demon killing scythe. There he began his traditional work in what he did best, second to pissing off Veronica who watched with Xiao Lin from the balcony.

"Shouldn't you be helping secure the chains?" Veronica asked Xiao Lin, who sat eating grapes. "This is your boss AND the reason we are here." Louis was close behind and already springing into action.

"Don't mind if we do." he said jumping from the balcony and into the arena. He landed on the back of the cyclops and rode in like a raging bull. Xiao Lin summoned her long sword wanting to fit in with the theme of the killing. She did a tiny war shriek of her own and went berserk the way no one knew she could.

There was a balance in the arena. Though there seemed to be no end to the hoard. They hoard began to climb up the walls and attack the audience. Bodies were flung to the sand as the patrons were defenseless and did not see the overturn of their seats in their foreseeable fate.

To Vincent's surprise, Adras made an appearance from the underworld. He was skinnier and wielding some demonic weapons. After his death he was sure never to be seen again, let alone to be on the evil side of things. Vincent wondered what kind of a man he was to be sent to Hades and come back a demon. Now was not the time to ask however.

Louis was thrown from the back of the Cyclops and with extreme agility, he landed on his feet. He used his staff to absorb some wind and then blew back a few on the skeleton demons. He whirled it around gathering force to knock off a few heads like a pro baseball player.

Xiao Lin was parrying some blades back like a tiger. She was delighted to have so many opponents. It was why she liked working alongside her boss in the field. They found trouble together just the way they liked it. Naturally they were tipping the scales in their favor.

Arrows were being shot by some demons from the edge of the arena. Patrons were being slaughtered by the unexpected onslaught. Veronica became surrounded by a few demons and she was defenseless as she was not a huntress. She stepped slowly backward until she reached the edge of the balcony. Then a soldier of Athens made short work of the demons. Athena sent her army to the rescue. Soon blue caped warriors filled the seats of the gory arena and the tide was soon to be settled.

Vincent began to fly with the sandals he received from Agatha. He circled the behemoth cyclops in attempts to confuse it and knock it off balance. It swatted at him but he was too elusive. He slashed at it, cutting off one of his arms. It flopped to the ground and the chains were up for grabs. He landed next to the appendage and picked it up. It was heavy, but nothing less was expected when dealing with such an ebon.

He then cut off the head of the cyclops and it shook the sands as it fell. When the final sword was sheathed it was the blue capes and the gladiators of the sand that emerged victorious. There were countless bodies in the pews, but Vincent was not responsible for any casualties that had suffered at the hands of Hades' army. The purple flames burned out and the second round of the games ended. There was a battle shout that saw it off.

The center of the arena began to glow and a lovely woman with her hair long and flowing materialized from the light. It was Athena and she looked at the arena in horror. She had not expected Hades to put such breach in Athens. This was to be dealt with. It was clear that her army arrived in time as they all knelt st what they did best. The gods would be at war for such folley.

"You there, warrior." Athena called Vincent. "What manner of weapon is that?"

"This?" he whirled his scythe. "This is a good fashioned death scythe."

"You wield it with great skill. From whose house do you fight for?"

"That would be me." Xiao Lin stepped forward. She was mesmerized by the beauty of the goddess. She simply had to have her for herself.

"Your house had fought well. Your ludus has shown promise. Is there a warrior among them whom you would give to serve as commander in my army?"

Faustas stepped forward. He considered it an honor and chose to take command against the forces of Hades. Xiao Lin approved as there was none she offered that would put his sword to greater purpose. She thought for a moment then offered all of her gladiators. In exchange she was offered one favor. She wanted a kiss she admitted to Vincent.

"Don't be ridiculous. If you get that you are paying for all of our plane tickets home." he said in scornship.

"I will transport you to your destination, but should the need arrive I will bring you here to fight the underworld." Athena said.

"Hey," Vincent said, "as long as you're paying."

"Fortune will be yours."

There was a flash of green light and soon they were back in the garage. Chicago never felt so sweet. Veronica immediately went to work on turning the chain into a rune so that it could be called at any time. Vincent left the flying sandals with Faustas. He figured it was a better deal for him having better chances as fighting the underworld army. The phone was ringing and who other than Incognito to be pestilent about punctuality?

"Do you have any idea how many times I have tried to call you, fool?" he sounded rash and upset.

"How long has it been?"

"Three weeks. You could have hauled your ass back here days ago. What the hell took you so goddamn long?"

"Well there was this practice in the ludus of Xiao Lin. See, it is the only ludus ever run by an asian woman."

"What kind of joke is that?"

"I don't know, we were getting popular. I am an official gladiator of Athens."

"Just get over here as soon as you can. You have to catch this witch before she takes over. No slacking, fool."

With that the conversation ended. It was thirty minutes before the new ebon was inked in. The crew showered and cleaned the sand from places sand should not have been. Their work would not end so soon. There was a witch to capture, or kill. The odds again were not in their favor. Beatrix was sure to have more minions. Xagos was shielded against their best fighter. It would be a fight to remember.

Vincent could not help it. He would need to call Dimitri. That rifle of his would give them a tactical advantage. Now they could capture the witch with the chains. There was sure to be a large bounty on her. She did start a bunch of waves.

Rachel arrives in the screeching wheels of Tags, the ebon warmachine. "Get in, we have a lot to go over." They climbed in and sped off toward the nightclub where they all sat at a round table while the music was playing. "We don't have a lot of time. Beatrix is planning to increase her powers. If she does that she will be able to open portals to let some mean demon though. If we thought she was trouble before, this would take the cake she was having and eating, too."

"How much time are we looking at?"

"Three hours, tops."

"We had better get moving, then." Vincent called Dimitri. He would meet them at a gate in the subway. There they would have a standoff in the dominion of a witch. That was dangerous. A witch's power was increased in their dominion. And there was Xagos to consider. There was also her scarecrow minions that were sure to be there for a fight. It was out of the frying pan and into the fire for the demon hunting crew.

Louis was on his computer as they drove. He looked into anything that could make his gate tracer that he made from Veronica's blood increase in its radius. He found nothing. He would have to be near her in order for it to read. The small beads that would normally whirl at a frequency were still and inert.

"Louis, we have to be focused, now may be the only time we can stop Beatrix." Vincent said, holding on to the railing overhead in the back of Tags.

"I'm focused. Just putting the finishing touches on some work. I can handle this."

They parked next to a stairwell on the street that led to the subway where their target was said to be hidden. They were prepared for the worst. "I hate the subway." Xiao Lin said. The team would separate to cover any of the exits. Radios were equipped so that they could keep in contact. The witch would not escape. She would be captured or eliminated.

The subway terminal was empty which was odd. Definitely a sign that they were in the right place. Vincent touched his ear. "Everyone keep your eyes peeled and be on your toes. We are expecting a heavy firefight."

"Roger." Rachel said first. "What is our game plan? She is weakened."

"We move to capture. This way we can return her to Solomon." Vincent said, expressing orders.

"I don't have any capture tools." Xiao Lin said, chiming in. "What if I run into her?"

"Then you let us know and we will converge on your location."

"I'm only good for a fight. Maybe I can put a gravity bind on her." Louis said.

"We need more tools." Xiao Lin was right. They were ready for a fight. They needed to move quickly as this was an opening. If Xagos were near it would only make matters worse.

Louis pulled out a gauge that would track magic. He snooped around the empty subway terminal but there was not much response from the ebon. "It's too quiet."

"I have a quiet front too."

"Are we sure this is where she is hiding?"

Rachel felt offended that her primary work was in question. "I am certain this is where the origin of her leyline exists."

A figure moved toward Vincent, its heels echoing off the walls. It was a familiar shape with its coat and hat. It was the man that crashed his car. "If you are looking for Betrix, she is already gone. You are much too late."

"I'm sorry, I didn't catch your name. Didn't I hand you a piece of yourself a while back?"

"My name is of no importance, and in time neither will you and your disrespectful witch hunt."

"What are you? Some sort of lackey? Are you looking for an ass kicking for destroying my ride? I owe you for that."

"I am only here to put distance between you and Beatrix. You can keep talking if you would like."

Scarecrows began to crawl from all over. Blades decorated their limbs. "Vincent, we have trouble." Louis said over the radio. "There are a ton of Beatrix's minions emerging."

"I have one of her soldiers in front of me. Team, what's your status?"

"Bogeys all around." Rachel said. Xiao Lin was in a similar situation.

"What are you planning? What does this witch want?" Vincent asked the nameless man.

"We want the destruction of the demon hunters. Your presence is as profane as it is a nuisance."

"Too bad you think you will win this one. Why don't I just put an end to you right here?"

"Come and try."

Vincent summoned Ammit. He fired and the spray of bullets shot out like a firecracker. The man was no amatuer to combat it seemed. He dodged the spray by jumping up and sticking to the ceiling. He ran toward Vincent with extreme speed before another shot would be fired. He leapt vertically and a hidden blade knocked Ammit from Vincent's hand.

Vincent responded by summoning his scythe and whirled the lethal and crafty end. He caught the overcoat of the man and ripped it from his being. The man leapt backward and removed his hat revealing his face which was a little unorthodox. He had stitching on him that proved he was no longer human. He looked like the work would prolong his life and he would serve demonkind in exchange for the procedure.

"Man you're one ugly son of a bitch." Vincent said.

"You are a bratty one. No wonder Xagos wants to kill you."

"So you admit to working on the losing team. That demon's head is mine."

"You do not realize the folly in which you speak. Xagos has the power beyond the likes of your understanding. The bind that your mother put on him is the only thing saving you from his infernal grasp. You should be grateful that you are fortunate enough to be protected."

"I will be the one killing him. That is just a matter of time."

"You may be protected, but the ones you brought along are not."

That set an alarm off in Vincent's head. "Vincent, we have a problem." Louis called. "That demon is here and he does not look like he is willing to play little league."

"We have to pull out. Everyone retreat." Vincent ordered.

"You think we will just let you leave?" the scarecrow man said. "Your soul will be added to the army in which we shape. Demon hunters be damned." He charged at Vincent with the blade pointing at vital. There were sparks when the blades collided. Vincent could keep pace but the reflexes of his opponent outclassed his strikes. Xagos shot bone shards at Louis, all he could do was take cover. He could not get close to the demon for every time he tried it was a literal trial by fire. Xiao Lin and Rachel had no luck against the scarecrow demons as they followed retreat orders and made their way topside.

Escape was Vincent's opt as well. He could stay and fight but he was worried about his team. Leaving them to the lack of mercy that was Xagos was not covered by their health insurance. Soon the terminal had overwhelming numbers of minions and Beatrix had already moved her hideout. They were too slow and there would be no reward for empty hands.

Vincent made it up the final stairwell with a hoard of scarecrows just at his heels. One of them dropped at the sound of a rifle. The bullet passed just over his shoulder and then he looked from the direction in which it came. It was Dimitri in the nick of time. "You look like you could use a hand, partner."

"We could have used you a second ago."

"Sorry I am late to the party, traffic was a nightmare." Dimitri fired again, knockinge one of the scarecrows off balance, then another to make its head explode.

Vincent turned to the opening of the stairwell and began to swing his scythe and bits of straw flew about. He summoned his Ammit and fired it keeping the hoard at bay until Tags showed up so that they could make a very narrow escape. When the wheels screeched and the back hatch opened it was nothing but a simple dive into the back before rubber was burned.

There were more scarecrows lined the streets. The gatling gun was manned by none other than the heroine Xiao Lin. Rachel sped through the streets looking to find a place to stop the roaring earmachine. It was a trap. Beatrix knew she was being followed. She set up a hoard of her minions so that the demon hunters should perish.

"Hold on to your hats. This is going to be a bumpy one." Rachel called out. She was running the demons off the road, bushels of straw scattered everywhere. The demons would jump onto Tags and began to cut into the walls of the warmachine with serrated limbs. Louis would beat them back with his rod. Vincent cut them with his scythe.

"There are just too many of them." Xiao Lin said.

Dimitri sped along in his sporty vehicle with a flamethrower, burning the straw as he passed. "Any plans to get rid of the infestation?"

"None that I can think of." Vincent called back.

"I have a detonator that can wipe out the field of scarecrows." Rachel said. "But it will take some time to load."

"You wait to tell me this now?"

"Better late than never." Rachel smiled.

"Yea, but never late is better."

They plummeted through more of the demons with bullets flying in a line and rubber kicking up straw. Xiao Lin had to duck under a blade of one of the demons that managed to make it on top of the roof.

She summoned her sword and managed to cut off a leg so that the demon tumbled off at the speed in which they were going.

The back door flew open as it was pierced by a black and then snatched off its hinges. "How long before detonation?"

"Thirty more seconds!"

Ammit gave enough kick so that the demons would fly backward when struck. A few moments later there was a pulse explosion set to convert anything that was not human into embers. When Tags was stopped and the crew hopped out, there were piles of burning staw all over the streets of Chicago.

"I can't wait to see that one in theaters." Vincent said out loud.

"See what now?" Rachel asked.

"He is convinced that his life is being narrated by an author. He curses him every time his life is in danger." Xiao Lin explained.

"Sounds a little nutty if you ask me." Rachel responded. "Those demons did a real number on Tags. It is going to take some real repair work before this puppy is set to ride again."

"Let's get back to headquarters. I am hungry from all this fighting."

Xiao Lin agreed. "Me too."

There was no luck in capturing Beatrix. Who was her lackey and how did her influence on him affect their cause. Vincent was sure to get to the bottom of this. It was just that the witches powers grew too quickly. They were ages behind her in terms of fire power. Dimitri was not enough to stop the hoard, but it sure did help. When was the witch planning to strike and who was her next target? These were things to consider. But first, chow time.

Veronica joined the crew for dinner. She did not want to spend time alone with her thoughts about the future. She let up on Vincent and decided to take it easy on him. Maybe there was promise in her agreement with Louis who kept his plans altogether from the rest of the crew. If he could not destroy the gate he would be forced to capture her and she would be executed. It was an option to save her life, but if he was ordered to he would commit.

The rest of the group was none the wiser. Veronica could not tell her family secret for fear of what the demo hunter would commit to doing. It was their duty to bring abrupt ends to events such as this. But their fates were the ones that hung in the balance. What would Vincent do if he knew? What would he say? She was certain she was loved but shied away from the reality of the coming storm that came with her father's avaricious return.

But the crew ate and repairs were set for their warmachine without any suspicions of upcoming events that pertained to the world to hang in the balance. They ate the food Xiao Lin made in the lounge's freshly remodeled kitchen. There was not even so much as a bruise to report. There was the matter of the witch and demon Xagos to consider, but there needed to be a large number of hunters perhaps before they could take her on. She moved her hideout so there would be time before she could be found. Then there was her skill to consider.

But Vincent wanted nothing more than to kill the demon that killed his family. Xagos saw no need to spare the hunter as well. They were locked in on each other with nothing but intent on the other. Powerful binds prevented them from harm and Vincent's drive to unbind himself from his mother's protection was the only thing that would gain him what he wanted. With one bind released they were both free to hack each other to pieces. For now the crew would enjoy each other's company. That was until the demon hunting council sent a summons to Vincent's door.

CHAPTER ELEVEN

A short woman in round glasses stood with a clipboard and blowing bubbles of gum. She had headphones and slowly nodded her head to whatever tunes kept her occupied.

"Can I help you?" Xiao Lin asked, looking her over in carnal delight. It was an instant attraction. The woman walked into the lounge uninvited so it was clear that she was not a vampire. It was fitting to blonde hair and that little diferencial disappointed the asian huntress.

The woman waltzed over to Vincent who was looking over a rune on Louis's computer. They were searching for any combination of magic that would put an end to the bond between him and Xagos. It was a lead though it was not a promising one.

"Vincent Delvine?" the woman asked.

"In the flesh, and you are?"

She did not hear him on the account of the music but she knew it was him. The council kept tabs on all the hunters. She only asked out of the formality of the errand she ran. "I am Donna Knowland. I need you to sign on the dotted line."

He took the clipboard and read it over with a quick glance. "What is this?"

"It is a summons to the council for an infraction of demon hunting law. Apparently you killed a human?" Donna popped a huge bubble.

The entire lounge moaned. "I didn't know he was malicious, I swear." Xiao Lin said, flabbergasted.

"How on earth did you guys find out?"

"The council knows all. We keep tabs on hunters and hunters alike. It is easy for us to track the damages, I will be representing you while you plead your case to the council."

"Are you a lawyer?" Louis asked. He was familiar with the council as they tied him to his mission to capture the gate Veronica. These were the same persons and they meant business. If they were heading to the council for court he could chat with them about the parameters of his mission. "Aren't you a little young?"

"Yea, the council is full of old geezers. You don't fit that description."

"I am infused with an anti age charm courtesy of a warlock that fell in love with me." Donna said.

"Anti age charm? Is that legal?" Rachel wondered.

Xiao Lin let a long face creep over her gaunt. "You're married?"

Donna corrected any predisposition at once. "It was completely one sided. He was stripped of all magic and is being held in a triple maximum security prison for crimes against humanity."

"Then how about a date!?" Xiao Lin exclaimed. She did not hesitate when it came to pretty women. Women did not seem to mind the childlike adoration she would give them.

"I am only here to keep your business up and running. If Vincent is convicted you all will be out of work and looking for a new boss."

Vincent needed to know more. "How bad is it?"

"It is not as bad as the council is making it seem. Our primary defense is you were not issued your demon hunting license by them as you were not ever a part of the academy. Since Incognito trained you himself he will need to make an appearance to the council as well. I trust he still owns the nightclub?"

"You know my mentor?"

"I was his partner some years back, yes. I found a job helping those with promise escape the clutches of the will of the council. I took the job after he retired."

Rachel chimed in, "I bet you are chalked full of stories."

"None that I wish to tell." Donna was reading lips. Xiao Lin was a little too close for comfort. Donna was not the affectionate type but Xiao Lin was sure she could make her sway.

THE DEMON HUNTER'S LOUNGE

"Anything else I need to know about how we are going to keep me out of demon hunting jail? I have a witch to catch and she has a powerful demon at her disposal. Time is money quite literally, I'm afraid."

"Since," and Donna was just going over some notes she had written down, "Adras was converted to Hades and still roamed the earth as a demon, he was not actually killed, rather relocated from living to demon, I would say the odds are in your favor."

"I get to see the council headquarters?" Xiao Lin asked Vincent.

"Somebody has to track Beatrix. I don't really see it as a field trip, anyway."

"I sat the last one out. I need some new sites in my life." Rachel said.

Louis offered a solution. "If we take Tags we can still do work while we keep our boss from being babysat behind bars." His solution was a tactical one. He did not want to be chosen to be left behind. It was a chance he would take on trying to remove the gate from Veronica. The council would have her head if he did not make any progress. It was likely and of course Vincent would have his head as well as his job.

"Splendid!" Xiao Lin exclaimed.

It would be some time before Vincent had to make an appearance in front of the council. It was the first time he had to deal with the official ordinance makers of the demon hunting world. It was the same as he viewed it with the academy, a big waste of time. He had a personal vendetta and skills to see its bloody fruition. They had no real connection with him so their grip was seen as something he could escape.

Donna sat at Vincent's desk asking him a load of questions as to how the event of killing Adras had come about. There was no mention of the nightmare of Xagos as he did not want to reveal too much about why he joined the unofficial ranks of being a demon hunter. He did not need the council sniffing around. Who knew what they would do if they knew of his personal engagements?

Every so often Xiao Lin would be caught staring into the corner office. She was practically drooling over the woman with the clipboard. She wondered what kind of ebon Donna carried. Since she worked so closely with Incognito in the past it had to be one worth asking about. Xiao Lin wanted to know the secrets of the lawyer. She had to have her for herself.

It turned out that Clair was over two-hundred years old thanks to the charm. She had been fighting demons before demon hunting was cool. She did tell some of the tales of her demon hunting woes to Vincent as she wanted to establish a connection on a more personal front. She told him that she at one point wanted to marry Incognito. Of course he turned her down for reasons she did not say.

She had many cases but none as open and shut as this one. There was one drawback that did not sit well with Vincent, however. He would have to register as an official demon hunter and would have to share information with them and be at their call when it came to demons, witches, and warlocks. He would be assigned work and pay would be short. He was not looking forward to the commitment.

He would lose his chances at battling Xagos. There was no way the council would approve of the demon hunt. He would miss out on capturing Beatrix. That was also unfavorable as he implored the challenge. It was not often that an enemy could hold their own. The bureaucracy that came along with registering was tedious and not the way he intended on continuing his work.

Donna assured him that such an acceptance was the only way he would be able to continue hunting. There was to be no more freelance work. That just did not sit well with him. It was the best he could do though. She had him sign a contract that said would work for them. He would have to maintain contact and wait for contracts that the council deemed for him. He told the news to the crew and they were all indifferent. Except for Louis.

Louis volunteered as the coordinator. He would be the one to accept the jobs and be in contact with the council headquarters. It fueled his own intent. He figured it was better this way, if he was going to save Veronica's life and stop an apocalypse from rearing its ugly head. He contacted the council via projection stone.

"Louis, I trust you have news for the council?" the figure said from the stone. Louis hid in the basement while conveying the message of his connection newly found by Vincent's new commitment.

"I will be able to communicate with the council as I am the coordinator of future excursions."

"What is the meaning of this?"

"Vincent will plead with the council for an official demon hunting license. He will be tied to us and we can force him to give us information about the gate." Louis kept his voice low.

"We were unaware that he knew of the gate's existence."

"You can order him to find out. It is nothing short of an assignment."

"We will consider this. Any new information about the gate?"

"I have an apparatus that will allow me to check the status of the gate, though it is close range. Veronica is not always around for me to monitor her."

"We will consider this." The projection ended.

Louis was now in a position of control. He could influence the crew on where to go and what jobs to take. All he needed was time to save Veronica before the council ordered him to end her life. All he needed was time. Time was something he did not have as the gate behaved unpredictably. He needed to get closer to Veronica. He was not sure how to do so without raising suspicion.

Incognito's was quiet in the day. It allowed him to pour over pages of the things he saw fit for information and trade amongst other hunters. Every so often he would make a deal for an artifact, the way he did for the artifact of the afterlife in egypt. It was different than actually participating in demon hunting. It was more of a hobby. There was a slight unrest when he saw Donna at his door. It was some years since his retirement. Nothing seemed to change when it came to the old times.

"Well if it isn't Donna." he said stepping into the outdoors. He sparked a cigar, an old anthem.

"I can't say the years have been kind, but I'm still alive." she said. It was like they never parted. Aside from traveling the world vanquishing those of an unsavory variety, feelings of affection rose with her.

"To what do I owe the pleasure of your company? You know I don't do any hunting of my own. So don't even bother to ask."

"It is nothing like that."

"Still looking to make me your man?"

"Not withstanding. Those days I feel will never be. I know how you feel when it comes to my age. I know those kinds of magics don't sit well with you. This is more about your apprentice, Mr. Delvine." She took a few papers from her clipboard and showed it to him. "He has fallen under the radar of the council and it would mean a great deal if you assisted him in his plea."

"What did he do this time?" Incognito inhaled deeply expecting some witch hunt that had gone wrong, not that it was not far from the truth.

"He would have to register with the council if he wants to continue to hunt. You are a well respected member of the coalition and it would be easier if you did."

"You mean I used to be. Those days are behind me."

"You would leave him high and dry? That is unlike you."

"I never said that. I just want you to know you shouldn't expect too much from me. I don't even so much as summon my ebon. I have people to do that for me."

"Classic you and your ever expanding influence."

Incognito flicked the ash from the cigar. "How is the life of an immortal? You should be running the council by now. Don't tell me you plan on serving papers forever, quite literally?"

"I will make progress when the time is right. You know my ambition. For now it is clerical work. Maybe I will have you back to work when the time is right." She had the influence in the proper channels and could force him out of retirement. It was just her character traits from having felled love that made the prompt.

Incognito would have none of it. He was his own man and his days of hunting were just a glimpse in the rearview mirror. If she were so sensitive seh should not have even come to Chicago. There was nothing but another rejection waiting for her, but she could pull the strings. Hell hath no fury like a woman scorned.

Calls were coming in from all over. The crew was not permitted to answer any of the incoming jobs until such times with the committee had passed. It was rather unfortunate. A week went by before they heard anything from the council about the summons. They would have to wait and Donna was policing the situation with an iron grip. She specialized in taming situations down to a dull roar and she did so with grace. She would be terrifying to have as an enemy. Luckily she was on Vincent's side.

Incognito hung around and signed paperwork that said Vincent would corporate and that was against his better wishes. The luxury of having the lounge gather objects would definitely come to a halt. Their freedoms were limited to the beckoning call of a bunch of hunters that did not see the beauty of fighting for what they wanted.

It was one thousand years ago when the council was formed. There was a genocide of humans by witches and walocks that saw their powers as something to rule over the earthly plane. There was one among the villainous lot that led the magic bearers in their crusade against mankind. His name was Vadin and he tore up the lives of countless bloodlines in an attempt to reign supreme.

For a time he was victorious in his endeavours and it was without the use of demons that he did it. There was only the raw power that one was born with that sufficed as adequate ammo to the defenseless people. Vadin killed without mercy and took no quarter. Wave after wave of dauntless people suffered if they did not obey. There were only two options back then; convert or die.

There were few that began to practice magic in secret while they were servants to Vadin. They practiced in the woods, conjuring up minor spells led by a brave Talia who used magic of light so that one day they might be free. She gathered only one-hundred insurgents to vanquish the tyrant Vadin. While they did not kill him, he was only sealed away by binding light, their victory gained them freedom and then countless others joined the cause and soon perilous times turned into that of reverie.

All those years ago and now the organization that was formed sent the soon to be council member Donna to Vincent's doorstep and the only way he was free to hunt Xagos was to join them. He would have to do what they said, take whatever jobs they gave him, and altogether keep him as a dog chained to a leash. It was the only option and it was a grim one.

But tales of old were not going to save the position of the young demon hunter. It was a very modern day problem that could not be avoided. He would serve the council, his crew along with him. They gathered and asked how such an event would even come about. Vincent broke the silence and told them the tale of his origin and the brutal murder of his parents. Though he was not sure what Xagos wanted with him. It was rather simple. Xagos needed a tie to the human world so that he could travel between verses and collect souls that would increase his power and lifespan. Xagos found that in Beatrix who was very human and becoming very powerful.

Did the council know of her? They had to. Maybe Vincent could ask their permission to find her. There were some that operated as a special task force that targeted special interest profiles. Only time would tell, that is if he was not put under lock and key. Donna assured him they had a good chance of keeping him free if he agreed to what the council demanded. She was unaware of the origin as Vincent told the story absent her presence.

When the time came to go and make his appearance before the council Vincent gave explicit orders to the crew to hunt down Beatrix and Xagos. It would be the final order that would need to prevail while he came under the order of those that sought to ensnare him for the minor inconvenience in Athens. Nothing would stop him from exacting bloody vengeance. All he needed was the bind to be broken so that Xagos would be on the same mortal playing field.

The crew piled into a cargo plane that was roomy for the trip to come. They flew in between dimensions as the council headquarters was placed between wards. Low level magics could not find it. It was a passage only to those with clearances and some were given passes so they could enter. All in all it was a hidden fortress with the most adept of hunters. One should not make a foe of the council. Timeless powers and ebon equipped the hunters of convenience that could topple great cities in a matter of hours.

"Is this your first time with the council?" Rachel asked Vincent.

"I never really was an official demon hunter, so yes. This little trip will be complete with a registry, among which I comply with all of their demands. It will keep us in business."

"I have seen the council's magnitude before." Xiao Lin said. "They have explosive skills that are second to none."

"When?" Vincent wanted to know all about the blowhards that would be sucking away his money as well as his entertainment value.

"It was when I was younger. I was saved in my refugee camp by a hunter with a gun that looked like diamonds. It fired rapidly into demon skin back when the world needed saving."

"They don't move often." Louis said with extensive knowledge of the council. "But when they do it is like a tidal wave of active fire power. Those guys are the reason most demons don't make it very far."

Donna chimed in. "It is for the preservation of mankind. The order was established at a point in time where humans were defenseless against powers that sought to enslave or destroy. Incognito, at one point was nominated to be one of the elite. Isn't that right?"

"That was a long time ago." Incognito said with the grim reminder of what he let go of. Donna saw him as powerful and wanted him back on the job. It was one of the reasons she responded the way she had before. She felt the world needed that kind of guidance. "I am just here to make sure my apprentice still has a job in a week."

That was true. Incognito had no desire to return to the workforce, He did well on his own. With the nightclub running with hunters by night he could count wads of cash in the morning, in his office, with his cigar. Returning to the council was a blood oath that was being broken but it was a small price to pay for who he considered one of the finest hunters he had ever seen. Vincent was quick with his work. The council would only slow him down.

The council headquarters was a site to see. It looked like a castle that was high enough above the clouds and sat like a fortress in the sky. They landed and began towards the large doors that would lead them to their chambers while they waited a day for the hearing. Xiao Lin, who loved seeing new sights, took pictures with a camera. There were guards on standby in uniforms that made them look like nights. The suits enhanced the powers of those who wore them. She even took pictures of the still seemingly inanimate warriors.

"You are to retire to your chambers and wait for word of the council for further direction." Donna informed Vincent. He agrees and was granted permissions to wander around as long as he did not cause any trouble.

The grandeur was enough to give the young hunter a headache. He could sense the paperwork piling in his head. What would he be if he was not free to act when the moment suited him. He would have to follow orders. Was there nothing he could do? The rest of the crew were not so doom and gloom. They took in the sites that looked like they were fit for the royal variety. Louis went off to see those that tasked him with Veronica, who stayed in Chicago tending the nightclub.

Louis needed tools to extract the gate. It was his proposal to the council so that Veronica would not die, or at least it was not in his nature to kill someone that fell victim to her warlock father. When he approached the council member that headed his operation he was a little taken back by the lack of surprise when he prompted his offer.

"Can I have this opportunity?" Louis asked.

The council member would also oversee Vincent's hearing and was aware that given the timeframe such an action to destroy the gate could be achieved.

"You are solely responsible for carrying out this mission. I trust you have the intentions of a nobleman. Should the gate open and release the warlock you will be stripped of all titles and removed from any affairs henceforth from the council's proceedings."

"Thank you. I will need time to assess what kind of seal the gate is."

"Do not falter in your research. Should the gate open the council itself will be forced to move against the powers that seek to destroy us. If that should happen all processes would come to a halt and we do not need such regressions that were made into fruition by the war one-thousand years ago. Do you understand the importance of your mission?"

"I do." Louis lowered his head. "I know if worse comes to worse Veronica should be eliminated. What of Vincent Delvine?"

"He will be too busy to interrupt. He is trained unofficially and will be handled accordingly. Do not worry about him. Just worry about the task at hand."

"Yes, your excellency."

Louis spent the day in the council library looking over runes that may break the gate in two. It was tedious work and was done with the most secrecy. If the crew found out who he was working for and why they were sure to get word back to Vincent. He did not need anyone to know. He found the story of Veronica's father in the old archives. He was held in a prison awaiting his fabled return. All he needed was for his daughter to falter. In time there would be no way to stop him. It would be a war, the likes of which would shake the foundation of demonic hunters.

Most demons were mindless creatures set to purpose by the one that summoned them. Veronica's father was fabled as a warlock that did not need to summon lesser demons. His powers were immense and did not cost him his soul. It was paramount that he should never arise. Louis was all that stood between him and total damnation.

The night was a quiet one. Vincent stayed up all night with Donna as she briefed him on the etiquette that he should adhere to when in the council's presence. It would be best that he comply if he wanted to fight Xagos. The council members were stern when it came to such proceedings. They did not have time for anything that did not do their dirty work. Vincent was no exception.

Chapter Twelve

The council hall was as gaudy as the rest of the complex. Donna and Vincent walked in side by side to face the will of the council. The council members were that of former demon hunters that moved up in the ranks. They were seasoned veterans when it came to that chaotic life. Vincent would become a gear in their quintessential construct against his better wishes and judgment. That sat on a tier dressed in robes that signified their absolution.

The rest of the crew and Incognito stood on the balcony just above the event hearing. Xiao Lin waved as the two entered, hoping for the best. The hearing could go one of two way: Vincent would be accepted and have to work as a cog in the machine or he would be held for his murder. Donna was his first line of defense in those measures and Incognito would only speak on the former.

They walked until they reached the center circle that was overlooked by five of the most powerful practitioners in all the known land. It was them that would decide Vincent's fate. Vincent only needed to adhere to the council's demands. Should he be found in their favor he was a free man with strings attached.

Donna opened the conversation. "Councilmen, I am here to speak on behalf of Vincent Delvine in the matter of murder of the human variety. I understand you all have been briefed on these proceedings?"

One of the members took the lead. "We understand the case as it was presented and stand firmly on a decision that has been chosen by the council as of yesterday. The hunter Vincent Delvine stands accused if murder in the first degree while carrying out unsolicited matters of ebon collecting and demon hunting. The council recognizes that you have a proposal to present on his behalf."

Donna stood ready as this was nothing but a flit in her many talents. She stood like an iron spire to those she had the intention of joining in her future. "I prompt the council to the conversion factor of souls as is in Athens. There was no murder. The victim in question was transmogrified from one verse to the next due to the magics used by the gods."

"The council does not rule in favor of such stirrings. The act of killing a human is prohibited and punishable by relinquishing all rights to demon hunting. What was done was done. There are no technicalities that would permit the defendant any quarter in the traditional verdicts notwithstanding."

Donna's first attempt at getting Vincent off the hook was a failure. It was stonewalled by the rules that were known to him. He did not know what he would do if he was not permitted to hunt Xagos. Perhaps their plea for him to become an initiate was the way to go.

Another council member spoke. "I am not hearing a proposal, Donna."

"I make a motion that Vincent become an initiate as one of the council soldiers as since he was never endocrined as an official demon hunter he can not and shall not find repercussions as dictated by the laws of the council."

The council members began to speak in hushed whispers to each other. That threw them through a loop. They had not seen the appeal and it did not sit right with them. But it was true, Vincent was not one of theirs. The best that they could do was to throw a leash on the rogue puppy and make him obey the rules.

"Are you proposing that we take him in as one of our own?" a woman on the council asked. "His unofficial titles could not possibly reach the standard of or requirements."

Donna was stern in her word choosing. "Consider since he has enough resources and manpower to function with an entire complex of his own that he is very capable and may be that of above the requirements to enlist."

"Is the defendant aware of what we are dealing with? That we are at war with demon generals that seek to mame if not enslave all of humankind? He may be skilled but he is an amatuer when it comes to taking orders. His negligence and aptitude to commit a crime such as what he is accused of is proof of that enough."

It was clear the council had no intention of enlisting Vincent. But it was time that Vincent spoke for himself. "I don't mind you all bickering about me. Hell, it might make a best seller someday. But if you aren't going to hire me then you have to let me go. I have other matters to attend to.

Donna quieted the brazen words of the demon hunter. She assured him that there was no need to antagonize the council. They could have him thrown in jail or worse. "I strongly urge you to move to enlist." she said. "It is better than having him roam free. It is the least to consider. He is going to do what he wants. Better have him serving in the frontlines." They took their leave.

The council spent the rest of the day deliberating on just what to do with Vincent. He had his crew to consider. Where would they be if he had to go and fight some battles in a war they had never heard of. Would he be able to hunt the demon that killed his family? There was the bind to consider. There was Beatrix. There was Louis and the gate that Vincent knew nothing about. All he knew was that their relationship had been rocky without the slightest idea that she would bring about the end of the world.

It would be a few days before a letter was slid under his door. It was from the council and it stated that he was to become a member of their military along with some paperwork and that his stirrings would be under their watchful eye. He would go where they told him to go and he was not to take any freelance work as he was a part of something much larger than himself. He would have to undergo an aptitude test to see where he would be placed in their ranks. He would have to take it alone. There would be no schemes for his crew to follow, no orders to give.

Donna saw it as a victory and offered to be the one to report back to the council if anything Vincent did was deemed insubordinate. She had a plan of her own. If she could make the hunter presentable she would put her name forth on the ballot that would have her ascend to the council seats. She would live in Chicago and Vincent would report to her so that the council would not miss a note on their new found bargain.

Though Vincent did not agree wholeheartedly with taking orders, he saw it better than being completely useless behind bars in Solomon or worse. He would have to keep his orders to his crew a secret but he would at least have something to do. Maybe he would find out what this war was about and be the one to end it. It was ambitious nonetheless. It was better to make the best of the agreement. At least that is what Donna kept assuring him.

Vincent was given a uniform that would display his allegiance to the council. It fit snuggly and gave an extra bounce to his mostions. The suit was built with the aspect of taking on multiple opponents, large scale battle routines were in mind. He would find out the savage powers that came with his new enlistment. It was nothing he faced before. Donna gave him a tour of what he had clearance to see. It was not much but it was definitely worth the appeal.

"There are armies and then there is us. We specialize in combat of that slay the demonic variety. Don't go and get yourself killed." she said.

"This isn't my first rodeo." Vincent retorted. "I have handled myself well thus far, haven't I?"

"That was before you joined us. These soldiers are top notch. I vouched for you during your trial but the combat status we have is far beyond your average hunter. Training will test you. I am sure you are aware of your placement test?"

"What am I to do, show off my supreme skill to a bunch of know it all council members?"

A voice came from behind the two of them as they walked the gaudy hall. "That is something that will have to wait. I am afraid the council will not see you as an opponent worth their advance."

"And you are?"

"I am Gideon, one of the council members that has overseen your trial." Gideon was dressed in similar combat gear as Vincent except it was a tad bit more flashy around the trim.

"I did not recognize you without the intolerance and robes."

Gideon responded with cordial intent. "A formality that casts us as a mysterious and dark force. I assure you it is just as we stand on ceremony."

Donna seemed impatient. Whenever the council made an appearance it was because they wanted something to their own end. They never mingled with those in lesser ranks if they did not stand something to gain. "And to what do we owe this dubious pleasure, Gideon? I am sure the council doesn't waste their time on new recruits."

Gideon smiled a sly smile, half his face wrinkled with excitement. "I was appointed to the tests and trial of the murderer Vincent. I am sure he will be a disappointment."

"Alleged murderer. And I think you had better watch your tone before I shove my foot up your-"

Donna cut him off before he made improper enemies, though the council member did make himself an easy target. "I see. I would like to be the one that submits the notes on his results. I am sure you can accommodate."

"Do as you please. I am only here not to see what he has to offer to us. First things first, a psychological analysis. Would you two oblige me by heading to an interrogation chamber?" Gideon half turned and gestured down the hall.

The room was dark and there was a glass window that Donna stood behind, a two way mirror so that she could see. She scribbled on her clipboard as Gideon asked questions to learn just how experienced the young hunter was. Vincent was not living up to the standard and the pressing questions only seemed to set him off.

"It seems as if you are skilled but are limited by your inexperience." Gideon taunted.

"I have experience. I have fought countless demons. You don't know what you are talking about."

"You have run wild and hoped for the best. That will not constitute you as a well seasoned soldier. We have rank, order, strategy. From what I've gauge, not in guessing, is that you will get yourself killed. I don't see why we even agreed to have you enlisted."

"Why don't I just show you. I can kick your ass in a matter of minutes."

"There will be time for that. In fact I will put the requisition form in myself to test what meekness your ebon can produce. But before I close that mouth of yours and all of its arrogant trappings, there are other regulations that you must be put through."

"Bring it on. I can handle anything."

Vincent could not handle it. He battled some of the other initiates and their skills were far above his. The use of ebons were not permitted in training which set him back yards behind the standard. The council had other weapons for them to use. They had to move in unison, something Vincent was not used to. He was used to doing things his way, winging it so to speak. He fell behind. Donna watched and wrote what she could but the outcome of her paperwork just was just ugly.

There was a time trial obstacle course in which a pair of soldiers had to climb and sprint across narrow planks while a team of other soldiers took the role of demons and tried to knock them off course. It was practice for escape and that was something Vincent saw his chance to shine for combat. But the soldiers outmatched him and his female partner was pissed that he did not stick to the task.

Vincent fell behind and his numbers were outclassed each and every time. Then it came to the battle with Gideon. Vincent was sore and exhausted. It was only a few hours into the tests when he realized he could not put his money where his mouth was. There was disdain in the ranks. A mass of soldiers gathered around the center area. Gideon did not take off his cloak, a sign that Vincent took offensively.

"Are you prepared hunter? To meet my grand design?" Gideon said, knowing his skill was far beyond ranking to the average hunter.

"Are you prepared to lose? I will make you a wager."

"You think anything you say can tempt me?" Gideon said smugly. "Go on let's hear it."

"If I win, I take your position as council member and you proceed to be my boot licker."

Gideon scoffed. "I am sure you would make a fine council member. However, you will find that I am wine best not mixed with milk."

"I don't think readers will understand that one."

"I beg your pardon?"

"Nevermind it. Let's get this show on the road." Vincent was armed with a power pole. It had a blade that was blue plasma made for cutting demon skin. Gideon flipped back his cape and gestured a taunt that Vincent took as an insult.

Vincent charged and swung his weapon. He was too slow for Gideon. The blows were met with side steps that were artfully managed. Gideon spun on his heel and kicked the demon hunter in the chin, sending him doubling backward.

"Bootlicker, you said?" Gideon was sure of Vincent's imminent loss.

Vincent threw the power pole like a javelin. It was caught as if Gideon knew of the carelessness that Vincent wore on his sleeve. He was now unarmed against one of the toughest opponents that he did not care to admit. He was outmatched. Gideon would punish that arrogance in a lesson not soon forgotten.

Vincent threw a few punches that were blocked and countered with a knee to the gut. When he keeled over the power pole met his jaw and Vincent was on the floor, barely managing to breathe.

"I assume you know when to admit defeat?" Gideon said proudly with those under his command watching.

Vincent coughed up blood. "We are barely getting started." He climbed to his feet and struggled to breathe. There was some sense that Gideon was merely toying with him. Vincent held his stomach trying to knead the pain into fasting away. "Besides you haven't seen me at my best." He summoned his scythe and did not hesitate to press the attack.

Gideon held out the power pole in an artful manner that just ticked Vincent off. He had a sense of pride that he was to maintain and did not want to be thrown all over the floor at the mercy of those that would stifel his freedom. He slashed at Gideon. Gideon allowed the ban on ebon to be lifted just to see what skill the hunter had. It was no match for the seasoned veteran. That was to be proved again, and again.

The scythe was blocked with the blade of the pole and electricity bursted from the point of impact. Gideon thrusted, pushing the young hunter to his heels. Vincent leapt in attempts to at least gain some ground. He attempted to bunt Gideon with the blunt end of the scythe. Gideon forced the weapon to the ground and shoved his forearm into the hunter's throat. Vincent collapsed on his arm and was unconscious. The strike was so fast that Vincent was knocked out before the cape came to a rest at the base of Gideon's boots.

Vincent woke an hour later in the infirmary with his crew watching over him. "Did I win?"

"Far from it." Donna said. "You took it in the rear like you were paying for it."

Vincent sat up in the bed. "Damn him. Who in the hell taught him how to fight?"

"You should learn from him. He has speed where you have ambition." Incognito said. "That hot head of yours landed you on the low end of the ranks."

"What? I am entry level?"

"You failed all of your tests and Gideon isn't even the strongest member of the council." Donna informed.

"Now that you are a member of the council's military force, what happens to us?" Xiao Lin asked.

Donna answered before Vincent could wrap his head around the idea. It was not something he considered. "You all now fall under the council's control and I will function as the messenger on all businesses that you undergo."

"What?" Vincent said angrily. "You mean the council controls my team as well?"

"Not so much them as they now control you. If your team chooses to continue to work for you, which I assume they shall, your work is now directly linked to the cause of the council." Donna was informative but it was nothing Vincent was willing to hear. His world came crashing down and now he had to kneel to some that proved arrogant and skilled as much as he hated to admit it to himself. There was no way to win.

He was handed some papers by another soldier that informed him of the conditions of being a fresh on the till recruit. He read it over and he was moved to a sense of despair when it said he was not to perform any acts of demon hunting that was not appointed by the council. They had their own motives in the war that was at hand and the only thing Vincent would look forward to was being on the front lines.

Then there was another paper that sent him even further to despair. Since he had failed all the criteria for the entrance exams he was stuck conditioning himself until he was fit for combat. His crew would be without their leader and he was stuck in the nest like some baby bird that had no permission to fly.

Vincent was left alone to lick his salty wounds. He roamed the halls until he reached the corridor that housed lunch for any of the soldiers that had an appetite. Vincent's was defeated when he lost the fight with Gideon. He had it in his mind that he would defeat him. There was a soldier that saw his wounded pride.

"Don't look so gloomy." the soldier said. "It is bad for morale."

"You didn't get your ass handed to you by an elite. This place isn't really my style."

"I have heard all about you. Hell, we all have. You are the first that ever had the opportunity to fight one of the most gifted. I don't think they like your attitude much."

"That was not a fight, it was a slaughter."

"Either way you are one of us now. You don't get to be so high and mighty. Here it is the team before yourself, you hear?"

"Looking forward to it." Vincent said sarcastically.

"Let me show you around." Vincent accepted just to ease his tense mind. They went into the mess hall and the soldier began to point out the various soldiers and their battle types. "Here is where all the initiates eat. You have your recon, your markman, stealth ops, and like me, the berserkers. You scored so low on your tests you won't be doing much beside entry level investigation. You get to ask questions while the rest of us have all the fun."

"Can't wait."

"I am sure with some training you will rightly move up. Ebons aren't permitted. We use special weapons to do battle, so you are going to get used to that. You have to anyway. Law of the land and such."

"What's your name? Or do they take that away from you, too?"

The soldier took off her helmet revealing a stunning face. She whirled her hair in the light which was a turkish black. "The name is Shawna. I trust you to remember it."

"Are you in charge of anything? Do I answer you? Why do I need to know you?"

"Because you are proned to die in combat, rookie. I think that is clear."

They went through the line and got a tray of food. The silverware was oddly shaped. It definitely stuck out in Vincent's mind. Shawna led him to a table with her partners that Vincent felt more welcome than he had since he reached the castle.

"Crew," Shawna said, addressing the table. "We have a new recruit, introduce yourselves."

There was a man with blonde spiked hair. His voice was clean and it seemed to have a lull that might have gone over well with female counterparts. "The name is Ezekiel, special weapons and frontlineman."

Another that was pure brawn answered with a deep low voice that carried a lot of power. He commanded respect. "Corbin, elite berserker. I have been around for five years. Please make your acquaintance."

The last one sat without food in front of him. He was the squad leader. HIs hair was long and flowered over his eyes. "I am Adriel. I am the voice of this team and I suspect you of being too unskilled to join us. But if you do there are some perks. Vincent, right?"

"Yeah, that's right. What is the deal with everyone calling me a rookie? I have handled my fair share of demons, you know?"

"Don't take it personal, everyone here started low in the tier. You are just the first to have to fight a council member to reach such low scores." Shawna said. It was enough to make the table laugh. All except for Vincent that contemplated a rematch.

"What does it take to become a council member?" Vincent asked generally.

"There are two ways." Adriel said, while the rest of the table ate adamantly. You could tell being a soldier was a profession. "You could be elected by soldiers or defeat one council member in combat. You shouldn't worry too much about that. You have a long way to go Vincent. That is a road that is a long and treacherous one."

"I don't know, I kind of want to stick it to the rear end of that smug bastard."

Shawna swallowed some bread. "Gideon wiped the floor with you. You sure you want to set your sights so high?"

"I have business that I have to get home to. Coming here was an agreement so that I was not stripped of my ebons and thrown in jail. I can't stay forever. I have a team that expects me to lead them."

"What exactly do you have to do?" Adriel asked.

"I have to get revenge on a demo that killed my parents on my thirteenth birthday. If I spend my days around here it will never happen."

"That may not be out of range." Ezekiel said, cleanly.

"What do you mean?"

They all paused what they were doing and looked at Adriel. "It depends on how it is presented to the council. Make a proposal and it could turn into a mission. Though they won't settle easily on something like revenge."

"What if that demon is teamed up with a witch and is terrorizing a city?"

"That may get you a little wiggle room." Shawna said. "But if they are not directly connected to the root of our enemy chances are small."

They ate and chatted while Vincent attempted to find out more about how to make a claim so that he could head to Chicago and finish what he started. He gave orders to the members of the lounge to go find out what they could about Beatrix. He would figure something out. He simply had to.

Chapter Thirteen

Vincent spent days training with Adirel and his squad. He officially became one of them and needless to say it took a toll on his body. He never knew he could learn so much when it came to combat. His progress was starting to show. His time on the obstacle course shortened as he trained with Ezekiel. Ezekiel's focus was agility. He loved the power pole which was nothing like Vincent's scythe. The uniform was good for mobility and Ezekiel pushed the young hunter to ride the suit rather than use so much muscle. Vincent was scaling walls and made impossible jumps with practice and repetition.

Shawna showed him the ropes when it came to using the phase gunner. It was a lightweight cannon that gave a huge kick. Vincent used the cannon's burst to jump higher as he pointed it at the floor and rocket propelled himself skyward. The cannon was also good for its intended uses. It burned the cardboard targets in the firing range to crisps when fired accordingly.

Corbin taught him close quarter combat, something that Vincent was familiar with. The hulking man served as the opponent Vincent needed to expand his knowledge when it came to fighting. Corbin's forearms were huge and he used them to block the dull end of the power pole. Vincent did not best him in combat, however. There were still some kinks and holes in Vincent's defenses that Corbin simply put, took advantage of.

Adriel was a different story. He was a savage when it came to fighting. He floored Vincent every time in a matter of seconds. "You have to understand, I have held my own against powerful demon generals." Adriel said, helping the young hunter up from the battle hall floor.

"Yea, but I have never seen anyone fight like that. Why don't you fight Gideon and take over the council seat he so smugly wears on his shoulders?"

Adriel smirked and patted him on the back. "Not everyone is as ambitious as you. I have no need to fight the council. My loyalties lie in the heat of combat."

"So what's your story? How did you come about joining up with the council's army. There were never any enlistment recruiters where I am from. They don't seem like the types to have open invitations."

"The stories of us are mostly the same. Demons ravage lands and people are orphaned. Families are torn apart leaving some with the burning disdain from the enemy. We fight to end the suffering. One day we will win. On that day we can do as we please." Adriel said as they put their weapons back on the racks.

"Who is the enemy?"

"There is an ancient demon named Vadin. He is rumored to have resurrected and began his assault on mankind the way he did one thousand years ago. He plans on enslaving mankind or destroying it."

"I have similar problems back home."

"You mean outside of your revenge on the demon that killed your mother and father?" Adriel wondered.

"My problems vary in the many."

"I suppose joining us was just a tally on your wall."

"At least I'm not bored. I was born to fight demons."

They locked their hands into each other's forearm. "That brother is where you and I are the same." Adriel said.

Vincent retired to his quarters and tried to get a hold of Veronica who he had not spoken to in days. It was not from lack of trying but when he had told her he would not be home for a while due to the outcome of his trial she was more than irritable. She had not returned his calls or even answered his message. There were only messages from his crew after they went back to Chicago to hunt for Beatrix; updates on their progress and hope to hear from you soon.

But he longed for his bride to be. How could he have a life where she was always so upset with him? Little did he know she wanted to be with him, too. The secret of her family was what made her so distant. Things in the dark always would damage love. In this case it was only in the way of the young lovers. When she finally did answer she was affectionate.

"I would very much like to visit you at Incognito's."

"That's going to be difficult now that you are a soldier against demonic forces. Will you ever get down time to come home?" she asked softly, weary of love.

"I'm sure something can be arranged. If I don't take this place over and have it under my heel by December, I am going to make a break for it. They can't hold me forever."

"It isn't like you to run. You have to win Vincent. I know that it is what you are good for." There was hope in her voice If she could not stop her father's return then maybe Vincent could stop him when he arrived. "Just don't forget about me in all that warfare. I am fragile nowadays."

How could he forget the one he intended to marry? Vincent assured her that she was all he thought about. It was not just her skill at ebon mechanics or her vast knowledge when it came to such weapons, but her and her bad ass self would make him a happy man. He told her he would be home as soon as he could. They would spend the day together. He would get her a new teddy bear if she promised not to burn it, which she agreed not to.

Beatrix had not made any move but the report in anticipation was said that her powers were to increase dramatically. Chicago had gone quiet but the rest of the world was in turmoil. Demons, warlocks, and witches were at an all time high. The lounge had calls from all over. Vincent gave them orders to proceed with measure as they were permitted to take any of the jobs they chose in his absence. Bills needed to be paid and there was no sense in closing the lounge when they were a capable breed.

Vincent wondered when he would get a mission of his own. Was he ready to do battle with what these elite soldiers like him were handling? Granted he made progress, but was it enough. I would be a shame if he was etched onto the memorial wall as a fallen one the first assignment he got. It would truly be a tragic end to his tale. For now he stuck to his training and ran down the numbers and battle strategy with Adriel's squad. Where he did not lead he followed loyally.

Donna advocated on the behalf of Vincent since his result did yield better outcomes. She took the position of Adriel and his squad into consideration and made it her sole responsibility for getting them to the battle front. She had faith in the young hunter and considered him a chess piece to fuel her own ambition. It was an even trade seeing as how she got him into this mess. It had to be better than hunter's jail or so she assumed. She was a huntress as well. She had an ebon. The turn was that she did not work for the council and wanted to project the idea that ebons are not the enemy, merely tools for eradicating their enemy.

She would have to campaign to one hundred thousand soldiers for a seat on the council and take the fight directly to the heart of their enemy. It would just be one of the many renovations she would put forth. All she needed was one cooperative soldier, a hunter of sorts. That is where she would rely on the new initiate Vincent Delvine. But first she was to see if he could survive what the war was savoring.

"You show true promise, Vincent. Are you prepared for war?" she prompted.

"I can handle anything except for the food here."

"I'm sure you won't die to goulash as well as the enemy forces that have been spotted in Nevada."

"I get to go to Vegas?"

"Well, yes actually. We assess that a demon there is biding time for a full scale assault and I want to send Adriel's squad as you have become familiar with them. I want you to go as well."

Vincent looked puzzled. "Is the council approving of the renegade branching off with a stronger squad just so he can get back to doing that which they wanted to stop him from doing? Killing demons I mean."

"Don't worry about them. The worst they will do is complain. I have measures set against their absolutions. I specialize in finding loopholes. Since your records are improving I am deeming you a soldier ready for battle. Just don't go dying out there."

"I can't die. The author wants a series."

"A series?" Donna asked.

"You know, maybe something longer than a trilogy."

Donna looked confused. "Is that a reference or something."

"Does no one understand catchy dialogue."

"I use rhetoric in my reports." she added.

"Close enough."

Adriel's squad was briefed. The mission was just a confirmation value. They were to find out if the demon in question was there before an assault would be cleared. They did not have permission to engage. It was strictly recon: photos, recordings, absolutely no fighting of any kind. Donna figured it was a great first mission for her project in these soldiers. They would be the orchestra and she the conductor. She would be close enough to give specific orders but she would not get into the danger of being close to the demon.

It would be the young hunter's first time in the gambling city. He wanted to see some sites. Xiao Lin would have no choice but to be jealous when he told her. She sent him a picture of her frowning when the news broke. She had work to do though; find the witch Beatrix and report back. Not send mopey pictures when the boss went on vacation. It was not really a vacation, but Xiao Lin considered the job killing demons while she went sightseeing. It is just the way she was and thus far she was a happy camper.

They were in a cargo plane on their way to Las Vegas to do some good old fashion demon hunting. They went another briefing on who the demon was pretending to be. A woman by the name of Katherine Avory. Her hair was short and she wore a suit. That was the extent of what they knew of her. Other than she swallows her victims whole. That was something they needed to watch out for.

They hovered just above the city near the target's location. They couldn't get a clear view through their sonar system. They had no idea exactly where Katherine was or what she was doing. They only had vague references to her routine and attempted to put those pieces together.

"I am sending you all in." Donna said, roughly. "Be sure that you are not to engage the target under any circumstance. This is just a confirmation mission. We want to know what she does. If she is part of a larger picture she will show herself."

"Wouldn't it be easier if we just killed her?" Vincent asked, not sure of how the council and their men behaved. It was very different from his routine, that was get in, get paid, and get out alive.

"You are going to have to follow protocol." Donna said. "We don't do things the way you are used to. This is for a bigger picture, a much larger fish."

"How is this going to further the campaign against demonkind?"

"We only need to know if the grip that Vadin has has spread."

"If not, do we just leave her to wreak havoc all over the devil's city?"

That was not what Vincent wanted to know; weather or not to leave the demon alive if she did not fit what they were planning to do. He wanted to know what the council planned in the event she did not. What was the council really after if it were not the eradication of those they saw as enemies. "That is no concern of yours."

They ziplined from the hovering craft down into the devil's city. The bright lights were blinding. Vincent wore a visor that enhanced his vision and allowed him to see past all the gleaming towers. They landed on top of a hotel without problems. Next was to infiltrate the complex and find out just what the alias Katherine was up to. Vincent was ready for a fight and he would not hesitate to break protocol if it meant an act of heroism.

They popped off the grate to a ventilation shaft and it was into the walls like spiders. The uniforms came with very nifty gadgets that allowed them to stick to the walls inside and crawl around in complete stealth. Vincent was impressed by the makings of the suits. He trailed behind the others as they moved quickly and quietly.

Donna came in on the headset that Vincent did not know was there or even active for that matter. "Position yourselves for reconnaissance. The target should be arriving any moment."

"Are we just talking now?" Vincent asked, attempting to break the seriousness in tension of the team. He was not exactly making any progress in that endeavour.

"No games soldier." Shawna said. "This is a simple routine. Will you get that head of yours into gear?"

Vincent rolled his eyes and popped the vent from the ceiling. It fell to the center hallway. The others wondered what he was doing. "Vincent, what the hell?" Ezekiel said on the com link. "You are going to blow our cover."

Vincent went silent as he ducked behind one of the doorways. He sighted Katherine. She was walking the halls with a young man giving him orders as he wrote everything down.

"I have eyes on the target."

"Do not engage." Donna said.

It was so much easier if he had. Just kill the demon making the deals and he would return a hero. Why was that so complicated? Katherine went into one of the rooms and Vincent sat outside the door while the rest of the squad turned in the ventilation shafts to try to get a better look so they could see and hear just what Katherine was up to.

Adriel chimed in as the fearless leader. "You can go invisible in that suit, Vincent." That would make things easier. "Just twist the nozzle near the visor."

Vincent did just that and the hexagon stitching in the uniform flipped and he was gone to the naked eye. He crept into the room as quietly as he could and Katherine was still directing the young man.

"That will be all." she said and the young man gave a deep nod, turned on his heel, and left the room. He nearly bumped into Vincent who was in killing range the way he wanted it to be. But for now he would just have to be satisfied with following the council's orders. Saying that to himself made his gut feel like he drank a gallon of spoiled milk.

There was a familiar face when it walked into the room. The

stitched man that followed orders from Beatrix stepped into the room in a long trench coat and his face was an overexposed eye.

"I know that guy." Vinceet whispered into the mic.

"What do you mean you know him?" Shawna said.

"Well, I don't "know him" know him." He works with a witch that has been trying to kill me since the start of this book."

Donna chimed in angrily. "Will you keep your voices down? It is imperative that we find out what exactly is going on here."

Vincent moved toward an open window with his team looming overhead in the vents. It was beyond him why they were not going to go with an assault. They were in a position to. There was the element of surprise, they outnumbered them, and even had really big guns strapped to their backs.

"Are you sure your witch is strong enough to join the ranks of Vadin, Drolo? It would be a shame if we put her to work and she was to die the first day."

"I assure you her powers have more than quadrupled. I alone can handle what Vadin has to offer. All we require is that Chicago be placed under her dominion and her powers are yours to command."

"What in the hell kind of a name is Drolo?" Vincent asked himself. He was shushed over the com by Amela who was taking pictures for the file.

That was confirmation enough. Vadin was resurrected in all his villainy and was moving again for efforts of the most heinous and vile. That was the proof they needed, right? Vincent began to sneak out of the room for extract and the team did the same.

"There is a curious matter we should address, Ms. Avory." Drolo said, moving toward Vincent who was now stopped in his tracks.

"There is no money involved in this. I am only here as a disguise, an agent if you will."

"Money was never any concern of ours. But it looks like you were followed. I will take care of this intruder as an act of goodwill." Drolo kicked Vincent across the room and his suit reverted back to its original can-be-seen regalia. The wall in which he landed cracked and then the young hunter fell to the floor.

"That uniform, he is with the Council of Talia." Katherine said. "Were we betrayed by the council member?"

"I highly doubt that." Drolo assured her. "I will make quick work of this one. You get out of here and relay our agreement. No need to sully your hands."

Vincent was dazed but was certain of his ears. Did the scarecrow man say there was a council member working as a double agent? He tried to use the mic to tell Donna what he had heard but the damn thing was busted. He stood to his feet as Katherine left the room in urgency. He quickly grabbed his phase gun and rapidly opened fire. Drolo was quick, as quick as he was in the subway. He was up the walls dodging fire and darted in blurs back and forth.

Drolo began to close the distance with speed and dexterity. He knocked the gun from Vincent's hands. It was too bulky for him to get a clear shot anyway. He switched to the power pole, something that was more his style. The electro end buzzed as he drew it and he was slashing away at the demon. He caught the demon's coat and whirled the rod around trying to slow the demon's movements. He pulled upward to attempt to ensnare Drolo but the demon simply slipped out of it revealing his face and body. He was made of sacks stitched together by his maker, a bald head, and teeth that looked like glass.

"Man, you're one ugly son of a bitch." Vincent said staggering back.

"You speak so haughty for someone who is about to die."

Vincent pressed the button on his visor and revealed his face. "I think this would be the third time you have tried to kill me. Drolo, was it?"

"Ah, the young hunter. Beatrix will be pleased once I have killed you. Tell me, what made you join the scum sucking ranks of the council of Talia. I think I liked you better when you weren't a trained military dog."

"It was a clerical error. I killed a guy, like I'm about to kill you." Vincent charged Drolo swiftly, remembering to let the uniform carry him the way he had learned in training. He pierced the demon's shoulder in attempts to pin him against the wall. He has some questions about which council member was the traitor. It was sure to get him a medal, or whatever the council had to offer for acts of heroism.

Drolo was not so easy an opponent, however. Drolo extended his arm so the stitches tore. He wrapped his arm around the power pole numerous times and pulled the demon hunter in close. "Do you think I would be so easily defeated?"

"For a second there," Vincent thought for a moment. "Yeah, I kind of did." Vincent let go of the rod and began a flurry of punches and kicks. The suit was spring and gave his movements a sort of piston charge. Drolo bobbed and weaved until he had an opening to whip his arm and the deadly end of the power pole in the young hunter's direction. There was an explosion from the ceiling and in dropped the squad breaking the orders not to engage.

They surrounded Drolo and each of them attempted to pierce the demon with their power poles. They definitely connected. However, the demon simply slipped from the sacks as a snake might when shedding its skin and before they had time to react he was out the window, falling hundreds of feet to the ground below. Without the sacks he looked like he was made out of straw made of silver. He was gone in a matter of seconds in his dissension.

"You guys picked a fine time to join the fight. I almost had him."

"Better late than never." Adriel said. The cargo plane that they had arrived in lowered to the open window. Come on, we have to get out of here."

Donna looked pissed. "You had orders, Vincent."

"He made me somehow. He saw me or something."

"Now they know we are onto them." Donna signaled the cargo plane to get closer so they could climb in, they did. "This is going to make this very difficult."

"The demon that we fought, he said something I think you should know about."

"This had better be good." Donna said, not really wanting to hear it."

"He said that there was someone on the council that they were cohorting with. There is a traitor among your legion of goodie two shoes."

Donna's eyebrows furled. "Are you certain of this? Are you sure you heard correctly?"

"I know it to be a fact. Someone is pulling some strings and you need to find out why."

The plane took off and headed back to the council headquarters. "I have orders for four of you that must be kept in the most secrecy. I am going to have you investigate the council members and find out what's going on. Vincent, you and I are going to Chicago to find this witch and force her to tell us everything she knows."

"It has to be a big deal. She is joining this Vadin demon and wants to take over Chicago. We have to stop this before it happens."

They landed in just a few short hours going over the plans to find out just which of the five councilmen was in league with those of the demonic variety. If Donna, leading as the commander in this mission, were to join the council she would first have to sniff out the traitor. It was not going to be easy. This was because each of the council members had ebon that were that of the cataclysmic sort. One wrong move and they would be set off, forced to do the unthinkable. Anyone under Donna's secreted command could be killed. She could trust no one else.

For now it was a debriefing and a report. Donna only said what the council needed to hear. There was no mention of Drolo, only that Katherine was in fact and indeed in the ranks of Vadin. She even told them they were recruiting witches. They accepted her words. It was still no sign on which one of them sought to enslave mankind.

Chapter Fourteen

There was no trouble in faking the documents that were needed to requisition a trip to Chicago. The Council of Talia saw Donna as one of their most promising candidates. Donna wondered if she was a part of their plans seeing as how they so willingly gave her the freedom to move about. Vincent joined her in the cargo plane there. Donna would trust no one that was outside of Adriel's squad so it was Ezekiel that flew the plane. It was just a few short hours before Vincent was back on the witch hunt.

More hunters had gone missing from the area. It was assumed that those that went missing could not return to their bodies. They were to be treated and hostile, not as brothers at arms. That was the plan in finding her, the witch Beatrix. Since her powers flourished since they could not stop her at the subway, they would have to move quickly and fight harder than they ever did before. Donna gave a good chance for them to defeat her, or so Vincent thought. She was a shoe in for the council so she had to have a few tricks up her sleeve. Was she allowed to use ebon? They would soon find out.

"Vincent, you're home!" Xiao Lin exclaimed when the two walked in the door. She ran over and hugged him like he was gone for years.

"Nice to see you, too."

Donna was sure minded and stayed to the course of why they came. "There is a witch we need to find. I need you all to be optimal and hunting. Are there any other hunters in the area that can help?"

"Just name your witch and we will find her." Rachel said, pushing her chair up from behind her desk.

"It's Beatrix. We have to find her."

Louis chimed in while on a headset and typing away on a computer. "Any particular reason outside of the problems she is already causing?"

Donna held command of the lounge as she outranked the hunters in attendance. "There is a traitor among council members. She knows who. We are going to make her talk."

Eyes went wide across the room. "A traitor? Among the most elite of hunters? Woe is me." Xiao Lin said, surprised. "Vincent, what have you done?"

"Hey, I'm the one that found out that dirty little secret. Why do you always assume I had something to do whenever something goes wrong?"

"It's just like you." Xiao said, chuckling.

Donna wanted to get the room back to course. "Any possible leads?"

"Not since she moved her headquarters." Rachel answered. "We thought we had her cornered a while back but it was a trap. It was almost as if she was expecting us. She called up her minions, hell even a demon or two. She has been ghosting hunters ever since."

Louis took off his headset. "We have a network of runes across the city to track her movements, but they are of no avail seeing as she has not tripped any of the triggers. She moves quickly. But one mistake and we can track her."

Donna was stoic. "That all just sounds like excuses. I will find this witch myself. I am taking command of this office. You all work for the Council of Talia now."

"Is there a pay raise?" Xiao Lin asked. She was already eager to start her new career in the council. She put it in her mind to be the best.

"Not a chance."

Louis's desk was taken over by Donna. She, with some force, made him tell him all the secrets of the matrix of runes that were scattered across the city. There was a flaw in the set up. Donna was certain the witch was not using magic to capture her victims which was why she could not be traced. She deduced this hypothesis based on the footage from Vincent's uniform that Vincent did not know was recording.

There was so much magitech jam packed in the suit, Vincent's mind was blown.

The computer screen showed Drolo without his coat and hat. The entire lounge was glued to the screen and watched as Donna typed like she was playing a piano, such finesse. "We have to capture this witch or this demon in order to find out the truth about the councilmen."

"What are we going to do when we have that information? It is not likely that the council will not defend itself."

Donna had not thought of what to do when the truth was found. "We confront the traitor and find out what he or she knows."

"Aren't those guys wicked strong?" Rachel chimed. "I thought they could bring a city to its knees in an hour."

"That makes them all the more suspicious. No one needs that kind of fire power. Is there anyone you answer to that has that ability off hand?"

Donna sat silent for a moment, thinking. "There are two possibilities. There is Marcel, who led your trial proceedings. Then there is Jane, she is too straight and narrow for that kind of activity. She is the reason I may have a seat on the council."

"It must be Marcel, he's the traitor!" Xiao Lin said with no real lead as to why she said it.

Donna pulled up a picture of Marcel. "Oh he is a handsome son of a gun." Rachel said leaning in close to the screen.

"Rachel has a thing for bad boys." Xiao Lin teased.

Donna, not derived from her intentions, continued. "He is the very seat of the council. All passes through him. I don't think he is the one. He is too clean, on point, by the book."

"What about Gideon?"

"He doesn't know his elbow from his asshole." Donna said, mockingly.

"Who else is there?"

Donna scrolled through more pictures. "Forris, he is quiet. And Mikaeus, he is quick to call for war."

"Has anything ever tipped you off, anything ever seem odd with any of them?"

Louis sat quiet. He had thought to himself that he could be working for someone that had ill intentions. It was the first time it ever crossed his mind. It was Mikaeus that he had secret orders from. He could not say anything to Donna about his mission. Nor could he say anything to Vincent. Louis did not even know the extent of the plans of his true master, nor the intent. It was always kill Veronica. Now that he thought of it, his problems only thickened. Any mention of this might put him in harm's way.

There were no leads. All that remained was to have the witch tell them. It was only a matter of time before they would find her. Donna ordered that the crew go on an active hunt rather than wait for her to make a mistake.

Rachel and Louis rode in the warmachine, Xiao Lin circled large city blocks on her motorcycle, and Donna road passenger in Vincent's underused mustang. They were going to use themselves as bait and lure out the witch. Since she was after hunters it was sure to turn out to be a flawless plan.

The city streets were bustling with people. There was too much noise around. "How do things look out there?"

Xiao Lin and her dutiful sense for her new position among the council's army answered first over the mic and headset. "Aside from us missing whatever brought all these people here, there's no sign of the witch."

Louis looked through the camera attached to Tags. "No visual here either, boss. We'll keep looking."

"Eyes and ears people, and if you get yourself in a bind alert the rest of us."

"Roger." the three of them said in unison.

Donna had an expression of rage upon her face. She was sitting in deep thought and wanted to know the truth of the council. The story was with Vadin's defeat the council was formed to keep the peace throughout the lands. It was unthinkable that among them was someone that betrayed that faith, the faith that came with giving mankind hope against those that had sights to do harm.

"Have you ever fought a council member?" Vincent wanted to break her from her enraged trance.

"I have not." Donna said, brooding.

"I can't say Gideon is an easy one. He did not even use any of his weapons against me. I hope you have something up your sleeve for when the time comes."

"The traitor will face trial and most likely be put to death." she said. She sighed and then rubbed the bridge of her nose with her index finger and thumb. "It is important that they stand for their crimes. This isn't like hunting demons, Vincent. There is an order to this."

"I don't think the traitor will go quietly. First we find out who, right?"

"That is correct. If this witch knows who, our job is to find out why and how to go about dealing with this situation. All actions that the council has is directly compromisable. I won't leave you in the treacherous zone opted by the plans of someone that is working with demons. Vadin is a dangerous enemy. If the rumors of his resurrection are true, we are the ones that called him back from the other side." Donna explained. She was as tense as she was informative.

"I have something in mind. In order to trap the witch." Vincent stopped the car. He opened the door and stepped out.

"What are you doing?" Donna asked. She stepped out of the car and began to follow him.

"The witch wants to kill hunters, right? I still am one. All we have to do is use myself as bait."

Would it be so simple? Vincent summoned his ebon and waited. There was not much to do but wait. Chances are Beatrix's minions would show. It was unlikely that she would show herself. They wanted her but since the chances were so low if minions showed Vincent would allow himself to be captured, revealing the witch's hideout so that she could be dealt with. It was a long shot but it was worth a try.

"If you are captured there is a distress resonance that will tell me your location. I will track you to where she is hiding."

"I trust you to save my life, Donna."

With that Donna went into hiding. She stayed close in case things got out of hand. There was a glowing alchemic circle that was purple and black. Soon the scarecrow appeared. It was dancing like a jester with blades in its hands. Vincent did not want it to look like he would be taken easily. If he had Beatrix might have suspected that he was up to what he was up to.

The scarecrow darted like a fish with his head down. Vincent tumbled to the right dodging the first initial strike. As he rose to his feet he hooked his scythe at the minion's ankle and ripped it. Tufts of straw spilled into the alley in where he stood. More purple alchemic circles appeared and soon the young hunter was surrounded on all sides. Donna sat quietly around the corner listening to the commotion.

There was a familiar voice that rang from the low rooftop. "Ah, if it isn't the hunter Vincent. You have chosen poorly on your outing." It was Drolo. He was back in his overcoat and his sack skin was back concealing the metal straw. "These minions are no match for you. That much I am sure."

"Maybe they are made from weak magic."

"That may be true for some. I however am made from something a little stronger." Drolo leapt from the rooftop and there was a small crater in his landing. The weight of the metal straw was enough to shake the very ground.

Vincent planned to put up a small fight but be defeated so that he could be taken to where he would find the witch hiding. "You talk a big game for someone who lost a gamble taking on a member of the council's military."

"You all are just fodder. Allow me to demonstrate." Drolo took off his coat and tossed it to the ground. He then outstretched his arms and lengthened them. "Soon you will be nothing more than a puppet for Beatrix."

Drolo threw his arm and it stretched the length of the alleyway. Vincent dodged for fear of what would happen when he was struck. He slashed to make it look like he would not be taken easily. There was a spark and the arm looped around Vincent's throat. The metal hay was too strong to cut. Drolo was more advanced in his machinations and design. Vincent was being choked into submission.

"You were lucky back in Vegas, hunter." Drolo said, tightening his hold of the young hunter. "But you can see I am out of your league. I was to keep my cover then. Now you will be captured and turned into one of Beatrix's finest puppets, strings and all."

Vincent began to lose consciousness. He had to act quickly if he wanted to attempt to extract information before things got too risky. He ran toward Drolo, the grip of the metal straw arm loosened and then Drolo retracted it. There were a short trade of blows before Vincent was kicked into the wall of the alleyway and he stopped short in his tracks. Vincent pushed off the wall and attempted to knock the demon off balance.

There was a pause as Drolo sat with a smile on his face. "Why struggle, hunter? There is no escape and your weapons are no match for me."

Vincent was cornered. He had the demon where he wanted him. Maybe he could have some questions answered. "Just one thing before you take me. I need to know who the traitor is among the council members. I need to know so I can kick their ass."

"Who? Mikaeus? You will see that he is nothing more than a pawn to the true cause of reawakening ancient powers."

Donna's eyes widened. There was nothing but the clue of the traitor that was erased. Mikaeus had hundreds of soldiers following him loyally. They would fight for him no matter the circumstance. It would not be so easy to overthrow him. There was no evidence of his treachery either. For now it was just word of mouth. But there had to be a way. For now Donna could only wait for the signal from Vincent's uniform to tell her that he was on the way to the hideout.

"Mikaeus? So that is the one? Don't know him."

"In time it won't matter. Soon the world will bend to the favor of demonkind."

"Did Beatrix make you? You seem a little stronger than the puppets she makes."

"That? No, I am a demon that helped spawn her power." Just then Beatrix appeared and pierced Vincent in the forearm with her large needle. Vincent pressed the distress button on his suit. Beatrix quickly stitched the young hunter's wrists together behind his back. Vincent's ebon was forced to recall itself.

"Now you will join my ranks, hunter." the witch said. They were transported by magic to the hideout.

Donna got on the mic and told the rest of the crew to convene. She was picked up by Rachel in the warmachine and then told them the plan. She also told them if they did not move swiftly their boss was going to have his goose cooked. The tracker was brought up onto the computer screen in the back of Tags and they were off following the blips on the scanner. It was not too far away but it was still a race against the clock.

Vincent was stitched to himself and a wall as he waited to be morphed into a scarecrow minion. "How does it work?" he asked the witch.

"It is simple. I use a polymorph ritual to convert your body and soul into one of my minions."

Vincent wanted to stall for time, anything so that he could be saved from the impending nature of the witch whose mercy he was now at. "What is it that Mikaeus hopes to achieve by deceiving the council?"

"The rumors surrounding that man are that he was implanted there years ago to amass as many soldiers as he could. The reason is unclear but it has something to do with Vadin, the demon that is whispered to conquer all."

"Demons can't take to the human world without a contract like you and Drolo. Is Mikaeus the one that Vadin is bound to?"

Beatrix put on some gloves and then pulled back a sheet that was hanging next to Vincent. A woman, probably a huntress, was unconscious and stitched to the wall just as Vincent had been. Beatrix continued. "That I do not know. But I do know that those suits that you soldiers are wearing are linked to Vadin's return."

"These things are ebon? I thought ebons were for hunters?"

"While that may be true it is not unlike the council to use them in mass numbers. The more those things are in use they will increase the initial powers of Vadin when he returns." Beatrix unveiled a small glowing red stone and held it in front of the huntress and then pressed it against her chest. She took a small blade and carved a hole into her chest. The stone sank under her skin and then she slowly morphed into one of her minions.

Vincent looked in sarcastic horror and he would be next to join the endless ranks of the scarecrow. "What is in it for you, Beatrix. You know those demons will do as they please if they ever gain all that power. Last I checked witches are still human."

Beatrix had a certain sense of deviant glee when he asked her that question. "I simply want to watch the world burn. I was born with this dark gift that I have demonstrated before you. I find a sense of rebellion when you hunters challenge me."

The beacon on Vincent's suit probably gave away more information to the council than he was willing to give. He would take off that uniform the moment he could. He could not speak for the rest of the soldiers, like Shawna and Adriel, but he would not contribute to the strength of his natural opponent. Slaying demons was his forte. This was just a sorry excuse for a fashion statement.

Beatrix unveiled another stone and held it up to the young hunter's chest just as she did the huntress before. "Any last words before I take your body and soul, hunter?"

"As a matter of fact I do."

"Incoming!" Xiao Lin shrouded as Tags and the crew came crashing through the brick wall. She was at the seat of the gatling gun. She fired them rapidly at the scarecrows that were hanging on the walls, incapacitating them before they were freed and could repel their rescue mission.

Beatrix turned to the commotion. She raised her hand to animate the scarecrows that were otherwise limp on the walls. The crew, including Donna, jumped out of the back hatch after the wheels brought the war machine to a screeching halt, the tires burning rubber. They began to fight off the minions but they would not last very long as they were outnumbered. Beatrix's labors made sure, if nothing, she could account for a small army.

Donna made her way to the beacon that Vincent's uniform emitted.

"You plan on taking what I have claimed for myself?" Beatrix said readying her giant needles.

Donna did not want to fight. Beatrix the witch was of no real concern. She more or less was there to rescue Vincent and wanted to find out what he found out about the council and their secrets. Donna summoned her ebon which was a fencing rapier. She apparently was an ace that moved just as swiftly as the witch. They were back and forth for a good minute before Donna found an opening and cut free the young hunter's hands.

Vincent summoned Ammit and opened fire on the witch. Drolo appeared with great speed and blocked the bullets with his steel straw arm. "You all are becoming quite troublesome." said the demon. "I suppose we shall have to do something about that."

Donna grabbed Vincent by the arm. "Your team won't be able to hold off all the minions. We go, now!"

"Man, I love a good smash and grab." said the young hunter. They made their way to the war machine and climbed in the back dodging a hail of daggers thrown by the minions. Soon they were out the way they came and peeled from the hideout, roaring in the streets of Chicago.

"It's Mikaeus." The team looked to Vincent. "Mikaeus is the one you should be after, Donna."

"He is a deadly one. But I need evidence." Donna said.

"There is something else."

"What else could there be?" Louis said. AS it turns out Mikaeus was the one council member that he worked for. There had to be more to his mission than Veronica. He wanted to find out just what he was being used for.

"These uniforms. They are ebons that will increase the power of Vadin upon his return." He began to take it off. "The more they are in use the more powerful he is said to be."

"Damn it." Donna said under her breath. "Mikaeus must be confronted."

"You seem to hold yourself up well in a fight. Maybe you could defeat him in combat."

"That is not the case. Mikaeus has tons of followers. Even if he is confronted he will be followed blindly by soldiers and potentially a few council members. He has too much pull in the militia. And if the uniforms are linked to him, he may know already that we are on to him." Donna was struggling to make sense of it. If she were to fight him head on she would surely die. On the other hand there was Adriel and his squad that needed to be checked on. If the traitor councilman was on to them she would surely lose what little forces she had stocked.

They drove back to the lounge and Vincent got the thread removed from his wrists. Soon he was back in his vest and overcoat, eating lo mein at his desk. It was nice to be back in the office again. He did not want to go back to the militia of the Order of Talia. There were troubles there that he could live without. Donna told him to sit tight and conduct work as he usually would while she went back to devise a plan that would expose Mikaeus and have him removed from his seat. There was not much she could do against the uniforms, of which may have been eyes and ears to all that were controlling them.

Donna told Vincent to keep the phone line clear in case she would call for any assistance she might need. There were only few she could trust and even fewer under her command. The young hunter agreed since she was the one that cleared him of jail time. It was the least he could do. So the young hunter and his crew began answering the phones and taking jobs of the demon hunting variety. Soon they would be off to gather large sums of money for the price of demon extermination.

Louis had to find out what was planned for him and the gate. If he was part of a demon resurrection scheme he would have to know. What was Veronica to them? Mikaeus could order her capture or have he killed. He needed to find out more about the gate and her father which the gate held. He was off to Incognito's to question the bringer of the apocalypse.

Chapter Fifteen

Louis did not have any connection to Incognito so the wait in line outside made him want to cry murder. There were hunters from all over doing what they usually do on nights much like this one. Louis wanted nothing more than to chat with his assignment in order to find out what she knew about Mikaeus, if she knew anything at all.

When he approached the bouncer at the door he was shocked by how tall he was. "You look new." the bouncer said. "Reason for being here?"

"I came for a drink." Louis lied, but the less he had to explain the better. "Just looking for a good time."

"This here is a private club. You have to have special qualifications to enter."

Louis did not know that Incognito's was a hunter's club. He tried to bribe the bouncer with a twenty. "How special are we talking?"

"Your money is no good here, runt." The bouncer folded his arms and made a very serious face. "This is a hunter's club."

Louis did not hesitate to summon his ebon when he heard the relieving news. "I am an official hunter with Vincent Delvine."

"You work for the kid, huh?" The bouncer stepped aside. "Enjoy your evening."

Domain stepped inside and the music hurt his ears. He was used to the quiet that came along with the council chambers, hell he could even handle a few plucky demons. This was just a little out of his taste. But he was there to talk to Veronica. In that expedition he could do no harm, except for his eardrum. He wandered over to the bar where he saw her sitting like she was not to spark the end of the world.

He approached her from behind and patted her on the shoulder to get her attention. "Hey, you got a minute?"

Veronica turned with a drink in her hand. "Well, look what the cat dragged in." She took a sip. "Did my boyfriend send you?"

"Actually, I'm here on my own. There has been some recent developments and I was wondering if you could tell me: what do you know about the council?"

"I don't know much. They have eyes everywhere and will kill me if they have the chance."

"That's actually why I am here. The one that sent me to help you with your apocalypse problem may be a traitor and he might also want me to kill you."

She sat her drink down on the counter, very very slowly. "Is that why you have come? To kill me before my father does?"

"Not exactly. I don't think it will come to that. I just need to know how he knows about your father. Can you tell me anything? Like, if there is some connection between the two?"

"Look, I am just a scared little girl in all of this. If you aren't going to kill me you are wasting my time."

The stone that traced the gate began to vibrate in Louis's pocket. He knew she was becoming unnerved. "Are you telling me you know nothing of your father's ongoings? Are you saying you went through life without a clue as to your father's imprisonment or why he is just so damn evil to begin with?"

"There is something. There was talk about a demon that was to be resurrected. My father may know how to do so. He may be a defining factor in that resurrection."

Louis sat quietly for a moment. He was thinking there was a pattern. So many warlocks and witches may have been being recruited for the demon Vadin. Their powers combined may have something to do with it. "Does the name Mikaeus mean anything to you?"

"That is the name of someone he worked closely with when I was younger. What does he have to do with this?"

"I am thinking if he orders me to kill you the gate will open and your father will be released prematurely."

"Why haven't you told Vincent about all this?" she said, picking up her drink and swallowing it all in one gulp.

"The same reason you haven't." Louis said.

"I am not a double agent out to maim, injure, or potentially kill his boss' girlfriend."

"There is always that." Louis said.

"Do you have any plans on how to stop the gate then, since you aren't going to kill me yet?"

Louis sat in the stool next to her. "That one is a bit tricky. There are ways to close it for good but it will stop your heart."

"Tragety after resounding tragedy."

"I am sure I will find something. But if I can't and Mikaeus orders me to kill you, you should know that I won't."

"You make for a terrible agent and a lousy articifer."

"I won't help with ending the world. That has to count for something."

"I suppose that makes two of us."

Incognito came down from his office that was just off the staircase next to the bar. He spotted Louis's familiar face and approached him wondering what brought the lounge in without first telling him. It was a little unusual for Vincent to behave out of character. "What brings you guys in tonight?"

"Actually, I am here on my own." Louis thought it would be best to cover his tracks. "Just needed a night to myself."

Incognito went quiet. That was an unlikely tale. Vincent would be notified, just as a question, on why the demon hunter had shown himself at his club of all places talking very chummy to one he should not be. Louis took his leave and Veronica decided to break the long silence that lingered thereafter.

"He knows."

That struck Incognito in a very irascible way. "You mean he knows about your father? What else does he know?"

"He said something about Vadin being on the verge of returning and that my father will have something to do with it."

"Maybe it is time you told Vincent the whole story, Veronica. Why keep him in the dark?"

"Maybe I should. I just don't want him to think he is going to kill my father. Family is still family."

"That complicates things quite a lot, woman." Incognito helped her from her seat.

"I just have to trust the agent of the council can find a way to stop the gate from opening without killing me. If I die the gate opens anyway."

Incognito shook his head. "Don't do anything reckless. That boy Vincent may be more open to helping you than you know. Give him a little credit."

"You know how he is. He is prideful and demanding."

"Don't I know it. But still…"

Louis high tailed it back to the lounge hoping no one would notice his short absence. He snuck in through the back entrance and went to his desk. Sparks were flying from where Rachel took a blow torch to the war machine attempting to adjust the wheels so that they could turn on a dime. Xiao Lin and Vincent were chatting on one of the couches about the next demon hunt. It would not be soon before they were back on the rails as a team. They were sure glad to have their boss back.

There was a phone call that interrupted the two on the couch. "The Demon Hunter's Lounge, you name them we slay them." Vincent fell quiet and his eyes slowly turned to Louis. "I see." the young hunter said. He then stormed over to Louis and grabbed him by the collar. "You were at Incognito's tonight, why?"

"There is something you should know." Louis knew his cover had been blown. "It is about Veronica."

"You have been talking to my gal behind my back? I should shiv you for that!"

"It's not like that. Though it would be easier if it were."

"You had better start singing a different tune, buddy. I have a short temper for those I can't trust."

"She is the bringer of the apocalypse." Louis was dropped in his chair. "I was sent as an agent from the council to close what would bring about the end of the earth or kill her."

"The council?" Vincent was pissed. "Who do you work for?"

"When I found out Mikaeus had other intentions aside from what was supposed to be protecting the world, I went to tell her the truth."

"You were sent to kill her?" Xiao Lin asked, breaking the tension. "You monster."

"My orders were to keep an eye on her and monitor the progression of the gate, the one bound to her heart. I was awaiting orders on how to proceed. Then I found out that the one that was pulling the strings was also the one that is a traitor on the council. That is the truth in whole."

"Vincent, you should go and talk to her." Xiao Lin said. "Find out from her."

"Damn straight." said the young hunter. He took his leave and made for Incognito's where he would find his lovely lady. Of course he did not know of the distressing damsel that she was due to her family affairs. He was more pissed that she had not told him this. They had known each other for years. This was just a wound in their already staggering relationship.

Veronica was binding an ebon to a demon hunter when he had arrived. She was known for that particular skill, and when Vincent interrupted she was a little uneasy about the way the young hunter carried himself in front of the others and her business.

"Veronica, can we go outside and talk?"

"I am in the middle of something. Or did becoming a soldier dampen your eyesight?" she said without looking up from the ink. Vincent grabbed her by the arm and began to pull her outside. "Jesus fucking Christ, Vincent." she said when they reached the line outside.

"What is this about a gate and bringing the end of the world?"

"So, Louis told you?"

"No, Incognito told me. Louis is in hot shit because he was sent to kill you. When were you planning on telling me? Don't you think I should have known?"

"I tried to tell you but you act like you are the solution to all my problems. How are you going to stop my father from ripping the world a new one? You care about money. Money isn't going to stop him." Veronica folded her arms. "What are you going to do, kill him?"

"What were you planning to do? Let him just take over? I can kill him if it comes down to it. But now I have to wonder, are you in on his plan? Do you work for the council?"

"You're fucking clueless. My life is on the line and you think I work for a bunch of good for nothing politicians that apparently aren't even straight? You have some nerve." Veronica began to storm away. "I can't believe you can be such an insensitive jerk."

Vincent got in his mustang and the tires roared as he rippled through the night road. He did not know what to think when it came to that woman that he held so dear. His phone began to ring. It was Incognito. Vincent was not in the mood to chat. He had just gotten into a fight with his girl about the end of the world, one of his underlings was now in the doghouse if not fired, and he was pretty sure he was driving way too fast to even answer the damned thing.

But he pressed a button to put in on the loud speaker. "Vincent, what the hell did you do? Veronica is weeping all over my club."

"We aren't seeing eye to eye on secrets and family affairs. I need time to clear my head before I talk to her again."

"Don't wait too long. I need her to be in top condition. She practically runs the show around here." Incognito hung up. He was trying to be the voice of reason. He wanted more than the club to be running smoothly. He watched the two of them become friends and then lovers over the years. He was genuinely concerned.

Vincent spent time near the lake when he heard a familiar voice. "You shouldn't be so hard on her. She carries a heavy burden." He turned to see to his surprise Agatha the arms dealer.

"Are you here to lecture me, too?"

"I only speak where I know love should not die. She needs you for a trying time in her life."

"What do you do when the one you love is a threat to all humanity? I am used to killing demons but this? This takes the cake." Vincent dangled his legs just above the water. "She could have told me."

"What would it have changed, young hunter? You still love her, don't you?"

"Is she evil? I mean she has always been evil to a certain degree." he joked, trying to ease his tension. "What if someone put a bounty on her. What do I do then?"

"You love her. You are supposed to protect her. You can't do that brooding all the way out here by your lonesome, can you? Besides, as long as you know, you can be there for her. Figure out a way to end her father's plans without alienating her for things she can not control."

"You knew, too?"

"Of course I knew. I am an oracle. I know all dangers impending and imminent."

"So what brings you here? Surely you aren't here to tell me not to give up on her." Vincent caught his reflection in the water. Anger did not look good on his face. Neither did disappointment of his own behavior. He looked away.

"No, I did that because no matter the threats that this world has to offer, considering my influence on them, I did that because I am still a sweet old woman. I am here with a request."

"Oh really? What does an all seeing oracle need from a demon hunter?"

"Isn't it obvious? I need you to kill a demon."

"Of course." Why would that not be the case?

"There was an unhappy accident in a lab involving an alachemist and he turned himself into a giant mantis."

"I think I remember that one." Vincent said recalling earlier escapades.

"He is now killing off people while hiding in a parking garage. You could say he is nesting there and just lies in wait for his victims."

"Do I get a kick ass ebon for this one."

Agatha sighed. "If I find one I will be sure to let you have it, but as for now you should do this out of the honor of being a demon hunter."

Vincent thought long and hard about the honor of a demon hunter. It was short words considering that there was a traitor among the elite. His mind had gone under a certain way of thinking since he found he was being tough on Veronica unnecessarily, and tough on himself. She had no control over her father. Maybe he should apologize for being himself.

He drove to the location that was specified by the oracle and went in with full intention of winning this one for the good old fashioned demon hunters. He was still enlisted in the Order of Talia but they never had any real fun. Here he could shoot and slice to his heart's content. And this was just a textbook assignment. Nothing like those jock soldiers, not that they did not have his respect. There was just a certain way the young hunter liked things to be done.

That is to say he went alone on this particular mission. He needed time away from the crew to decide what he would do with Louis, the double agent. He could send him back to the academy but that would not stop him from his orders from Mikaeus. He would go in the shadows to get to Veronica and behind his back was not some place he wanted that kind of mojo. He had to devise a plan. Maybe use Louis to get to the council. He would consult Donna to that end.

The parking garage's lights had all been blown out. It was dark and dangerous. Vincent left the lights of his mustang on just so he could see. The element of surprise belonged to the demon that held dominion on while it hunted for stalked prey. The young hunter drove slowly just to attempt to find out exactly where the damned demon was.

Then he saw it. It was hanging upside down in front of a sign that read "4-E". It was all the way up and eating, crunching and slurping as demons that ate humans often did.

"You have a parking pass there buddy?" Vincent called out. "The meters are running."

The demon jerked his head and swallowed a limb. "You dare disturb me. I will have your hide with butter, hunter."

"Man, you really should watch your calories. What am I saying? You are already an overgrown bug."

"Oh, it is you. I regret letting you slip away." The demon's legs unfolded and it was on the floor, standing around ten feet tall. "I will have you this time."

Vincent summoned Ammit. "Yeah? I would like to see you try."

The demon lunged forward, flapping its wings to gain momentum. It swiped its bladed arms but the hunter rolled to the side barely getting out of the way. He fired and its hind leg. The carapace was enough to stop the bullet. With enough munitions he could break through it and do some real damage. That meant he needed to keep up the barrage.

The demon jumped, flapping its wings to gain enough height to turn and land on top of the hunter. It then moved to strike. Vincent half rolled because he was in between the demon's legs. The bladed arm of the demon pierced the concrete and Vincent rolled backward to get out of the positioning disadvantage. He then dove at the following swipe the demon made. He fired a few rounds into the abdomen of the giant insect while walking stylishly to steady his aim.

The demon jumped back, then rushed forward. It knocked the hunter backward and he slid across the floor. "Damn, that hurt." Vincent said. He rolled over to his side and then was up on his feet. The demon was already making another move. Its legs were alternating in motion, closing the distance between the two of them.

Vincent whirled and summoned the chains and threw them around the demon's front legs. The chains wrapped around and the demon toppled over and smashed head first on the pavement. Vincent, not anticipating the weight of the insect, flew a few feet and slid on the floor again.

"You have some new tricks up your sleeve, hunter." The demon said as they both shambled to their feet.

"You could say I am well seasoned, now."

"I hope it makes you taste better."

Vincent sighed. He set himself up for that one. There was no time to waste on poorly placed one liners. Vincent summoned his scythe and prepared for a lethal dose of close quarter combat. The demon and himself walked slowly toward one another and the demon towered like the monster it was.

"I will strip your flesh from your bones."

Vincent slashed at the demon's face. It went up on its hind legs to dodge the strike. It came down with intent on piercing with its front bladed arms but Vincent was all the more cunning. He slashed the arm clean off and the demon wailed in pain. It went for a strike with the other arm. Vincent slid underneath it and dragged the sharp end of his ebon through the abdomen, spilling the demon's guts onto the floor. The demon fell to the ground and began to twitch.

Vincent circled his handy work to the demon's face. "What was that about you eating me?"

"You arrogant hunter. This world will belong to the demons. There is nothing you can do to stop that from happening." The demon spit out some blue blood. "The humans will serve in our hell or they will die!"

"You don't get to see the day." Vincent cut off the mantis' head. That was the end of that. There were more and more parables that led to the conclusion that the demons were going to make a move, and in all probability, very very soon.

Vincent got back in his car and revved the engine. He peeled out feeling the exuberance of completing a kill. This was nothing like the Order of Talia. They were under the grip of potentially a madman. This was the life Vincent wanted. The life of a hunter. There was no greater joy. All he needed was to kill Xagos and he would feel complete. There was no way he would get that sort of clearance in being a soldier.

He returned to the lounge and only Xiao Lin was ecstatic to see him. He told her of the mild skirmish in the parking garage and she was upset that she was not along for the ride. Vincent assured her she would definitely be there for the next one. It was high time they went out for a mission again. That was if Vincent could find the gusto to be in the same room with Louis. There may have been hope.

Vincent thought of a terrific plan on how to find out more about Mikaeus and his movement and maintain the semblance that Louis was still after Veronica without the council being suspicious about what he was up to.

CHAPTER SIXTEEN

Donna was determined to find out just how far the council she would one day be a part of trailed into the demonic secrets. She could not serve while the plots of those who may be in league with the enslavement of mankind. Her agents were only that of Adriel's squad but it had to be enough to find out the truth. She told them to get close to Mikaeus without compromising their intent. SKilled though they are, they would be no match for the raw strength that the council member had.

Donna decided it would be best if she had a council member on her side. She approached Jane who was known for her abilities and her aptitude for reading minds, or so she said. It was more along the lines of calculating the streams of events and predicting their outcomes. If Donna could not trust her, then no one was to be trusted.

"Jane." she called to the council member. "A word?"

Jane was busy in the fact that she was promoting Donna to one day serve the council as an elite. "Donna, long time no chat. Is this a good news visit?"

"Far from it. Is there some place we could talk privately? This is of great importance."

The two of them went into an office just short of the main chambers where the council would meet to devise strategy in the war that Donna assumed was orchestrated by none other than Mikaeus himself. This among other things were to be discussed with the elite fighter. There was no doubt in Donna's mind that Jane could be trusted. She needed to know if Mikaeus' plan was that of the entire council. She had to tread softly when it came to asking questions.

"What do you know of Mikaeus?" Donna asked as they both sat down.

"Aside from his cast influence among the soldiers he is one of the best. His raw destructive ability on the battlefield makes him crucial for the war."

"That is what I want to talk to you about, the war in its holistic sense. There are some rumors going about that he may have a hand in it on the enemy side. The lives of soldiers and the very state of humankind may be all in danger due to his influence."

"Are you suggesting he is more than he says? That is a bold accusation and could be counted as treason. Donna, you may be tried for such convictions."

"It is a risk I am willing to take. I need to know that you aren't of a similar accord. Forgive me of my suspicions but I need to know the truth." Donna folded her hands trying not to seem like the evil one.

"I am not a traitor. I am sure there is just some miscommunication. However, such a statement should not be overlooked. How did you come about this information?"

Donna explained the interaction with the demon in Vegas. Jane listened to that tale with the intent of reading it to the possibility of it being true. Jane was a level headed one, not ruling out the chance that Mikaeus was in fact in league with the enemy. She told her of Vincent and his reckless nature but assured Jane that his story was legit.

"I see." Jane said. "That means you need evidence. What is your intention with Mikaeus? If it turns out that he is in fact practicing demonic arts with the intent of summoning an old foe, what do you intend to happen?"

"He should be removed from the council and interrogated so that he reveals all sources pertaining to Vadin and his return."

"If he is in the confirmation of your suspicions he will not go down without a fight. He has thousands of our soldiers at his disposal. There will be a war."

"We are already at war, Jane. This is just a battle worth fighting. Will you help me?"

"Bring me proof. I will assist you then." Jane stood up from the table. "Until then keep this under wraps. Your life may be on the line. It would be a shame to see you fall attempting to do good in the world."

"Thank you, council member. I will do what I can."

———∿∿∿———

Vincent pulled Louis aside and told him what he wanted done. Since he was tracking a gate of a warlock for a twisted elite there was no reason why he could not devise a plan of his own to make sure Veronica was not in the clutches of doom and treated like a useless pawn in a war he was not a part of. Well, Vincent took it personally. He was not interested in the war, just the well being of the one he doted on.

"You are going to tell the council member that the gate opened and the warlock is free."

"You mean lie to someone as powerful as Mikaeus? That only puts my life in danger." Louis said reluctantly.

"Lookk, I have every right to kick your ass for infiltrating my establishment with the intent of targeting someone I intend to marry. So just for kicks, you know to keep you employed here, you will do what may expose Mikaeus to Donna and put an end to the war."

"I can do that. But what will you do to ensure that the actual gate isn't opened? I have not found any rune that could stop it and there is only a matter of time before it opens. I am sure Veronica will disappear into nothingness as her father emerges. You will lose her and there will be more problems in the world."

"We have to do what is best right now. Stick to your research. I will make sure you don't die in the process."

Vincent wanted to stall the death of his beloved any way possible. He wanted to target Mikaeus for death for even beginning to use his love in whatever war he started. There was no getting around, though. The council was full of strong fighters. Their soldiers were better trained. It would take a miracle to bring down that kind of mojo. But for Veronica, Vincent would lay down his life.

There was a call. It came from Donna and she had a mission for the young hunter and his crew. It was imperative that he follow the orders he was still ordained to carry out, no matter if he wore the uniform or not.

"Vincent, I have orders for you. It is imperative that you follow them to a tee."

"I have plans that you need to be notified of as well. It involves a lie that is to be spoken by our friendly double agent."

Donna listened to the young hunter over the phone intently. "I'm all ears." she said.

Vincent explained the plan in hopes that it would draw out the next move of Mikaeus. If she was told to monitor his moves and if anything seemed out of order she should make a move to arrest the traitor.

"That is a masterful ploy Vincent. It may be of some use. You will serve the council well with that kind of logic."

"I am not doing it for the council. I am doing it to keep Veronica alive. I don't trust the council. I never have."

"Hopefully that way of thinking is changed once I am an official member. This is your war as it is mine, I understand your intentions but as a hunter you cannot overlook the simplistic enemy that is yours as well."

"If it isn't about money, then I don't want to hear it."

"Surely you don't mean that?" Donna had hopes for Vincent. She could not understand the attachment to money. Was Vincent so egotistical? Aside from the commonplace sobriquet of demon hunting, Xagos was a target of his. That was just a selfish slew of words that should have stifled the hope of Donna, though her aspirations did not falter.

"What are your orders?"

"I need proof that Mikaeus is in cohesion with our common enemy. So I need you to return to Vegas and capture Katherine."

"The demon that knows of Mikaues' plans. That won't be a problem."

"If I can get her to confess to what she knows about Vadin and the agents that seek his resurrection it should be enough to have Vadin arrested and tried for crimes against mankind."

"That would be the end of it, and possibly the war?" Vincent kicked his feet up on his desk.

"I am not so sure that it would end the war, but it would put a damper on the resurrection, slowing the process a little. Maybe we could find out who else is involved and they would be brought to justice."

"I hear you. Alright, we will move out as soon as possible. That demon is as good as in your hands."

The phone hung up and Vincent called all personnel in his small regime to arm. He briefed them on the mission and its importance. Despite their leader's indifference to the war, they were enthusiastic to help against the demonkind that sought to do harm to the people of the earth. Xiao Lin, as usual, was excited about the trip. Once they were told all that Vincent and Louis knew they were eager to capture the demon that masqueraded as a human.

They began to load up in the war machine to fast travel to the devil's city. Jam packed into the vehicle it was only a matter of minutes before they were transported by rune magic to the streets of gambling. It took a few short minutes to get to where Vincent knew the demon was operating.

The crew waltzed in like they owned the place and asked a few questions regarding the whereabouts of the demon they sought to capture. She was up high in the suites doing god knows what to whatever human was unlucky enough to cross paths with her. They moved into the upper halls where they heard the slurping sounds where a human was most likely being eaten.

Vincent gave a gesture for the team to wait outside while he went in to see if the demon would be more or less cooperative with what they were intended for. Vincent bursted through the door.

"You look like you need a new batch of friends."

"And you are?" the demon asked. The upper half of her body was that of a human but the lower half seemed that of a snake. Her stomach was settling from whoever she swallowed whole. "My next meal isn't for another couple days."

"Well, I don't have to worry about being eaten. That is quite the relief. I am afraid I have business with you, Katherine was it?"

"That is just an alias I use to navigate the human world undetected. Do I owe you money?"

"More like a confession. Are you familiar with the Council of Talia?"

"Did Mikaeus send you? I assured him that the power of Vadin was well accounted for. Or is he considering me a loose end?"

Vincent laughed. Mikaeus couldn't even be trusted as a traitor. "Oh no, I am sure you would be just that. For now I need you to come with me so we can incriminate your boss and send him to a hell that would pretty much end the war between us. You know how that goes don't you?"

The demon hissed. "I would never betray Vadin."

"I am afraid that is exactly what you are going to do."

The demon shot passed the young hunter and slithered into the hall where her path was halted by the rest of the crew. Vincent turned and ran after her but by the time he made it to the hall, the demon had jumped over the ambush and went for the stairs. She was meaning to run away. Where to was beyond reckoning.

"Louis, after her." Vincent ordered. "The rest you take the elevator." The crew moved swiftly so they would trap the demon.

Vincent broke through the glass window some thirty stories up. He used his chain ebon to swing downward very artfully to the ground, blocking the entrance. He swung through the entrance and kicked the snake square in the chest. He then flung the chains and wrapped around on their target. The demon was immobile. The rest of the crew showed up out of breath.

"You don't strike me as an all powerful demon." Vincent said, kneeling over the demon. "Why are you around in this war?"

"I have information. I know things." the demon said. "I know you will die just like the rest that stand in the way of Vadin."

"I am actually getting tired of being threatened."

"This is a promise." the demon hissed.

Soon they were back in Chicago. The demon sat in the basement still chained as a prisoner so that it would not do any harm. The demon though, was not a fighter and did not put up much resistance.

Vincent called Donna and she brought along the council member Jane to interrogate the demon. They arrived a few hours after they were told the demon would not give up the information without being promised she would be protected from Mikaeus. It was the only way it would say anything. It wanted freedom, not to be kept in a place like Solomon where she was destined to go.

Donna began the interrogation. "How is Mikaeus involved with the resurrection?"

The tail of the demon coiled. "He is not the architect of the demon's return. He is just a pawn much like I am."

Donna's brow furled. "There is another?"

"There are many that are involved with the resurrection. Milaeus promised the numbers in which to be sacrificed for the Vadin. There is an entire group that promises to bring order by way of warlocks controlling demons to enslave mankind."

"Sacrifice? What is the nature of this?"

"Thousands will be purged to free the demon. Soldiers, witches, warlocks, that will all be mortar and fodder for the demon's power."

Jane chimed in. "How long before they make their move?"

"It will take some time. Old powers need to be brought to the light. Some you may know of. The warlock that haunts Vincent's love is one of them. There is no stopping Vadin, you all should know. No matter if you bring down Mikaeus, there are others willing to take his place."

Jane turned to Donna. "This is enough to convict councilman Mikaeus. He will most likely abandon the council and take a few thousand soldiers with him. He will most likely use them to wake the demon."

"What do you want me to do?" Donna asked.

"It will take me some time to convince the other members of the treachery and treason. I am sure they will hear my plea. Don't do anything without my word, Donna. This is a delicate manner."

"What will you do with me?" the demon hissed.

"You will be sent to solomon. It is the only place we can be sure you stay alive and cause no further hells in the resurrection of Vadin."

The demon rose up on its tail. "You betray your words. I will not be sent to the hell that is Solomon."

There was a flash in Jane's eye. The demon toppled over and fell still. Donna was surprised by the sudden stop in the demon. "What happened?"

Jane replied. "I have an acute sensory that allows me to render a target motionless and unconscious for a short amount of time. Just one of the reasons the council will prevail. I can use it to subdue Mikaeus in the event he wants to issue a coup."

Vincent chimed in. "Remind me to stay on your good side."

"Aren't you the hunter that killed a human? You are already on my bad side." Jane said.

"It was one little mistake. Just don't use your eye voodoo on me. I promise it won't happen again."

They sent the demon to Solomon thanks to a few minor tweaks in Tags and Vincent knowing the prison's location. Jane questioned the young hunter about his lack of uniform and was surprised when she was told that the suits were ebon. Soon Donna and Jane would head back to the council's headquarters to make the arrest. Everything would go smoothly due to Jane's hypnosis. Mikaeus went under without a hitch. Vincent even attended the trial where the traitor council member could confess. Not that Jane needed him to. The demon's confession was enough to convict.

Mikaeus was wheeled in on a type of standing gurney. He was strapped with cuffs that would halt his demonic weapons. Ebon were not forbidden among the elites so the council could take no chances.

Jane made the opening statement and led the trial. It was mostly just a sentencing but no one expected the trial to end in chaos. "Mikaeus Hollow, you have been found guilty in crimes against humanity by way of cohorting with demons. You have been found guilty of planning to resurrect Vadin of the ancient order. You have been stripped of all council titles. Your verdict is death. Do you have any final words?"

Vadin raised his head. There was a projection from a badge that remained on his person. The script was cast on the table in front of him. It was Louis. "The gate has been opened. Veronica is dead."

Mikaeus smirked. That was what he was waiting for, the opportune time to strike. "I say to you all; Death to the council. Evil shall prevail." Compulsory rifles began to ring shots. The henchman of the traitor began to attack the council. A few of Mikaeus' agents swarmed him and cut loose his leather restraints. They could not undo the cuffs, but they made for their escape.

The plan was to link up with Veronica's father and then they would be one step closer to their planetary devastations. The council members would begin to fight off the henchmen but they looked too similar to those that remained loyal. There was an order for those who had not betrayed the council to remove their visors for the duration of the skirmish.

Even Vincent joined the fight. He aimed to stop the escape of the convict and repelled down from the upper balcony with the ebon chains. "Just where do you think you are going?" the young hunter said to the escape artist.

"To plan your demise. Really Vincent, you are no match for me even with these restraints." Mikaeus said.

"Perhaps I could give you a worthy opponent." Donna stood with her rapier ready and stood on the poise of her toes.

"Perhaps later? I have other things keeping me. Maybe we can fight at the end of the world." There was a huge plume of smoke that was meant to distract anyone that tried to stop Mikaeus. He was swarmed by loyal soldiers but by the time the smoke cleared he was gone.

The view of the fleet of traitors was an omen of things to come. Hundreds of fleet planes left the clouds thick and dark with smoke. "Are you going to go after them?" Vincent asked as they looked at the ascending brigade. "They just stole all your ships."

Jane scowled. She was not so petty as she was preparing for war. "Let them go. We need to replenish our ranks and prepare for an assault. If we find him, we eliminate him and his entire army." She turned to Donna. "I leave you with the task of finding him. Let me know as soon as you know. With his death comes your seat on the council."

Donna saluted. "Roger that."

Some of the soldiers were killed by the surprise strike. Vincent had to go back to Chicago to tell off Louis for his poorly timed call. Though he was just following orders, the execution may have gone on without any real problems. Those chances were low, it seemed to Vincent in hindsight that the scolding was ineffective.

———

Mikaeus went to see the maker of his sinister plot. It was at the base of an active volcano where he landed an entire sky fleet. There was a masked man dressed in white robes that welcomed him.

"The gate has opened. One of the marked ones has been released. Collecting all six will be easier. The dark one will be resurrected soon."

The masked man gently put his fingers on the cuffs. They popped open and fell to the ground. "There is a problem with your information. The gate has not opened. I would be able to sense Malekai, but there is no trace of him." His voice sounded as if he was talking through an electronic device.

"I have been fooled? It is that human agent of ours. He must be dealt with." Mikaeus was livid.

"Eliminate him. It is clear he has betrayed us."

"I will do just that. He has sided with Vincent. He has not yet tapped into his powers in which you say he has. Shall I kill him before such a truth can be realized?"

"Leave him to me. I will see what he knows. If I can sway his mind I can stop him from summoning the next seraph. Taking over the world will be that much easier."

Mikaeus dipped his head. "Yes, my lord." He then began to shout orders to all of his soldiers. They were to prepare for the hunt for the marked ones.

It was said that the marked ones knew the secret of Vadin and when their powers combined all hell on earth would break loose.

They were skilled humans that together could break open the prison in which the ancient one Vadin was held. Vincent knew nothing of the seraph. It would be too late when he did. But it was time for the orchestrator of the apocalypse to meet the one that could end him.

Chapter Seventeen

"You say them, we slay them." Vincent hung up the office phone. "Alright crew, we have been issued a challenge."

"Come again?" Rachel said wheeling her chair into the hall where she could see her boss with the new office mission.

This one was not a classic tale of demon hunting but a chance to brag about how well Vincent was doing in his business escapades. There was the phone call that was just hung up about a battle that was to take place should Vincent or a member of his team accept. Someone wanted to meet. The prize was an ebon.

"Just pay attention Rachel, I'm just getting started. There is an ebon at stake and we could use some advancement here in the office. I really feel like I have been carrying most of our mission. I would like the chance to get a new piece of equipment on board."

Rachel rolled her eyes. "So us saving you from captivity counts towards your skills?"

"I feel I played an excellent hostage."

Xiao Lin laughed. "Or like that time you were gone for almost a month serving the council as a military dog."

"That was a one time thing. Besides it helped with the investigations. I am one of the best soldiers.

Xiao Lin swore in chinese. "That is not what Jane is telling me while we send partial nudes back and forth."

"I did not know they could carry phones."

Louis chimed, "And I'm pretty sure Veronica hates us."

"That is purely incidental."

Damain flipped his pencil in the air and caught it behind his ear. "How do you figure?"

"As soon as I make it up to her she will only hate you." The scowl of the young hunter's face dissipated. "So who wants to fight a well trained student from the academy for glory and a new ebon?"

Xiao Lin ducked behind the wall, suggesting that she hated the idea. As glamorous as the oriental was, she did not like to brag.

"I'm out." Rachel said, wheeling her way back to the garage.

"That leaves you, Louis."

"Shouldn't I be working on the gate? You know, to stop the progression of Vadin?"

"This new ebon will guarantee that I get the chance to face Xagos without the binds on us. Just think of it as making it up to me for snooping into my commission with false pretenses." Vincent wrapped his arm around his employee's shoulder. "You owe me for your job."

"Fine. After this we are square."

The two of them left for the academy immediately after they settled into the mustang. They sped down the streets with Vincent very confident that Louis could handle anything that the academy could throw at him. It was that or Louis was fired.

They registered at the front desk just shortly after their arrival. There were students in the hall. They were in between lessons when they heard of the challenge. It had apparently been spread by psychics that saw it in their future and spread the word.

There was a twist. The masked villain that Mikaeus serves was the student. He appeared young enough but wore his mask to cover his identity. He made a future where he could meet Vincent just to find out his strength. He planned to see the young hunter sooner or later. He wanted it under his control.

The mass of bodies went out to the courtyard. The masked student took his time for the skirmish yet to happen. Vincent and Louis went over battle tactics as Louis whirled his rod and Vincent was giving him pointers in front of the whole study body. Then the crowd began to part when the white robes streamed by.

The masked student's voice was still sounding like it came through a com mic. "So good of you to accept my challenge. I am eager to see what talents you possess."

"I am not going to be the one to fight you. It will be my novice student excellante." Vincent said, almost knocking the thin Louis over by patting his back just a little too hard.

"You must understand that my challenge was for you."

"That was not specified. We came all this way. The least you could do is accept my defeat and hand over the ebon."

The student turned to walk away. "I forfeit the match. You will not get an ebon from me."

"Just hold it." Louis said. "Don't tell me you know you can't handle either one of us." he said, taunting. "I think you should see what you are up against."

"Very well." the masked student said. "Show me what you are made of. If you can land a single strike on me you get your ebon."

Louis readied his rod.

"Not that ebon Louis. Use the seraph sword." The masked one said, abruptly.

"How do you know my name?"

"I know a lot of things. I know you worked for Mikaeus. He knows the gate has not been opened."

Vincent and Louis both gasped. There were no others that knew of the mission. It led the two to believe that he was no ordinary student. Vincent became as an inquisitive detective would be if such an alarm was set off with such words used by the one impersonating a student.

"What is so special about the blade?"

"I will be taking it of course." The masked student said. "That has to be the most interesting thing that could ever make you wonder as to why."

"Louis, care to fill me in?"

"It is a sword of the seraph. It was rumored that Talia was the first to communicate with a holy order of valkyrie." Louis began. "It is said to be the weapon of the one warrior that would end the war between the Order of Talia and Vadin's evil forces. I have kept it as the personal savior of mankind and since this guy knows about it as well I can only assume that this is what it was meant for."

"And you think that guy is the one to defeat?"

Louis nodded. "Yes, I do." He readied the seraph blade. The hilt was a set of wings carved into steel.

"Good thing we showed up here today. Go us. We get an ebon and you can save the world."

The air grew denser. There was nothing but whispered tones on the school grounds of students. They were using all of their battle aptitude reading skills to determine who the victor would be before the match began. Louis was the first to make a move. He swiped the sword with elegance. Vincent could tell that Louis had practiced thoroughly with it. It shimmered in the light which gave off beams that made the sword look like it was on fire.

The masked student was no amateur to battle, or so it seemed. He artfully and quite melodically moved out of the way of the blade and its wielder hit nothing but air. Damai even brought out some of his finest combinations; one where he jumped in the air and spun for three slashes, and sweeping low, then making a rising cut that was supposed to be undodgeable.

The masked student was quick to end the match. There was no entertainment in the skirmish for him. "I will be ending this little demonstration of your, Louis. You are not the stuff of legends. You will not be the one to stop Vadin." He moved like blinding blurs when he snapped Louis's forearm. He held his arm as he forced Louis to his knees and slowly pulled the blade from his grasps.

One he had it he let Louis fall to the ground in pain. Vincent said. "Well it looks like you have a lot of work to put in, hero." He walked over to the distressing warrior and helped him to his feet. Then looked over to the masked student. "Now that you have it, you're going to use it to bring back that demon? Everyone has been going on and on about it and quite frankly it's all I can think about and I'm sick of it."

The masked student held out the sword and looked it over from behind slits in the mask. "Very exquisite. The steel, the sharpness alone is enough to want such a precious item. In the hands of a valkyrie it may have bested me. But in the lonely hands of a human…"

The student took his leave and Vincent had to report this new character that knew of the demon Vadin, Mikaeus, something called the seraph, and possibly the war to Clarie: the only person he knew that this information would be of value to. He called her up and she came over right away.

"Yeah, this kid straight whomped Louis and took his sword."

"Did you think to ask his name?" Donna asked, decently.

"Can't say that I did. I drew a picture of the mask he was wearing."

Donna took the piece of paper that Xiao was holding and combed it over from h=behind her glasses. "That is Vadin's face."

"So the guy is wearing that demon's face. Bold, looks like he isn't hiding it."

Jane crossed her legs. "I'll say. If you come across him again be sure to get as much information as you can. Chances are that he is the ringleader with that face."

"That guy was too young."

Louis rolled his arm slightly testing the way how much leeway he had with his wrist. "And good, there was no way he should have been dodging all my moves. They were top notch."

"Oh yeah, big savior of mankind. You lost to a student impersonator."

"Just the same." Donna said. "Those stacked against us are gathering in force. We can not rule out their strengths."

"Just look at the poor hero." Vincent teased. "How are things looking at the council headquarters?"

"You would know if you ever came by." Donna said, seeming edgy. "You know we are replenishing the numbers. You are technically an initiate. Maybe I should order you back to the headquarters."

"Not really my style, you guys work for free. I am not about that saving the world legacy you guys seem to have."

"I want to save the world!" Xiao Lin called from the other room.

Donna laughed, which was completely out of character. "You could learn from her, Vincent. Where is your demon hunting enthusiasm?"

"I have all the problems I need."

Donna stood up and began to make her way out of the door. "You still work for the council. I am just giving you freedoms. Would you answer the call willingly if I called you to war?"

"Not for free."

With that she was gone. It was back to business. "People say they think they seen a pterodactyl in Arkansas." Rachel said, going through memos.

"Too prehistoric. We already pulled an Indiana already."

A Sakura, Hand of Yakuza called. She would like to visit Xiao Lin." Rachel continued.

Xiao Lin leapt in from the office area. "Princess Sakura!"

"Xiao Lin, think of the fans."

"I'm going to text Shin." The huntress said. Her thumbs moved like lightning, one could almost hear a melody.

"I guess we see Empress of Japan." Louis said leaning dangerously back in his chair?

"A long story about demons and witches in the Shinto Province of Japan. You had to be there."

"Are we indebted to her? Did you somehow end up owing the mob?" Louis asked.

"Nothing like that. She is actually someone that Xiao flirts with. When I saw them last
They were making out on the riverside."

There was a week that went passed before Sakura showed up in Chicago, It was a ceremonious endeavour. When Xiao Lin saw her friend it was a leap into her arms and it was like they had never left each other's life. They spent the first day catching up. Xiao Lin filled Sakura in on the ongoings of the lounge but mostly Sakura wanted to talk about how she took over the Japanese underground.

Vincent was taunted for power when he saw the massive ninja army that courted the Japanese huntress. It was like he knew he wanted an army of his own. There was no consideration in working in the Council of Talia which would have granted him just that if he had applied himself. It was something about working for someone other than himself that never sat right with the young hunter. Though it would have been the most logical thing.

There was a job that was taken in France. A missing hunter that was a part of a team had gone missing while chasing an ebon and their leader wanted her back. The story was that the huntress went into the territory of a warlock that had the ebon brought in from the underworld and he wanted the ebon for reasons that were unknown. The warlock was not doing anything sinister but the disappearance of the huntress did spark some alarm.

Xiao Lin wanted to run as point runner on this mission. Vincent did not even go. He wanted to save his first trip to France for his honeymoon so he let Xiao and Sakura take on the mission himself and even keep the pay if they were successful in finding the missing huntress.

Sakura had a private plane that took them to the hunter Cloe in a sorority of huntresses. It was like Xiao Lin had died and gone to heaven. The huntresses were things of beauty and it did not take long for her to become acclimated to the figures of the women.

Cloe spoke with a heavy french accent. "There are a few key points when it come to finding our lost Abella."

Xiao Lin listened attentively. "What do we know of the warlock?"

Cloe continued towards the prompt. "His anime is Adami and he is skilled in poisons. He uses very potent flowers to taint the senses and it can be quite troublesome. Though Abella reported him as a non-threat it was her encounter with him that is so interesting."

Sakura chimed in as if she was an expert. Her time with the Yatagarasu gave her insight. "So he isn't wanted?"

"No, we just want Abella home." Chloe said. The sisters of the sorority were close. They were elite assassins but the poison from Adami could have taken sister Abella.

Xiao Lin became determined. "How do we find this warlock?"

"He is in midtown. It is not hard to spot his garden. It is fenced in by a large back gate with a sign that is marked "Potent Flowers.""

They were off to find the potential killer. There was no telling if the ebon that was in question was ever found. The only information that was given was that Abella did not return and it was Adami that was last heard of her in contact. Just as Chloe described there was the garden. There were dangerous looking flowers that bore purple thorns. It was clea it was a threat to health so the two huntresses decided to take the direct approach and ask some questions.

They ambled inside arm in arm and saw a short haired skinny man toying with the sap of a flower that was as beautiful as it was deadly.

"Are you Adami?" Xiao Lin began.

"I am. Welcome to my craft shop. How can I be of assistance? Do you need such an amazing flower to help you fall in love? Or one that can kill your foe quite secretly and painfully?"

Sakura began to snoop around, pretending that she was looking for a certain type of flower all the while summoning her armed ninja force to surround the shop in case the warlock tried to bolt.

"We were thinking of a beautiful french flower by the name of Abella. We heard you were the last one she spoke to before vanishing." Xiao Lin pressed. "You wouldn't know anything about that would you?"

Adami did not look up from his work. "I can not say that I do mademoiselle, I have many patrons that come in and out looking for love or worse."

"She is a huntress." Xiao Lin pulled out her pistol and pointed it at the distracted worker. "Looking for an ebon."

Adami laughed. "Really there is no need for such irrationalities. I am sure we can come to an agreement. I do remember such a young woman coming and asking about a demon weapon. I told her I knew of no such thing and sent her on her way."

"Is that right?" Xiao Lin said, aiming the barrel at the warlock.

"You don't believe me?"

"I have reason to believe elseways. Demon hunters and warlocks aren't exactly known to be so cordial with one another." Xiao Lin said.

"That is because I am a liar, love." Adami pulled a vial from his sleeve and threw it to the ground. A yellowish haze took the air very quickly.

Sakura shouted, "Don't breathe it in!"

Xiao Lin fired a shot in the direction of Adami. The bullet caught him in the shoulder as Xiao drew in a breath to hold so that the poison of any variety would not invade her lungs. Sakura moved expeditiously to the back of Adami and took him almost hostage. "Don't move or you are dead, warlock."

Adami raised his hands. "Are you sure I can't get you anything, sweet rose?"

"Where is the huntress?" Sakura demanded.

"Such a shame." Adami said. "No one ever really appreciates a bouquet of thorns the way I do." He made a sweeping motion with one of his fingers and vines came from the ceiling and snaked their way around the wrists and ankles of Sakura. She was lifted into the air and entangled.

Xiao Lin, turning purple from holding her breath moved to free Sakura as Adami ran for the door. He was met by more than a dozen blades from Sakura's ebon and was halted in his tracks. Sakura's ninjas cut her free and then they noticed something peculiar from a large budding flower in the center of the room.

In the cup of the flower's petals was a face. It had to be Abella. She was dead and the flower was sapping the blood from her body. The flower rose up and moved with tentacle like vines as it sauntered to Xiao and Sakura. Adami used a vine as a whip as he tried to make an escape through the Yatagarasu warriors.

"Don't let him get away!" Sakura yelled to Xiao. "I will free the body of Abella."

Xiao Lin was out of the door raining shots into the streets after the warlock. He was not particularly skilled but he did put up a decent chase. Sakura dodged swipes from the sentient flowers and cut away at some of the vines. But for every vine she cut another grew in its place.

The flower attempted to grab Sakura. Sakura summoned her armor in fear that the spikes the flower carried were poisonous given the nature of the shop. The flower was slow however and there seemed to be a soft spot underneath where the flower set the vines it was standing on.

Sakura rolled underneath the plant and gave a clean cut to a glowing sack that seemed to be filled with water. The plant keeled over and the naked body of Abella slid from the pistol of the plant. It fell over and turned unhealthy shades of brown.

Xiao Lin and the ninjas had no problems cornering Adami. He was captured and sent to a prison for the misuse of flowers and the death of a huntress. The two, Sakura and Xiao Lin, returned to Chloe with the body of their sister. The entire sorority was in tears at the sight of one of the fallen ones. The two huntresses stayed for the burial rights and paid their respects in a show of sisterhood.

It was Xiao Lin's first trip to France and it had been a gruesome one. She got permission from Vincent to stay there for a couple more days. She wanted to snap pictures and spend a little more time in the love capital of the world with Sakura. They spent time with the sisters of Abella, mourned and Xiao Lin persuaded them into exchanging phone numbers.

But soon she had to return home. Sakura had to do the same. For once one became the queen crime boss in Japan one would find herself very busy. Xiao Lin was flustered that someone had died. Could it have been prevented? Who would know? There was the ebon that was in question. It was never found. Adami was sent to warlock jail for the rest of his natural life. That did not satisfy Xiao Lin but it was something she had to live with.

The rest of the crew gathered around as she told the tale of Abella. She told it like she was a part of the sorority itself. She showed the pictures she had taken over in the country of love. It was an all around harmonious moment for the lounge. It was not often they could sit and relax and swap stories.

For Vincent it was an endearing moment. He decided that he would allow more solo missions between the members of the lounge if it was not too dangerous. More money would flow in as more work would be able to be done if the labor was split between the four of them. Himself handling a giant mantis and Xiao Lin taking on warlocks with the Japanese princess was a good start.

Louis was next to do some solo work. His mission was to find out an informant that could expose those responsible for Vadin and the cruelty the demon would bestow on the planet. He accepted but had to get more done to aide Veronica. Malekai, her father, should be stopped before he arrives. That was Louis's logic. It was not far fetched. He just had a small kink to work out before he could return to his research. How hard could asking a couple questions about the bringers of the apocalypse be? He was sure to find out. Before he set off he pitched the stone that allowed him to speak to Mikaeus. He did not want to live that kind of double life.

CHAPTER EIGHTEEN

Vincent wole at his apartment: a place where he never spent time. It was a slow morning with a pot of coffee and a demon hunter's newspaper. There were articles that posted pictures of Mikaeus and it raved about the demon's return. It was primarily the story of the hit that the Council of Talia suffered at the hands of the agent that worked there. Vincent wondered if Donna had anything to do with the article. She probably had since she was one for making facetime. She was ambitious and wanted herself to be known among all the hunters.

It was a slow drive to the office where Louis had taken leave to gather more information for the council since he had turned over a leaf. Xiao Lin was jamming in a large set of headphones and Rachel was still in the garage tweaking the war machine Tags. Who besides Rachel knew the maintenance that such an ebo required.

Vincent hopped to his desk after Xiao Lin waved to him. He sat in his chair looking at his cellphone where he spent a majority of the morning trying to get a hold of Veronica. After their last encounter it was good to say she was more than a little pissed at him. Had he overreacted? Maybe. There was nothing that was resolved when it came to that little lover's quarrel. Veronica was still the anticipated gate of her father Malekai and all Vincent had now was a cold phone.

It took him a while before he came up with the inner strength to apologize though he was sure it would not do the trick. He drove to the nightclub only to find that she had called in. Incognito said there was something that she needed to take care of for herself.

"She said you weren't being supportive." Incognito said while puffing a cigar behind the bar. "She said you were being an insensitive jerk."

"She always says that."

"Love is give and take. Knowing she has troubles with her family should spark at least a little light in that dim head of yours. Can I get you anything to take the edge off?" Incognito taped the ashes off the stogie when he offered.

"Maybe some rum. Is it on the house?"

"Given your troubles I should say so." Incognito poured a shot into a glass.

There was more to Vincent than just a hard head that was out of money and vengeance. He wanted Veronica to know that. There was no way he could if she was not to be around or not to answer any of his calls. He sat and drank a few shots of rum before he set out to find her.

"We may show up tonight, the crew and I."

"Any special occasion?" The nightclub was dead in the mornings. There was some business so Incognito stayed open then. "Should I reserve a private section?"

"Definitely. It is Xiao Lin's birthday." Vincent chugged the last shot of rum and was off to do a little shopping for Xiao Lin. Incognito gave a slight not and then the young hunter departed.

He went to an oriental shop and bought a ceremonial robe for Xiao and packed it into the trunk of his car along with some tea and candles that he just knew she would use to decorate the office. He still could not get a hold of Veronica. He wondered what she could possibly be up to. He hated that their interaction was a fight. He wanted her to be there so they could celebrate the day together. A surprise party was what he had planned. Xiao Lin loves dumplings and Veronica made them the best. That is to say Vincent did not want Xiao to make them herself.

Night fell and mum was the word to Xiao Lin. Vincent told Rachel to take Xiao Lin out and arrive at the nightclub in a few short hours so that there could be a surprise at the party. There was a private section in the nightclub that was reserved for just that. Free drinks, free food and whatever the birthday girl wanted to play for music was just a few perks of having a birthday the way they did in downtown Chicago.

When Xiao Lin arrived there was red confetti showering her.

Xiao Lin was so happy. "I thought that you had forgotten!"

"How could we? You are our best huntress."

Rachel frowned. "I had better get a horse for my birthday then."

Xiao Lin changed into the robes and sat on the VIP couch as the special hostess for the night. Everyone sang happy birthday to her and even the other hunters joined in. She received several compliments on her music choice which consisted primarily of electronic dance music. All of the club was in the throw of celebration. Xiao Lin took the stage with a few huntresses and they danced like they never have before.

After a few hours of merriment they crew, minus Louis, sat back in their special section. "This is the best birthday ever!" Xiao Lin sipped some tea while Vincent had more rum. Rachel had some whiskey. Vincent ordered some special dumplings from an asian grocer and needless to say they were delicious.

"I have something else for you, Xiao." Vincent pulled out an envelope and put it into her hands. "Don't spend it all in one place."

It was a wad of cash. "I can finally upgrade my bike." Xiao Lin leapt into her boss' arms. "You are the greatest ever."

There was a silence at the door. The bouncer had gone down. A familiar figure waltz into the nightclub. It was Drolo. The door was bombarded with the scarecrow minions and demon hunters were at arms. Incognito looked from his office and saw the commotion. He was on his way to the main floor.

Drolo appeared in the VIP section as if by magic. "How nice to see you again, Vincent. I hope I am wrong about not getting an invitation to the party?"

"You have to be fucking kidding me. You are a fool to attack here where we demon hunters gather. What's your agenda?"

Drolo smiled. "I have orders to take this club and tear it asunder. All demon hunters are to be killed with you especially in mind."

"Don't tell me. Your Vadin bosses sent you?"

"Indeed." Drolo said. "You aren't to draw another breath."

Vincent summoned his scythe to prepare for the coming storm. Hunters from the club were already trading blades with the minions. There was chaos everywhere. Chairs were being used to block blades, the glass tables had minions slammed through them, it was a scene that procted the coming war.

"You dare crash my party?" Xiao Lin said, angrily. She drew her ebon pistols and opened fire on Drolo. The demon raised his arm to stop the projectiles from harming him. The steel straw was enough to stop any bullet.

"You think you can stop me with those low level ebon? You are in for a rude awakening." Drolo extended his arm and knocked the huntress back a few feet. She fell back onto the couch with a slight ring in her chest from the impact. The VIP section was soon crawling with scarecrows armed to the teeth with blades ready to do the unthinkable.

When the minions began to charge at Vincent with precision he whirled his weapon and clashed cold steel with the witch's minions. She had to be nearby. Vincent sent Xiao Lin and Rachel to find her for if the witch was stopped her minions would cease to function. Vincent would handle Drolo on his own.

The minions worked in cohesion with one another. They moved better than they had before. One went low to swipe at the young hunter's legs in attempts to immobilize him. Vincent pressed the staff end of the scythe to the floor and pressed on the top of the dull end to jump over the scarecrow. While he was mid air another minion darted at him with blades taking advantage of the momentary stall in the hang time of the young hunter.

Vincent rolled over the minion and spun so the minion was on the lethal end of his ebon. When he pulled the crafty rod portion of his ebon the minion was ripped in half exposing a white soul.

The souls acted as the batteries that powered the minions and brought them to life. While it was altogether impossible to kill the minion, harvesting the soul made them useless. Vincent sliced the soul and the minion's straw dissipated into the air.

Vincent landed gracefully. "I am sure you run on the same mechanics." he said to Drolo.

"Maybe. But I am far more skilled than these underlings." Drolo threw off its overcoat to the floor and challenged the demon hunter head on.

A minion attempted to pierce Vincent from the side. The young hunter used the dull end of his ebon to stop the strike of the minion. He then lifted the scythe and spun it cleaving away the straw exposing the soul. He then made a single sweep to eliminate the scarecrow holistically.

Drolo began to sense the pattern. He sprang forward and kneed the young hunter in the chest. He was far beyond any of the minions in terms of power and speed. Vincent caught his balance and slashed at the demon. The demon ducked below the lethal end of the ebon and extended his arm into Vincent's gut. The hunter countered by bringing the ebon above him and going into a downward strike.

The demon caught the blade flat palmed in its hands. "You are naive to think you can win this, hunter."

"A little soon to be talking like that, don't you think?"

The demon yanked the scythe from Vincent's hands, pulling him closer as it did so. The demon then threw a slew of punches into the torso of the hunter. The demon kept into the air and gave a roundhouse kick straight to the jaw of the young hunter. The hunter fell back onto the glass table that sat in the center of the room and shattered it.

The hunter stood to his feet, recalling his ebon to his possession. "I see you have some moves on you."

"That is not all I can do." Drolo said. "Would you like to experience the full extent of my capabilities? Or should I just kill you slow?"

"I think you and I both know how this is going to play out. Do your worst."

The demon held up his hand. "As you wish." Then a stream of steel straw shot from the demon's palm, piercing the demon hunter in a multitude like the spine of a porcupine.

Vincent was surprised to see the projectiles. He had to react quickly or succumb to the dozens of needles. He quickly whirled his ebon and blocked as many as he could but he did not stop them all. "That is what you had me waiting for?" Some needles were sticking out of his jacket. "I'm disappointed."

"You talk a pretty large game for someone that is about to die." Drolo said, charging at Vincent. The young hunter did the same and they were both through the window on the second floor that overlooked the dance area. There was a brawl between minions and hunters down there. They cracked a glass table.

"You're paying for that." Incognito said as the young hunter rolled to his feet.

"Aren't you covered by some sort of hunter's insurance?"

"Not by a long shot. That stuff does more harm than good." Incognito gestured toward the demon that now stood in front of him. "What is the story with this guy?"

"Vincent pulled out some of the needles from his jacket. "That guy has metal throughout his body, makes it tough to cut through." Vincent grabbed Incognito by the shoulder and they ducked behind a couch as more needles rained in the club. "He can also do that."

"Well lets see how tough he is against my ebon." Incognito said. He stood from behind the couch with a reddish gold grenade launcher.

"Whoa, is that the cerberus?"

"Damn skippy." Incognito fired a round at Drolo. There was a small explosion and one of Drolo's arms was shredded. Steel straw flew in all directions. This alarmed the minions. A few of the hunters were no match for them and they were free to target Incognito. Vincent opened fire with Ammit, exposing souls through the straw. Grenades from cerberus eliminated them in whole.

Drolo was running out of options. He was no match for the explosive power of the ebon that Incognito carried. Vincent wasted no time in pressing the attack against Drolo with Incognito aiding him. He dashed forward to the demon and began to distract him with a flurry of slashes that knocked the demon off balance. The strategy was to leave the demon open so that Incognito could blast it and expose any of the souls that held it together.

It was working fluently. Incognito kept the aim for when he saw an opening. Vincent, who kept a watchful eye on the club owner, was flipping through the air causing sparks every time the blade collided with the steel straw. The demon lunged when he had opportunity, the swiftness of the young hunter simply outplayed the efforts of the demon.

Vincent connected to the demon's head with the blunt end of his ebon and then leapt backward. Incognito saw that as the opening he was waiting for and blasted the demon through the front window and into the street where demons were fighting hunter's galore.

Vincent stepped through the opening of the window and Incognito took to the door. "Looks like you are out of ideas."

Drolo was half the demon he used to be. "I have a few more tricks up my sleeve. That ebon will have its work cut out for it." Drolo said, referring to Incognito. Drolo then extended the mangled arm and wrapped it around a few minions. He then pulled them in and absorbed them. The demon reconfigures itself to have four arms and was bulkier.

"That's some serious shit." Incognito said.

"I'll say. You are going to have to keep up suppressive fire while I find the soul that is keeping that demon alive."

Incognito smirked like he never does. "Just don't get in the line of fire. You might get your head blown clean off."

Drolo used two of his arms to pick up a car and flung it at the young hunter. Vincent cleaved through it and began summersets to blunt the arms of the demon so that it could not use lethal force. Incognito fired more grenades but they only knocked off a few bits of straw. Drolo was a bit more powerful in terms of defense.

"You are becoming a nuisance." Drolo said to the young hunter.

"And you are becoming a problem." Vincent hopped on the back of the demon and used Ammit to attempt to beat away some of the straw. He fired repeatedly until there was a hole in the demon's back exposing the soul that gave the demon power. The demon reacted by extending one of its four arms, grabbing the young hunter and whipped him into one of the nearby buildings. Then the demon dragged Vincent across the pavement, mostly ruining his favorite coat.

Incognito was surrounded by minions on all sides. He fired rounds at them blasting them into oblivion. Some got close enough for the club owner to punch back so he had a clear shot without being in range of the explosions. It took Vincent a moment to recover from being whipped around like a ragdoll before he came to assist his mentor.

The demon was relentless, however. Drolo bagan to fire more of the needles at the young hunter. All Vincent could do was take cover. There were more of the projectiles now that the demon was larger. The needles pierced the car so deeply that it was only a matter of time before they made their way through. Once Incognito had a clear shot he blasted the arm of Drolo back so that he could not fire in a straight line. Vincent recovered and threw the chain ebon around the demon's arm and swung his way closer to the demon.

Drolo reared back and the young hunter was flung upward. He artfully took the force to a backflip and struck downward and used the force to cleave off one of the demon's arms. There was an exposed soul in the shoulder where the arm used to be.

"There!" the young hunter said. "Fire now!"

"You don't have to tell me that, fool." Incognito fired and the explosion collapsed the soul. Drolo could not regenerate the limb after that.

They kept up the barrage of attacks, knocking off limbs and blasting the exposed soul. Soon the demon was nothing more than a pile of mangle straw on the street. The soul that kept the demon alive was in its head, exposed as it layed on the asphalt. Vincent stood over the demon with the barrel of Ammit pointed for a lethal blow.

"Not going to lie, you put up a hell of a fight. But I was made to slay things like you."

Drolo laughed demonically. "Looks like I have found my match. You will find Beatrix no easy foe."

"You have a hit put out on me. I take that as an insult." Vincent fired into the soul and the demon was dead.

"You have to find that witch and put an end to this. If that demon was that strong then your underlings may be in trouble."

"Yeah, what kind of boss would I be if I let them die?" Vincent was off speeding in his mustang while on the phone trying to find out if

Xiao Lin and Rachel found the witch. If they had it was sure to be one hell of a scene.

There was no answer the first few times he tried. Then when he finally got through it was the witch on Xiao Lin's phone. "Is this Vincent, the fabled hunter?"

"Beatrix, you bitch. What have you done?"

"Nothing I can't explain as simple stitching. Your underlings are quite brave but lack the intuition to fight an opponent such as myself."

"If you killed them," Vincent paused. "I swear to god."

"They are alive for now. If you want to keep them that way you will meet me at the train station where I will trade their lives for yours."

"I have a better idea. Why don't I just show up and kill you just like I did that shit kicker demon of yours. You know, send you to the depths of oblivion and let you meet your maker."

"Bold." the witch said. "I will see you meet an agonizing end."

The phone was hung up and the young hunter was speeding to the subway. His car was ambushed by some of the witch's minions. The tires were slashed and the car spun into a stop sign. Vincent got out of the wreckage and it was a fight that was anticipated. He made quick work of the minions and there were more along the way. He had to fight his way to the underground tunnels of the subway.

At first there was no sign of them. Then, after traveling in the underground, he saw that Xiao Lin and Rachel were stitched together on a pillar. "Vincent! It's a trap!" Xiao Lin called out.

Vincent stopped in his tracks. He saw a gleam and there was a slash that Vincent barely managed to elude. When the young hunter saw what attacked him it was a shock to even see. It was a scarecrow version of himself. It came complete with a scythe and even had his jacket.

"That witch is trying to manipulate you using a magic mirror." Rachel said.

Then, a ways down the tunnel, there was the silhouette of a woman that turned out to be Beatrix. She emerged from the shadows holding a black mirror. "Surprised to see you?" the witch said.

"What kind of bullshit are you pulling now?"

The scarecrow made another swipe at the hunter before there was any more rapport. There was a clash of sparks and an exchanging of strikes. The young hunter and the scarecrow were an even match. Every move that the young hunter made the scarecrow could match evenly. Vincent had to be creative. His normal attacks were stalled and pressed back.

The scarecrow moved like a wisp. The more Vincent fought the smarter his doppleganger seemed to become. He slashed at the minion and the minion dodge and gave him a swift kick to the jaw. He slashed again and the minion jumped over the strike and kicked him in the chest. It seemed pointless to try and do battle with it.

When Vincent saw an opening he moved to free his subordinates from the pillar. "Thanks." Rachel said. "That wire was really starting to dig in."

"Why don't you two help me corner that thing. A few heads are better than one?"

"Got that right." Xiao Lin said.

Xiao Lin summoned her long sword ebon and Rachel brought out her knife. It was three against one. They charged the minion. The dexterity of it was enough to call it a decent foe. It dodge everything they threw at it. It was a clever trapping that had its back crash against the wall. Vincent saw this as an opportunity to strike. He slashed at the arm of the minion and when he did there was a sharp pain in his arm.

"What the hell?" the young hunter said to himself. There was a stream of blood pouring down his arm.

"You like my magic?" Beatrix saidm still holding the mirror. "Once your reflection is caught in this mirror a voodoo doll is made. Anything that happens to it happens to you."

"Looks like we can't just cut it to ribbons or the boss dies, too." Rachel said.

"Maybe if we break the mirror." Xiao Lin proposed.

The three hunters made a battle formation. They concocted a plan that was simple: Two of them would distract the doll and one would go for the mirror while not dealing any lethal damage to the doll for fear of what it might do to their leader.

It would be tricky because if the fight dragged on the chances of them dying would be greater. They could not give the witch what she wanted. That was the death of Vincent, maybe the three of them in general. Careful tactics and abrupt timing would be needed if the plan were to be found in succession.

They stood ready with their target in their sights. It was proposed that Xiao Lin deal the blow to the mirror. They charged in unison to break Vincent free of the voodoo curse.

CHAPTER NINETEEN

The copy was well an adept in close quarter combat. He was faster than the three of them and seemed to welcome open attacks as if to cause damage to Vincent. They battled carefully and tried to gain ground as the witch sat at the end of the tunnel. She propped the black mirror on the wall and waited to see the progression of the skirmish.

Vincent pushed the voodoo doll backward without so much as giving it a scratch because his life was on the line. Xiao Lin hung back to find an opening to attack the mirror. When they were finally close enough she went for a clean strike. Beatrix would have none of it. The witch protected the mirror with her giant needles and parried the long sword of Xiao Lin.

Xiao Loin stayed in range and battled the witch as she tried to break the cursed mirror. Rachel and the young hunter kept the voodoo doll occupied.

"You really think you are a match for me, huntress? I have captured you once already." the witch said.

Xiao Lin scowled and readied her blade. "It's not you I am after. The boss will take care of that. I only want to break your unholy toy."

"You will have to get past me. And I outclass you in this type of fight." The witch pressed forward and attacked. She had speed but Xiao Lin had cunning. Xiao's elusive maneuvers gave her position to gain ground and get close to the mirror. When she was close enough to strike it the arm of the voodoo doll stretched and gripped her by the throat. It pulled her backward so that she lost the inches that she had gained.

Rachel, assuming the worst, kicked the doll in the ribs. Vincent felt the brunt of that swift action. "Can you be careful with that? Those are my ribs, too."

"Sorry boss, just looking out for my partner." Rachel said, resetting her form.

The doll set its eyes on Xiao but could not get through the line of the young hunter and his underling. "Oh no you don't." The doll made a sweep with its scythe and it was metal for metal when Vincent blocked it. Rachel pounced and got the doll in a headlock, careful not to choke it too hard.

Xiao Lin was exchanging metal with the witch but she was no match. She was tethered by the limbs with wire from the witch's weapon. The witch then pulled the strings to control Xiao's body. It was another trick that the witch had not revealed until now.

The doll broke free of the choke hold by wrapping its arms around Rachel and filing her to the ground. There were only minor scrapes and bruises from the toss but it was still very forceful. When Vincent moved to strike the doll before it could kill Xiao, who was rendered immobile by the wire, Beatrix moved Xiao into the huntress into the line of fire. Vincent stopped short so that he did not hit his underling. He instead whirled his ebon and cut her free of the wire that bound her into a human shield puppet.

The doll was on Vincent before he could make his next move. It kicked him in the jaw and he went doppling backwards. Xiao Lin was making elegant moves to strike the mirror and Rachel joined in. The attempts on the mirror had the witch's attention while Vincent battled the doll.

There was an even match between the two. It even had his face stitched in cloth. The doll summoned a version of Ammit and the young hunter took cover behind a pillar as the doll shot a barrage of shotgun shells directly at him for lethality.

"So this is what it feels like."

Rachel parried the needles of the witch and barred her arm in a grappling maneuver that rendered the witch in her clutch. Xiao Lin saw it as a chance to make the move on the mirror. She took out her pistol and shot it. It cracked and then shattered into pieces.

"Vincent, now is your chance!" Xiao Lin shouted from down the tunnel.

The young hunter sprang into action. He whipped his chain from behind the pillar and it wrapped around the voodoo doll's leg. He pulled it and the doll fell flat on its back. There was no pain that Vincent felt so the curse had to be broken. Thersubway was approaching. Vincent dragged the chain and threw the doll in front of the moving railway car.

Beatrix swept Rachel's legs and flipped her to the ground. "You all are becoming a burden." she said.

Xiao Lin put her pistol up to the witch's head. "Don't move. It will be the end of you."

"Testy." the witch said, raising her hands to show defeat. "It is a shame that demons act of their own accord. Elseways I would have Xagos burn you to cinders."

Vincent closed the distance between him and the witch. "Xagos is going to die and you are going back to Solomon."

"Solomon? You can't send me back to that hole. I can help you acquire what you desire most." The witch had schemes. Vincent was sure she was spouting nonsense.

"And what, pray tell, is it that you think I want?"

"To kill Xagos. I can help remove the charm."

This was against the demon hunter code; to help a witch. It definitely had the young hunter's attention. "What do you know of the charm?"

"I am one of many of the Sisters of Taltos. We know charms, binds, and enchantments far and wide. The ones that bind you two are complex but nothing that can't be overwritten. I can make it so that you and the demon are vulnerable to each other."

"What do you want in exchange?"

"What I want is simple. To be freed. I will make an agreement that my powers will be used for good."

"What about all the hunters you killed to make minions? Will their lives be restored?"

"I can not say that they will. Solomon is no place for a witch; stripped of all magic and left to rot in a cell. Free me and I will give you the chance to kill Xagos." The witch was desperate.

"You can't take her word." Xiao Lin said. "She is evil."

This was the only chance Vincent had to kill Xagos. It had to be taken. It would be the only way to get his revenge. "Xiao, just trust me. I know what I am doing."

There was an arrangement between Vincent and the witch that if and when he killed Xagos she would work for him at the lounge. She would be free afterwards. She would work tirelessly to break the bind so that the demon could be killed. They went back to the lounge and the witch was chained in the basement. She was given all that she needed to break the bind, though it would take some time to prepare.

Everyone else in the lounge thought it was a mistake of an idea. The one track mind of the hunter was in secret questioning. It was imperative that the bind would be found and broken quickly as the demon still had ties with the witch. The demon could find her if summoned and there would be hell in the lounge.

Incognito called when the fighting was over and was fumed that his nightclub had been ravaged by the minions. It would take a fortune to rebuild. Money was the problem. Vincent agreed to pay for most of the damages but restocking the bar would fall on his mentor.

Vincent went to the basement to talk with Beatrix to find out more about the bind.

"It is that of seraph protection." the witch said. "It is almost impossible to be undone."

"Seraph? The angels that everyone is going on about?"

"Indeed. It is stated that they only appear when the world needs them the most."

"Times of peril, armageddon, the works. I know that but what does that have to do with me?"

Beatrix took a moment as is preparing to tell an ancient secret. "You don't know?"

Vincent shook his head. "Care to tell me?"

"It is stated that the seraph can only give birth to girls. It is part of their bloodline. You are just an anomaly in that regard. Your mother should have told you. You are born of angelic properties. You are the one who is to save this world."

"I thought that was the promise of the weapon that imbued the seraph. It was destroyed by a masked freak that proclaims to want to awaken the demon Vadin. You know, the demon everyone has on the tips of their tongues these days."

"That one is dangerous." the witch said.

"What do you know of him?"

"He goes by the name Zakaire. He is most powerful when it comes to physical combat. His magic is unparalleled. If he summons Vadin it is the end of days." The witch's tone lowered. "I would be one to be weary. If you want to save this world I suggest you stop him before that happens."

"I'm not out to save the world. That is the least of my worries."

"What sort of hunter are you." Beatrix asked. "You're not the least bit concerned given your bloodline. You would be the only one that can stop him."

"There is a lot of promise of the end of the world. I have even stopped you. Why were you trying to kill me anyway?"

The witch was embarrassed by her defeat in the subway tunnel. "Because Zekaire knows you are the one that will kill him. Killing you before you got the chance would promise me more attachments that would enhance my powers. If you thought my minions were strong before, you should see what they would have become."

"You aren't to make any more of those."

"I am aware of those trappings if I want to be freed."

"What is the plan for helping me defeat Xagos? I assume you have one."

The witch began by taking out a small book etched with runes. "There is a dimension where there is no magic. All powers are made to null. I can transport you there but there is one problem."

"And what's that?"

"You are not strong enough to defeat Xagos. With your current ebons and the threat of mortality you will most likely be defeated. You will need more if you are going to kill Xagos."

"You just let me worry about that."

Now it was only a matter of time before the young hunter got what he wanted. Xagoa would be a distant memory and Vincent would have avenged the death of his parents that were killed on his thirteenth birthday. He only had to find the patience and not go back on the dark bargain he made with a witch.

———

Louis took to the inner city where he would meet his contact about the location of Zakaire and Mikaeus. He was lured to an empty building that was being torn down. It was all in favor of ending the war before things got out of hand. He should have not gone alone. Even after the threat of the witch Beatrix being gone it was still more than he could chew.

Zakaire and Mikaeus were there waiting for him. The building was flooded with the traitors that ransacked the council headquarters. "I am surprised you fell for this." Mikaeus said. "It is such a shame as well. You would have made a fine sacrifice for our plans."

Louis knew this would be the end of him. He could only try to take them both down before he lost his life. Judging by the last battle he had at the academy the odds of that were slim, but he had to try.

"You didn't think we'd just let you go with all that information that you carry, did you?" Zakaire's metallic voice echoed from behind the white mask that carried Vadin's face. "You had to have known we would get you eventually."

"I knew you would come for me. But I am not going to make it easy on you." Louis said. He summoned his ebon and prepared for one last fight. "I am going to take you both down and end your plans right here."

Zakaire scoffed. "You really think you can defeat us? We number in the thousands. Not to mention I have defeated you once before."

Louis had a trick up his sleeve. An ace in the hole if you will. If he were to be defeated he would drag Zakaire into a realm and trap him there for all eternity. It was a short chance but it was the one he had. He wanted to be the hero that the seraph told about. It would cost him his life but the way he saw it, he was as good as in the grave already.

Zakaire raised his hand. "Go, my sentinels, show him our raw power."

The army that stood in the shadows emerged with power poles, though they were dressed in white this time around. Louis drew in wind with his ebon and sent it outward in all directions around him very chaotically. The force of wind pushed a large number of them from the building that housed them and they went flying out of the windows.

He could not get them all. Soon he was fending off a barrage of strikes from lethal javelins while bashing and breaking bones where he saw openings. Mikaeus began to enter the fight but Zakaire stopped him. "I'll deal with this weasel. You go and find the gate and bring her to me." Mikaeus took his leave and the masked marauder stepped down to face off with Louis.

"Bold of you to join the fray." Louis said. "This gives me a chance to end the war and kill you."

"Are those your last words, hunter? You would have done well in serving me."

"You are haughty."

"True victors often are."

"Let's see how much you talk when you are dead." Louis threw his staff to and fro in attempts to hit Zakaire. HIs attempts were met with the air as the masked man dodge the swings. When Louis was sure he would connect his staff only passed through his opponent. Things were looking grim.

Zakaire hit Louis in the stomach when his barrage of attacks failed. "Do you give up, or do I need to force you to beg for your life?"

"Fuck you." Louis said, keeled over.

"That is not how to beg." The masked man moved swiftly as he pummeled Louis. The sentinels that stood around them in a circle pushed the hunter back into the line of fire and he was knocked senseless.

It was time to act. Louis was on his knees, empty handed. Zakaire walked in range of the hunter's trump card. "Any last words?" Zakaire said.

"See you in hell." Louis took a stone from his pocket and crushed it. There was a vortex that pulled a large number of the sentinel in but Zakaire phased through the storm. When the cosmic dust settled there was the masked man standing where Louis used to be.

"Foolish young man." Zakaire said.

———

The lounge went dark. Everyone gasped. "Did you forget to pay the power bill?" Rachel joked.

"Not by a long shot."

Before they could scramble to the power box a projection had shown in the center of the lounge. It was Zakaire. "So this is where you have been hiding, Vincent Delvine."

"Oh look, it's the boy wonder from the academy. To what do I owe this pleasure?"

"I have come with news about your hunter friend. Louis was it?"

"What of him?"

"He is no more. You all will be facing a similar fate."

Xiao Lin cried out. "You killed him?"

Zakaire chuckled. "He killed himself trying to kill me. That is two for me and none for him."

"Bastard."

"Now there is no room for name calling. Where is your gentleman's pride?"

"In the ground where you will find yourself if you keep fucking around." Vincent said, growing angry for being targeted again.

"I will face you in good time, hunter. That much I can promise. But for now you will tell me where the gate is. I may spare your little team here if you cooperate."

"You mean Veronica?"

"Is that her name?" the masked one asked.

"You lay one finger on her and you are a dead man."

"I am afraid that your threat falls on deaf ears. Besides, you are no match for me and my pending powers, hunter. I will bring about the destruction of the world. Your Veronica is just a stepping stone for greater purposes. We will meet again, hunter. When we do prepare to spill your soul."

The projection evaporated.

"What do we do?" Rachel asked.

But there was no time to grieve. Veronica had to be found and protected against those forces that sought to do the undetermined. The entire lounge was after her. She would not answer her phone. They had to get to her before the masked one did.

She had not contacted Incognito either. He was working on repairing his shop. He did not have time to fiddle with the emotional damage Vincent had caused. His mind was elsewhere. She would turn up when she felt like it, the way she always had.

Louis was the closest person to remove the gate. With him gone Veronica was just a target. The forces that sought to end the world were just beginning to demonstrate their power. No one knew when the end of the world would happen but with each passing moment it seemed to be more and more likely.

Agatha had made an appearance to Vincent just before sunset. "Young hunter, you have a calling that I must share with you."

"You again? What is it this time?"

"You are to die by the hands of Zakaire."

"You mean the fool that is threatening Veronica? I can handle that small fry."

"It is to save the world. If you enter combat with him you will die. It is the only way to save the world."

"How is my death going to stop him?"

"When your bloodline ends is when the seraph will send a new warrior to protect this planet and all its inhabitants from the forces that seek to bring out destruction, perdition, and chaos." Agatha was sitting cross legged on the young hunter's car.

"I am going to kick his ass if he dares lay a finger on her. No sort of prophecy that you proclaim will stop that from happening."

"There is more." she said.

"Oh, let's hear it."

"You are to face death and decide if the world is worth saving. If you can find a way back the world will be as it was after Zakaire is defeated."

"All these end of the world bullshitters mean nothing to me. I care for Veronica and those that seek to harm her will feel my wrath."

"Is she worth dying for?"

"I believe so."

"Then we will meet again and when we do I shall have the means to aid you in the upcoming war."

She vanished and the search for Veronica was back on. Vincent searched high and low, damn near every crevice that Chicago offered. Where could she have gone? Was their fight so bad? Did she know she was in danger?

The body of Louis was never found. The lounge held a memorial service in the main corridor where they put up a picture of Louis to honor his memory. They would never know that he gave his life trying to end the war. He was an unsung hero.

Rachel felt it the most as the two had graduated together and joined up with Vincent around the same time. Rachel wanted the memory to rest easy so she made a silent vow to kill the one that murdered her classmate.

Xiao Lin wore ceremonial gowns every Tuesday as she lit candles to guide Louis's soul in the afterlife so that he may gain eternal rest. Vincent had to replace the fallen hunter. It was back to the academy. It would take some time. He had to file paperwork and explain what happened to his underling. The academy did not take too kindly to students dying under the supervision of hunters.

It was a few months before his paperwork was approved. When the academy sent over a new recruit it was nothing short of someone who would fit right in. She was a bright shiny face. She studied summoning: the craft of calling forth beasts and other creatures to aid her when needed.

"The name is Isabella. Looks like I am going to be one with the clan." she said

EPILOGUE

Veronica sped off with tears in her eyes. "He doesn't love me anyway." Incognito's was in the rearview mirror. There were those that were after her and she knew it. This was all to do with her father. She had known since she was a girl that she was being used by family. It was her heart and the gate it carried. Malekai the avaricious would be damnation.

She went to the upper east side to meet with an old connection. It was time to call in a favor. This was the way she was going to foil her father's plot. It was a short drive if you ignored the red lights. But when emotions run high is when the old saying says that rules were made to be broken. Streetlights were just one of those rules.

She was off to see an old friend so that she could take control of her life. Vincent was not so understanding which was why she kept the secret of her father from him for so long. She knew he would overreact. She did not expect him to grab her the way he did. She ignored all calls from anyone that had anything to do with him. But she did call Christian. She had known him for a while and it was time to cash in on old favors.

"Where are you?" she asked.

"Christian's voice was soothing the way you found in movies. It was as if he knew what to say. "I'm at the shop. I have been waiting for your call. You keep me in the dark all this time."

"You know the way I work. I am a mystery and a half."

Christian chuckled like a gentleman. "I think you just like people owing you."

"A girl has to keep her wits about her. Especially one in my case."

"What are you looking for?"

Veronica rounded the corner a block away from the shop named "Deep Earths". It was a warlock shop. This one was not antagonistic in any way. It just helped out people in need. In Veronica's case it helped with her wants. "Just a simple summons."

"Anything in particular? I could call a cat. Or I could call a god. Anything in between really."

"I should have that of a demon."

"Demons are hard. You know they want souls in the end. Not to mention the wrong kind could wreck my shop."

"How about we run the risk and any damages will square us. Given what you owe me you can sustain a little property damage."

She arrived just in front of the shop. When the warlock met her at the door he ushered her in and then turned his "open" sign to "closed". She dropped her bag on the counter and walked straight to the back of the shop where he usually charged extra for the magic to happen.

"Do you have a particular demon in mind?" he asked as she sat in the corner chair.

"As a matter of fact there is one. One my guy will hate."

"This is about Vincent? What did he do this time?"

Veronica took off her boots and slid them under the chair. "He has been an all around jerk. I know he is going to try to kill my father. I want to make preparations so that I can get even and destroy what my father values."

"What's the demon's name?"

"Xagos."

"Ah, the wishmaker of flames. He is like a genie but sends your soul to his furnace for dominion of the earth. That one can be quite tricky seeing as how he only comes to those willing to make the trade."

"I thinkI am more than willing."

Christian set out to his books to find a ley line that was strong enough to get the demon's attention. Summoning a demon was like making a phone call. All you need is a ley line strong enough to pull the demon's dominion to where you were. After that it was just chatting if the demon did not kill you before any talking began.

There were some interesting clues on the ley line that Christian had written down. This was not the first time he called this demon. Though it was the first time Veronica did, Maybe she knew what she was getting into. It did not seem to bother the shop owner at all.

They waited until nightfall to begin the ritual that would call forth the evil of all evils. The was a transmutation circle that would pull the demon from wherever it was to ask for a favor. Candles were lit in a pentagram to counteract the flames from Xagos in case he tried to attack. There was no telling what a demon would do. So there had to be precautionary measures.

Veronica stood in the center of the circle. Chrisatian was on the outer side and had to chant continuously during the ritual to keep the barrier that would hold back the flames so that Veronica would stay safe.

When the ritual began everything aside from Christian was dead quiet. The ritual was written in latin and he read the contents from a book that was well guarded in his shop. It was one that held the secrets of most demonic arts. This one was one that needed complete focus. One false move and veronica would be toast, quite literally.

There was a tremble in the floorboards. The flames began to wisp around. There was a slight wind behind the closed doors and paper began to fly in eddies around the room like the leaves of early November. Christian continued to chant.

There was smoke, black and thin slowly filling the room. After a few short seconds the room was filled with billows of thick black smog. The winds picked up. Christian chanted louder and more intensely. The wind spun the smog into the center of the room and then a barrier flashed around the sphere of smog then dissipated.

A giant face of flame appeared in the center of the smog. It was Xagos with the smile of all evil smiles. His horns poked like crags. "Who dares summon me?" the demon said. It was clear that he was enraged. The faces' eyes were red and alienated.

At first Veronica said nothing. The ritual worked and it was a sense of control that she had to keep if she were to make it through this alive. "I have called you here to ask for a favor."

"Speak and it may be yours."

"I am promised to bring about the destruction of the world. I offer you a gate and to souls to stop the degradation of my body and take the gate that will summon perdition to use as you see fit." Veronica said with the confidence of an amazoness.

"You are the daughter of a warlock. I know your tale. You offer his soul before his return?" the demon said.

"Yes, and that of mine."

"I accept this offer. For now you will roam as if I own you. When the time comes your soul is mine."

The face receded into the smog. Then it disappeared altogether. Papers settled back to the floor and the winds stopped circling in the room. There was a burst of magic that signified that the demon was gone and the ritual was complete.

"You offered your soul to save the world?" Christian asked, catching his breath from the incantation. "That will make you an unsung hero."

"It is the least I can do. The truth is we don't need the world to end. So many are after the earth being destroyed I figured I might as well do my part."

"I can't say I would have done the same."

The candles had streams of smoke where the flames used to be. The streams rocked back and forth like a ballerina would if she was one hundred degrees hotter and on the end of a wick.

Then, suddenly, the candles relit. The two that just finished the ritual looked in awe. "Did you do that?" Veronica asked.

"No, wasn't me." Christian moved to blow out the candles. The flames moved to his breath but did not extinguish. The flames instead bursted the back room into flames. Xagos was angry that he was pulled where he was from. The demon left behind some pyrokinesis and set the shop ablaze. "Let's get moving."

Veronica made for the door. "You don't have to tell me twice."

Flames licked along the wall chasing them as they moved. Veronica grabbed her boots and jacket on the way out. The flames were at their heels and looked like hands snatching in their trial. Xagos wanted Christian to burn very badly. It was clear by the way the flames grabbed at him. They nearly caught him but the worst was his jacket was singed on the way to the street.

The two of them stood and watched the shop burn to the ground. "Are you considering this collateral damage?" Christian asked.

"Don't think for a second I am paying for this."

"I think it makes us even then."

"I would say you are right."

There was a vibration in Veronica's coat. Her phone had been going off nonstop. She looked and there were twenty four missed calls. All of them came from the Demon Hunter's lounge or from Vincent's private phone. She did not want to talk to him. She did not want to see his face or hear his voice. She had already made a deal with a demon to do what Vincent did not seem all too concerned about.

"Is it him?" Christian asked.

"I don't want to talk about him." She then pressed "ignore".

Printed in the United States
by Baker & Taylor Publisher Services